The Killer Poet

The Killer Poet

YOSHE

www.urbanbooks.net

Urban Books, LLC
78 East Industry Court
Deer Park, NY 11729

ISBN 13: 978-1-60162-485-7
ISBN 10: 1-60162-485-9

First Printing January 2012
Printed in the United States of America

10 9 8 7 6 5 4 3 2 1

Distributed by Kensington Publishing Corp.
Submit Wholesale Orders to:
Kensington Publishing Corp.
C/O Penguin Group (USA) Inc.
Attention: Order Processing
405 Murray Hill Parkway
East Rutherford, NJ 07073-2316
Phone: 1-800-526-0275
Fax: 1-800-227-9604

Chapter 1

The Beginning of the End

It was early in the morning and the streets of Brownsville were practically deserted. Twenty-year-old Prince Poet Washington exited the gypsy cab in front of his building in the Langston Hughes housing projects. He attended a house party the night before, devouring shots of cognac and chasing the shots down with a Corona or two. Standing in the lobby of his apartment building, Poet slowly began to feel the side effects of the Hennessy that he had consumed earlier. As he wobbled toward the elevator, a wave of nausea came over him. While Poet stood against the wall trying to regain his senses, he was alarmed by an unidentified man who ran out of the staircase. The man brushed by Poet, almost knocking him down.

"Yo, man! Watch where the hell you're goin'!" Poet yelled loudly.

The man turned around, uttered a quick apology, and sped out the door but not before Poet noticed a dark scar on the right side of the man's face. Poet watched as the man ran outside and made a quick turn onto Sutter Avenue.

Pressing for the elevator, something about the man's hastiness made Poet uneasy. He figured that the man had been up to no good, but he was too tired to care.

The elevator seemed to be taking forever so the hungover Poet grudgingly walked up the flights to his seventh floor apartment.

When Poet got to the fifth floor stairwell, he heard a whimpering noise. The sound made him pause for a moment, as he silently prayed that he hadn't run into any criminal or sexual activity. Poet slowly peeked around the brick wall. He saw a teenage girl lying on the floor of the staircase, half-naked and bleeding. Although her body was fully exposed, she was hiding her face.

"Oh, shit!" Poet announced, covering his mouth. "Who did this to you?" he asked the girl in amazement, while cautiously approaching her.

The girl attempted to sit up and gradually uncovered her blackened eyes. Poet assisted her by propping her up against the graffiti-marked brick wall. All she could see was Poet's silhouette through her swollen eyes.

"It was that man," she whispered. "It was the light-skinned man with the scar on his face."

"What's your name, baby girl?" Poet asked, looking at her with empathy in his eyes.

"Erika," she meekly replied.

Suddenly, Erika began crying uncontrollably. Poet felt his face flush, embarrassed at the girl's half nakedness. He removed his hooded sweatshirt and helped her put it on. It was then that he noticed the other bruises all over her body. Her panties and jeans were in the corner of the staircase in a messy heap.

Light-skinned man with a scar on his face, he thought.

Poet's thoughts went back to the man who almost knocked him down in the lobby a few minutes before.

At this point, Poet didn't know whether to just walk away from the victim or call the police himself. He did not want to be blamed for or even questioned about what had obviously occurred in the staircase. But Poet's conscience wouldn't allow him to leave the distraught girl's side. He knelt down to comfort her as she immediately recounted what happened to her.

"I was goin' to the store for my Auntie and this man was downstairs in the lobby, waitin' for the elevator," the traumatized girl began. Poet picked up on her Southern accent as her voice trembled with fear and sadness.

Poet gave the victim his undivided attention as she continued. "I didn't pay him no mind until he grabbed me and pulled me in the staircase. I tried to fight him off, thinkin' that if I screamed he was gonna kill me. I realized that he wasn't gonna stop when he punched me in my face a couple of times. Then he pulled out a knife and cut my clothes off me. After that, he forced himself on me. I told him that I was a virgin but he wasn't listenin' to me. I kept tellin' him over and over again that I was a virgin but all he did was just told me to shut up and then he held the knife to my throat and . . . and . . ." Erika trailed off and her eyes seemed distant.

A few seconds later, her body began trembling as if she was having convulsions. The frightened Poet ran out of the staircase to the nearest apartment and asked a neighbor to call 911 for the girl.

Within seconds, Poet returned to Erika's side to check on her. She was still trembling and staring into space. She was unaware of her exposed vagina and the dried-up blood that was smeared on the inside of her almond-colored thighs. Seeing her in the state that she was in, it was then that Poet made the decision to hunt down the rapist himself.

In a fit of rage, Poet ran back downstairs and went outside. He frantically looked up and down Sutter Avenue, hoping that the mysterious man with the scar on his face would reappear before the police came. Poet was unsure of what he was going to do or say if he saw the man. He grew angrier by the minute as he thought about his two younger sisters, Porsha and Precious. He couldn't help but think that the teenage girl could have easily been one of them.

Poet was overcome with anger. What made him even more upset was that the rape had occurred so close to home. He had grown weary of living in the projects and was tired of feeling as if he was trapped in the crime-ridden neighborhood that most likely bred the vermin who had committed the heinous act. The rage that Poet was experiencing had him so amped; it actually made him want to kill somebody.

Poet looked at his watch and cursed to himself after seeing the time. "It's six-twenty in the mornin'. It's too got-damn early for this bullshit," Poet said with a loud sigh.

Coming back to his senses, Poet decided to walk to the store for a pack of Newports. Seeing the rape victim, Erika, lying in the stairway with bruises all over her body and virgin blood all over her crotch had blown his high. He figured that if he smoked a cigarette or two, it would help to calm his nerves.

When Poet arrived at the window of the bodega on the corner of his block, he just happened to notice a familiar-looking person walking down the street. Then there was a funny feeling in his gut. If his memory was correct, the man looked like the same person who had almost knocked him down in the lobby and the one who had raped Erika. Poet couldn't remember the clothes that the man was wearing but curiosity got the best of him. He just had to see if the man strolling down the street was really the person who Erika had described.

Poet saw several squad cars and an ambulance racing down Rockaway Avenue, toward his building. He lit a cigarette, then casually strolled across the street and began following the light-complexioned stranger. Poet walked behind the man for the next two blocks, still not sure if he was the person who raped Erika. When the man turned the corner at Blake Avenue near where he was standing, Poet noticed the scar on his face. The man fit the exact description of the man who Erika had described. It was then that Poet knew that the man was his guy.

"That's him!" Poet whispered to himself. His heart began to beat a mile a minute.

Poet noticed that the rapist began picking up the pace, as another squad car raced down the street. To Poet, that was definitely the sign of a guilty man.

Poet lagged closely behind the suspect. A block later, the man slowed down, obviously unaware that he was being followed. Poet slowed down too, and checked the inside of his jacket pocket. He wanted to make sure that the 9 mm he had on him was cocked and ready with a bullet in the chamber. When the man finally stopped to take a breath, once again Poet was able to catch a glimpse of the scar on the right side of his face.

As Poet prepared to approach the rapist, he began to feel a little anxious. Beads of sweat formed under his New York Yankees fitted cap. Poet gripped the gun in his right hand and began to mumble under his breath. He watched the tired suspect closely, as he attempted to get his own nerves together. His murderous instincts were kicking in and his adrenaline was off the charts. Poet had never killed anyone before but he realized that once he pulled that trigger, there was no turning back. "Thou shalt not kill" was one of the Ten Commandments that he said that he would never break, unless someone messed with his family. On that particular day, he considered the rape victim, Erika, a family member. Poet silently asked God for forgiveness because a life was about to be forsaken and it sure wasn't going to be his own.

Poet quickly walked up to the suspect. "Yo, what's up?" Poet asked with a frown on his face.

The man looked nervous, as if he didn't know what to do next. Poet's heart skipped a beat after hearing more sirens in the distance.

"What you mean, young'un?" the man replied with a smirk on his face. "You know me from somewhere or you got some of that shit on you?" he asked, referring to drugs.

"I don't have nothin' on me but this!" Poet exclaimed, putting the gun in the rapist's face. The man jumped back.

"What the fuck? I ain't got no money on me, homeboy! I just smoke the shit, I don't sell the shit!" he said with a fearful look on his face.

Poet chuckled. "Motherfucker, does it look like I would be out here robbin' you for some fuckin' crack rocks, man? You know what you just did to that little girl in the staircase back there! I'm the dude you almost knocked over while runnin' outta that same buildin', homie!"

All of a sudden, the suspect's body began to quiver. His eyes went to the gun in Poet's hand. The rapist thought he had made a clean break. Rape and sexual assault were nothing new for him and Erika had not been his first victim. Being that Erika was walking alone so early that morning, he figured that she was one of the many teenage runaways who frequented the area. He had managed to get away with raping a few other young women for the last couple of months without so much as a police report from the victims, and now this.

The scar-faced suspect was also an unregistered sex offender, who thought that as long as he stayed off the radar, he could get away with his offenses. But this time he was wrong. It looked like he was finally about to pay for his perverted indiscretions.

"I don't know what you're talkin' about, homeboy! I wasn't even in the—" the man began.

The suspect couldn't even finish his sentence. Poet held the gun tightly in his hand and grabbed the willowy man by his jacket. There was an abandoned building at the corner, not too far from where they stood. Poet forcefully dragged the frail suspect by his jacket collar toward the dilapidated structure.

"Come and take a walk with me, my dude! We have some things to discuss!" Poet ordered, looking over his shoulders.

It was six-forty-five on a Saturday morning. With the exception of a few cars passing them by on the one-way street, no one was in sight.

The man made a futile attempt to wrestle away from Poet's strong grasp but he knew that he was no match for the younger man. Plus, Poet's mind was made up. The man was as good as dead and he was the Grim Reaper. This one was for Erika.

Poet yanked the rapist into the building with his strong hand still wrapped tightly around his collar. Once they were inside, the rapist immediately began to wrestle for his life. Poet punched the man in the face and dropped him with one hard hit to the jawbone. Poet looked down at the ingrate, who was writhing in pain on the dirty floor. He felt victorious as the self-proclaimed crackhead begged for his life.

"I'm sorry, man! Lemme go and I'll turn myself in! Or . . . or you could call the police yourself!" the rapist pleaded with tears in his eyes.

Poet sucked his teeth and kicked the man in his ribs. He smiled as he listened to the perp howl in pain.

"Motherfucker, I'm not callin' no five-o!" Poet exclaimed, referring to the police. "Jail is too good for your perverted ass! And do you honestly think I should let you live while that girl is out here sufferin' for what you did to her? Do you think that I should let you live so that you can rape or kill somebody else? You must be a fool!"

"Please, man, please! I just need help, man! I don't want to die!"

"Nah, you have to die, my man," Poet whispered, as his lips trembled and tears dropped from his eyes as the realization of what he was about to do hit him. "I got sisters and a mother and I'm not about to let your punk ass live another day so that you can hurt them, too. So before I put one of these hot ones in your ass, tell me: why did you rape her, man? Why?"

Poet aimed the gun directly at his head and the rapist began to wail loudly. He looked at Poet's tearful eyes and he knew that it was over for him. At that moment, he figured that he might as well go out with a bang and confess to his crimes.

"Okay, okay, I took the pussy because I wanted to!" he shouted, with saliva shooting out of his mouth. "That little bitch wanted me to give it to her! She was the one walkin' around with them tight-ass jeans on and that fitted shirt on with her titties lookin' all ripe and juicy! To me, all of them bitches wanted it! All of 'em! Fuck 'em all! I ain't never like bitches no way, always teasin' and fuckin' with my mind, tryin' to get in my pockets and take my money . . . Bitches ain't worth a sh—"

The rapist's confession was drowned out by the sound of Poet's gun going off. The bullet ripped into the rapist's right leg. He screamed in pain but it didn't stop him from talking recklessly.

"Fuck you, you bitch motherfucker! I shoulda raped your momma, too!"

Before the rapist could say anything else, Poet shot him in the head three times. Poet watched in awe as the rapist fell backward and his blood and brains soaked into the rotted wood of the rickety floor. Poet stood there for a few moments, as if his body were frozen in place and his hands were stuck on the gun. He felt a weird chill go down his spine as he looked at the smoking weapon that he held in his sweaty palm. Poet was having mixed feelings about what had just occurred, unsure if he should be hailed as a hero or a murderer. After all, he did just take someone's life.

Poet walked to the doorway. He looked to the left and the right to see if anyone was walking by the building before he stepped outside. Dogs barked in the distance but he hoped no one had noticed the sounds of gunshots.

After making sure that the coast was clear, Poet walked out of the raggedy structure. And he didn't dare look back. He seriously hoped that by the time the police found the body of the rapist, the man would have made a nice meal for the rats in the old building.

Poet nervously shoved the murder weapon into his jeans pocket as he walked down Rockaway Avenue toward his building. Unable to relax with the evidence on his person, he decided to ditch the murder weapon into a nearby sewer. After shoving the gun into a garbage-strewn sewer at the curb of his block, Poet breathed a sigh of relief. He had made a decision that would change his life forever. A gun that he carried for his own protection was now the physical evidence in a murder. Poet walked home with his head held down, thinking about the consequences of what he had done and how much of hypocrite he had become.

It was 7:05 A.M. by the time Poet arrived back at his building. Scores of reporters, police, and EMT personnel cluttered the lobby but he managed to slide undetected by all of the paparazzi. Before walking into the staircase, Poet caught a glimpse of Erika, the young victim, being carried out on a stretcher. He made sure he stayed as far away from her as possible. Once they carried Erika's battered body out of the front door, Poet ran all the way up to seventh floor and practically ran inside his house, locking the door behind him.

Poet tried to tiptoe into his bedroom when his mother, Cheryl, suddenly appeared in the doorway of her bedroom. Cheryl Washington was raising three children on her own and the last thing that she needed to do was worry about them being in the streets at all times of the night. Unfortunately, her son, Poet, was her biggest concern.

"Poet, why are you just now coming in this house, boy?" she asked. "It's after seven o'clock in the morning! Where have you been, mister?"

Poet sighed. "C'mon, Ma, I was at my homeboy's crib! We went out last night and I had one too many drinks so I just crashed on his couch until this mornin'," Poet explained.

Cheryl put her hands on her ample hips. The constant sounds of the police sirens had her nerves on edge.

"Prince Poet, do you not see all of the damn police officers and EMT workers downstairs in the lobby of this building? And why didn't you call me to let me know that you were going to be spending the night out? What the hell do you have a cell phone for, Poet? When I got up to pee at about six this morning and I realized that you were not in this house, my heart dropped all the way down to the bottom of my feet! Then when I called you and your phone went into voice mail, I thought that I was going to die!" she said, putting her hand to her chest. "I'm not gonna allow you to come in my house at all hours of the morning, Poet. I won't allow it!" she yelled.

Poet loved his mother but as he thought about what he just done moments before, he felt a sudden surge of power. He had just put a man into an early grave and here was his mother yelling at him like he was some punk. The murder was weighing heavily on his mind and he needed to lash out at someone.

"Yo, Ma, just leave me alone, all right? I mean, I'm in the damn house now, in one piece, so you should be happy! Here I am, about to be twenty-one years old, and you up here sweatin' me about comin' in the house at a certain time and whatnot, like I'm on a curfew or somethin'! I know how to take care of myself!" he exclaimed and slammed the door of his bedroom in his mother's face.

Poet couldn't understand why his mother was on his back. He helped her out with the bills and his younger sisters, Porsha and Precious. His father, James, had abandoned the family sixteen years before and now that he was older, Poet considered himself the man of the house. With that title, Poet felt that he should be able to do whatever he wanted without any questions from his mother.

His mother didn't know what it was like to be a man. Being raised without a father figure had left Poet with his own preconceived notion about what it was to be one, and having to rely on the male residents of Brownsville to be role models for him hadn't helped matters much.

Poet took off his clothes and fell back onto his full-sized bed. He stared at the various posters of 50 Cent and Jay-Z that were taped to the wall. Looking at his hip hop idols made him feel proud about what he had done to the rapist. Jay and 50 always rapped about their shady pasts and criminal activities and he imagined the rap stars would have done the same thing if they were in his shoes. Before falling into a deep slumber, Poet smiled to himself, not realizing that it was only going to be a matter of time before he killed again.

Chapter 2

Secrets

Feeling bad about the way he talked to his mother on that fateful day, Poet had since apologized to her. Now it was exactly two Saturdays after the incident. Everyone and everything had resumed back to normal except Poet.

Poet was extremely confused as to why he suddenly felt unmoved about the execution-style murder of the rapist. What he did know was that after seeing the young victim in the state that she was in, something in him just snapped. That moment of insanity caused him to take the law into his own hands. Now he was afraid to tell a soul about what happened. And what had him even more fearful was that he could not stop thinking about how easy it would be for him to kill again.

"Yeeoooo, Poet!" a male voice boomed from downstairs beneath his bedroom window. "Aye, yeeeooooo!"

Poet smiled. He would know that voice anywhere. He stuck his head outside the living room window and saw his right-hand, Mekhi, standing downstairs. They were childhood friends but they had love for each other like brothers.

"What's good, Khi?" Poet announced. "Why are you yellin' up at my window when you could have just come upstairs?" He shook his head. "Damn, you're ghetto!" he said with a chuckle.

Mekhi waved Poet off. "First of all, your intercom is broken again and when somebody did let me in the building, I found out that your damn elevator is broken, too!" he said. "And I was not about to walk up no seven flights of stairs! I live on the second floor in my buildin' and I'm not used to that!"

Poet nodded his head in agreement. If the elevators were out of order, he knew that it was a serious hike to his apartment. Considering what happened to Erika, the teenage rape victim, it was obvious that the staircases in his building weren't the safest place to be.

"Okay, okay. You got that. I'm comin' down but I just want to let you know that you're one lazy dude, man!" Poet replied.

Mekhi smirked. "Call me what you wanna call me but I woulda been crazy to walk up those damn stairs!"

Mekhi stood in front of the building, waiting for his friend. They were an inseparable duo and trusted each other with their lives. But Mekhi had his own secret. Within the last year or so, Mekhi discovered that he was infatuated with Poet's younger sister, Precious. She was only fifteen and a half but she was one of the prettiest girls he had ever seen in their neighborhood. Precious was ready and ripe for the picking, too, flirting with Mekhi and whoever else would pay her some attention. Most of the guys around the way knew that Precious was off-limits because of her overprotective brother. But this didn't stop Mekhi from wanting her.

With his good looks and shy demeanor, Mekhi could have had any woman he wanted. His honey brown skin and piercing green eyes were enticing to say the least, and women of all ages were attracted to him. Unfortunately, Mekhi lacked the confidence to converse with a mature-minded young woman. He was intimidated by them.

Instead, he dreamed about having an intimate relationship with the pubescent Precious. Mekhi loved Poet but the affinity that he had for Precious was completely different. It didn't matter that she was the girl whom he watched grow up from an infant. It didn't matter that he was there when she cut her first teeth and even when she lost a few. Even though he was six years old at the time, Mekhi remembered watching her take her first steps. Now Precious had definitely blossomed into a beautiful girl.

Mekhi glanced up at the apartment window several times, hoping that Precious would at least stick her head outside so he could catch a glimpse of her long, silky hair blowing in the cool breeze.

Upstairs, Poet grabbed a lightweight jacket out of the closet. As he began looking around his small bedroom for his house keys, Precious appeared in his doorway.

"Isn't that Mekhi waitin' for you outside?" Precious asked, having already peeked out the window.

Poet ignored his little sister as he ransacked his dresser drawers for his keys. She sucked her teeth and held up the keys that were in her hand.

"Are you lookin' for these?" she asked with a mischievous grin on her face. Poet snatched the keys away from her.

"How did you get my keys? Why were you in my room?" he yelled.

"For your information, I wasn't in your room!" Precious retorted. "Your keys have been on the kitchen table since last night!"

Poet rolled his eyes at her and walked out of the house. When Precious heard the staircase door slam, she decided to flirt with Mekhi a little before her brother arrived downstairs.

"Hey, Mekhi!" Precious shouted out of the dining area window. "What's up?"

Mekhi looked up at her with a lovelorn look on his face.

"What's up, Presh? You chillin'?" he asked, with a bright twinkle in his green eyes.

Precious smiled from ear to ear. She knew that Mekhi had a serious crush on her.

"Yeah, I'm chillin'. You're lookin' good, Mekhi, and I like your outfit," she complimented.

"Thanks. You look good too, as usual," he replied, wearing a big grin on his handsome face.

A few seconds later, Poet walked outside and Precious quickly stuck her head back into the window. When she turned around, her older sister, Porsha, was standing behind her with her arms crossed and shaking her head.

"Why are you still tryin' to flirt with Mekhi?" Porsha asked. "Do you know that Poet would flip his wig if he knew that you were flirtin' with his best friend?"

Precious waved her sister off. "Please, Porsha. I am not thinkin' about Mekhi," she lied. "Even though I do think that he is kinda sexy."

Porsha looked at her younger sister and shook her head. She was glad that she was the complete opposite of her siblings. She was so far removed from her dismal surroundings. Porsha was too preoccupied with the thought of finishing up college and trying to get out of the projects than to be flirting with the likes of any young man in their neighborhood.

Meanwhile, Poet walked out of the building and gave Mekhi a pound. "So what's good for the day?" he asked.

"I don't know," Mekhi replied. "You wanna take a ride to Manhattan?"

Poet shook his head. "Manhattan? That would be cool but my pockets ain't really sayin' Manhattan. Let's just walk down the Ave. I need to pick up a few things anyway."

So they took off for Pitkin Avenue, the local shopping area. They walked through the throngs of shoppers who were out in full force on the clear Saturday afternoon.

"So what have you been up to, Po?" Mekhi asked with a concerned look on his face. "What's been goin' on with you? I haven't seen you in the last two weeks. You kept tellin' me that you were going to call me back but you didn't do that, neither."

Poet knew that he had been missing in action for a short time. He wasn't in the mood to talk to anyone about how he had discovered the rape victim in the stairwell. But it was more than the rape that was bothering him. After the murder, he needed that time to gather his feelings about what he had done.

"All I was doin' was just chillin' in the crib, playin' PlayStation 3, listenin' to my iPod, not doin' anything special," Poet volunteered. "I know that we usually hang out almost every other day but I was shook up after I stumbled on the rape victim in the staircase of my buildin', know what I'm sayin'? Had me thinkin' about how that person could have been Mom Dukes or my sisters."

Mekhi stopped in the middle of the sidewalk. "So you're the one that found the girl? I didn't know that!" They proceeded to walk again and Mekhi continued to inquire about the incident. "I had forgotten all about the rape in your building." Mekhi shook his head. "Damn. That was some foul shit, man."

Poet hesitated to talk about it. The grisly image of the bloody and naked Erika appeared in his head. He kept

seeing images in his head of her battered face along
with the dead body of the rapist in his dreams almost
every night since the day of the incident.

"I was so shook up after what happened. I just
needed a moment to get my mind right," Poet said.

"So what ever happened to the girl? Did you ever see
her again after that?"

Poet shook his head and began kicking an empty
beer can as they walked down the block. His nerves
were getting the best of him.

"Nah, I haven't seen her. I think her family sent her
back to North Carolina on the first thing smokin' after the rape," he replied. Poet frowned. "Why are you
askin' about her anyway? Did you hear somethin' else
about that?"

Mekhi looked at Poet strangely. "No, man, I'm just
askin' a question. I wonder if they ever caught the dude
that did it."

Poet swallowed hard. "I don't think that they caught
that dude yet. But I know one thing: if any dude, and I
mean any dude, even thinks about comin' near my little
sisters, I swear I'd kill me a motherfucker!"

Mekhi shoved his hands deep into the pockets of
his jeans. He knew how Poet felt about his sisters, but
that didn't stop him from yearning for Precious. Mekhi
thought about her day and night, but was he ready to
give up his friendship and possibly risk his life to be
with Precious?

Mekhi sighed. "I ain't mad at you, Po. I don't have
any sisters but I can understand how you feel."

Poet continued his rant. "Shit, I don't care if it's my
moms, aunts, grandma . . . I'd kill for any woman in my
family! But my sisters? Do you see how pretty they are,
Khi? That's a whole different ball game! They're some
good girls and I want them to stay that way. Part of my

job is to make sure none of these grimeballs out here fucks with or disrespects my little sisters."

Once again, Mekhi had to agree with Poet, but he couldn't help but notice that it was the first time he heard Poet talking about murdering anyone.

Mekhi nodded his head and, for a moment, there was a silent pause between the two. He changed the subject.

"So all you've been doin' for the last two weeks was hanging out in your crib with them loud-ass sisters of yours and your moms all day? I know the womenfolk in that house had to be drivin' your ass crazy."

Poet laughed. "Well, you know how they are. My family loves it when I'm in the house, especially Moms. Too much shit is goin' on in these streets and they worry about me. Plus, are you forgettin' that I'm the man of the house? That I'm the king of that castle?" Poet said, pounding on his chest.

Mekhi laughed loudly. "Are you kiddin' me? You know that Miss Cheryl runs that house! She's the queen and don't you forget that! And Miss Cheryl ain't no joke. When we were younger, you remember how she used to whip our ass?"

They laughed hysterically as they reminisced about their younger years and how mischievous they were.

Poet sighed. "That shit seems like yesterday, right? Those were some good times. At least we didn't have to be out here in these streets, tryin' to find ways to make money. Our peoples made sure that we were taken care of. Now it's about takin' care of ourselves and eventually takin' care of them, you know what I mean?" Poet said.

As they continued their conversation, Mekhi erased Poet's murderous rant from his mind. He was too busy thinking of Precious. But how was he going to get to her without her brother finding out?

Chapter 3

The Discovery

Meanwhile, a few blocks away, yellow crime scene tape blocked the entrance of an abandoned building. Uniformed officers and detectives milled in and out of the building while a small crowd of people gathered around, hoping to catch a quick glimpse of the dead body that was inside.

"Damn, it stinks in here!" stated Detective Shareef Oates. He held his nose as he stood in the abandoned building. The decomposed body had an overbearing stench to it. "All of these years on the job and I still can't get used to the smell of a dead body!"

"You and me both. Who discovered this body anyway?" asked Detective Rodney Lewis, while adjusting his latex gloves. He put menthol under his nose to kill the smell of the corpse and handed it to Oates.

"Some kids found this guy in here," Oates replied, putting the menthol under his nose as well. He bent down and looked at the body. Other detectives milled around the murder scene, looking for evidence.

"What the hell were these kids doing playing inside this building anyway? Their mommas need to start whipping some ass!" Lewis said, holding his hands up in the air.

Oates laughed at his partner. "What are you talking about, man? They're kids! We both grew up in the hood, man, and you know how it was back in the day when we were young. We used to play in some of the most fucked-up places. We were some exploratory little bastards, too! Shit like this was exciting to us."

Lewis shook his head and chuckled as he watched the other investigators take pictures of the scene. "Yeah, I guess you're right," he replied with a sigh. "You know what it is, O? I just don't feel like dealing with this shit right now, that's all."

Detectives Oates and Lewis of the Seventy-third Precinct in Brownsville were the lead homicide detectives on the case. Decorated officers of the NYPD and fifteen-year veterans, they'd seen a lot of murders in their tenure. The partners had solved a lot of cases but they had just as many unsolved murders too, much to their dismay. Being African American males, it was discouraging for them to see so many black men involved in the meaningless killings and deaths of their own kind, and other races as well. Now lying on the floor of an old, abandoned building in the heart of Brownsville was another black male statistic.

Sergeant Hayes, their supervisor, walked toward the detectives. He had an exasperated look on his face.

"What's up, fellas?" he greeted them with a frown. "I'm getting a little pissed off! Where the hell is the medical examiner? Where's the coroner?"

Oates shrugged his shoulders. "The medical examiner is inside the building, Sarge. The coroner should be here any minute now."

Sergeant Hayes rubbed his bald head. "Well, they're going to have to get on the ball. We have a lot of things we have to search for, like shell casings." Sarge looked around the crime scene. "As a matter of fact, did you guys see any shell casings around here?"

Lewis and Oates looked around, as well. "Nah, we didn't see any yet," said Lewis. "Maybe when they get this body up out of here we could get a better look." He patted Sergeant Hayes on his shoulder. "Don't worry about it, Sarge. We got you!"

Sergeant Hayes calmed down. "Hey, I know you guys got my back. You're the best on the squad." Sarge looked behind them and saw the captain coming their way. "Ah, shit!" he exclaimed. "Let me go and talk to this asshole. You men carry on." They watched as Sarge intercepted the captain.

"We need to get this investigation started as soon as possible," Oates said. "For some reason, I have feeling that there's a little more to this story than just some random killing."

Lewis looked at his partner. "I love it when you have an epiphany, man," he said with a fist pump in the air. He knew that every time his partner got that "feeling," the case was going to be a big one. "Well, do you think that this one is going to be newsworthy?"

"Yeah, I do," Oates replied, while his eyes roamed around the crime scene. "I mean, the average detective—who, by the way, we are not—will probably overlook a lot of things, just for the sake of catching their killer. I like to get to the story behind the killing."

Lewis shook his head. Oates used his sixth sense to solve many of their cases. Most of the time, he hit the jackpot. But after coming up with nothing at this particular crime scene, they both agreed that they would have to come back after the body was removed and look for physical evidence.

"Well, partner, just lead the way so that we can solve this case," Lewis replied as he knelt down to search the body.

The two detectives watched as the medical examiner rifled through the victim's pockets for evidence and identification. Much to their dismay, the unidentified man had no New York State license or non-driver's ID in his possession to prove who he was. Of course, they couldn't recognize his face because his body was badly decomposed. Now he would have to be identified through dental records or fingerprints. They would also have to wait for the pathologist's report to come back in order to find out when and exactly how the man died. This murder was going to be time consuming and they would have to be meticulous about the way they handled it.

The coroner arrived half an hour later and the body was finally ready to get moved from the crime scene to the city morgue. The crowd outside was disappointed about not being able to get a glimpse of the dead body and began booing the uniformed officers and the detectives who were on the scene. Lewis and Oates shook their heads with embarrassment as they walked to the car.

"Damn, Lew! Can you believe that these spectators are booing us?" Oates exclaimed as they hopped into their department-issued Chevy Impala. "They're booing us because they can't take a look at a dead body! What type of bullshit is that?"

Lewis beeped the horn at some people standing in the middle of the one-way street.

"Our people," Lewis announced with a loud sigh as they pulled off.

It was the end of a busy work day when Detective Oates climbed into his Lincoln Navigator and pulled off from the precinct. He was happy that the day was over, and he couldn't wait to get home so that he could shower the horrible smell of death off his body.

Driving on the Belt Parkway East, toward his home on Guy Brewer Boulevard in Queens, Oates thought about dead man whose body was discovered earlier that day. He wondered what the man's life had been like. He wondered if he had left behind any children. He also wondered what the man had done to deserve to die in the shit hole that they found him in.

Oates had to admit that being a homicide detective had its perks but sometimes the constant interaction with the deceased took a toll on the human psyche. That's why he made sure that he put God first, took care of his health, stayed close with his family, and, most importantly, enjoyed life to the fullest. Seeing the countless dead bodies only made him have an even stronger zest for life.

Born and raised in Harlem, it was there that Shareef Oates had made the decision to become a detective and, back in those days, it was almost unimaginable for a young boy from the ghetto to aspire to become a police officer. Having discovered a few dead people himself as a precocious youngster, he always wondered what it felt like to crack the case on a murder.

After joining the force and patrolling communities as a uniformed officer for several years, Oates had finally managed to make his dream come true by becoming a highly decorated homicide detective for the last ten years.

Oates slowly pulled into his driveway. After getting out of his vehicle, he walked inside his comfortable two-family home and put his keys on a table next to the couch. As soon as he made his way downstairs to his bedroom, his house phone began ringing.

"Yeah, who is this?" he answered, slightly annoyed and out of breath after running back up the stairs.

"Whoa, whoa," said the male voice on the other end. "Hey, man, it's me, Lew. I thought that you would be home by now."

Oates laughed. "Man, you was about to get cussed out! What's up?"

"Look, this weekend the Twenty-fifth Precinct is having a party at the Armory up in Harlem, your old neighborhood. You wanna go?"

Oates smiled. "Count me in. I need to get out and do something, man. I've been working too hard and not taking the time out to enjoy myself."

"Well, here's your chance to do it. So get your threads together and we're gonna hang out this upcoming weekend. You never know. You just might meet something nice up in there!"

Oates sighed. "I don't know, Lew. I'm tired of bumping and grinding with these random chicks. I'm losing interest in that shit. I've been thinking that I'm ready to settle down."

Lewis laughed loudly on the other end of the phone. "What? Shareef Oates, certified player extraordinaire, is ready to settle down?"

"Yeah, man. This player is thirty-nine years old with a daughter in college and even she is doing her own thing. She doesn't have time for her daddy anymore. That used to be my little sidekick. Shit, even her momma done got remarried! I'm just tired of wasting my time with these different women."

Lewis laughed. "Well, man, as for me, I've been married most of my damn life. Now that me and the missus are getting a divorce, I'm ready to party! But on another note, I can't get mad at the way you're feeling, O." There was a silent pause then Lewis sighed as he continued. "Anyway, my brother, put that shit in your mental Rolodex for Saturday night, man. We're in there."

At one time, he loved being single. With only one college-age daughter from a previous relationship, he was free to do whatever he wanted. Now that he was getting older, he yearned for a change in his current situation. Oates realized that he was a lonely man and something was missing in his life. For the first time in a long time, Oates felt the urge to settle down with someone.

But he couldn't be with just any woman. To him, women had become so superficial and shallow these days. The women he had previously dated seemed as if they were only looking for sponsors, not husbands or committed boyfriends.

Oates wanted to be with someone he could trust, someone who was genuine and knew how to love him and be loved by him. He was looking for more than just a woman with a nice body and a beautiful face. He made a promise to take time out for himself to do just that. Only he wasn't going to wait for love this time. He figured that it wouldn't hurt to open himself up to a prospective mate.

Maybe Lewis was right about meeting that special someone at the party that they were attending.

They said their good-byes and Oates hung up the phone. Exhausted from a long day, he went back to his bedroom to undress. After doing that, Oates headed toward the bathroom for a nice, hot shower before retiring to his bed for the night. Before his head could hit the pillow, he was fast asleep.

Chapter 4

Little Girl Lost

The Brownsville Houses courtyard consisted of a recently upgraded basketball court, newly painted benches, and of course, the customary cement animals for the smaller children to climb on. It was also somewhere for the young people to congregate and that they did until the wee hours of the morning, weekdays included. Hanging out in the courtyard became addictive to those who thrived off the latest happenings in the neighborhood.

Precious knew that her brother was not very fond of the courtyard activities due to the trivial shootings and fights that usually occurred there. Unfortunately, it was her favorite spot. Poet was uncomfortable with her being there and he told her more than enough times to stay away from the courtyard. In all her defiance, Precious proceeded to do exactly what she wanted to do.

Precious was going on sixteen years old and becoming one with her outer beauty. She relished the attention that she received from boys and men alike, and now she was becoming restless. She wasn't sure if it was because her birthday was quickly approaching that she found herself just wanting to be out and about even more than ever. She had grown weary of being under the watchful eye of her family. Being that she was the youngest, she felt that they treated her like a baby.

Although her mother's rules and Poet's overprotec-tiveness were issues for her, there was one thing that really got on her nerves. Precious didn't like being the only one out of her friends who was still a virgin. She was sick of having those sexual feelings without know-ing what the real thing felt like. She had to listen to her friends talk about how it hurt so bad but felt so good at the same time. She was curious to know what it felt like to be in the strong arms of a real man.

But Precious wanted to lose her virginity to someone she could trust. This was when she thought about Me-khi. She had been thinking that he would be the perfect candidate to be her first. Mekhi was handsome, older than her, and she was sure that he was sexually expe-rienced. Now the only thing she had to work on was getting Mekhi to actually agree to it.

Precious walked towards a group of girls who were sitting around talking over each other, purposely ig-noring the catcalls and requests of some guys.

"What's up, Presh?" her best friend, Malika, yelled out from across the courtyard. Their other friends turned around and greeted Precious with a smile. "You're just now comin' outside, girl? We've been out here for a while now."

Precious waved Malika off as she approached the bench. "You know that my brother tries to keep me and Porsha trapped in the house like two prisoners. I think he's a little nervous about us bein' hurt, especially after that girl got raped in our buildin'," she volunteered.

"Please!" Malika exclaimed with a wave of indiffer-ence. "Bitches get raped out here probably every damn day so I don't even know why your brother be trippin'. She ain't the first chick to get raped and damn sure won't be the last!"

Precious frowned. "Why are you so ignorant, Malika? Nobody deserves to get raped. That girl didn't deserve that and you know it!"

Malika shrugged her shoulders. "Well, I don't know the broad personally but I do know that she shoulda been on her A game and watched her back! Dudes can't creep up on Malika 'cause I got somethin' for their ass!" she said, pulling out an orange box cutter from her pocket. "I'll cut a motherfucker's dick off!"

Unfortunately, Malika came from a generation of people who were uneducated and ill-bred. She was a young girl who was fascinated with material things, money, and negativity. A decent education for her was irrelevant. Regrettably, Malika hadn't learned better because she wasn't taught better. Her mother was a fourth-generation welfare recipient and Malika was one of eight children.

Never knowing who her father was and having a negligent mother who was more of a friend than a parent, Malika did anything to get attention. Her upbringing caused her to grow up to be insensitive and cruel, unable to empathize with anyone. She had no compassion for anyone and had developed frostiness around her heart that no one could melt. Strangely enough, she was unbelievably loyal to Precious.

Everyone laughed with Malika. Precious didn't crack a smile.

"You're crazy!" she said, shaking her head with embarrassment. Precious sat beside her on the back of the bench. "What have y'all been up to lately? Anything good been happenin' around here?"

"Well, a few weeks ago, they found this dead man in one of them empty buildings on Chester Street," Malika announced. "You know, we was over there tryin' to get us a good look at the motherfucker, see what kinda damage the killer had done to the person," she stated.

The others girls laughed at Malika's statement and slapped her five.

Precious had a disgusted look on her face. "Why would you wanna see a dead body, Malika? Don't you think that's disgustin' and kinda strange?" Precious said.

Malika laughed. "Fuck that dude! I don't know him! He probably stole somethin' or he was a crackhead or a dopefiend," she said.

Precious sucked her teeth. She knew that Malika was about to go into one of her hateful rants, acting like she didn't have any drug abusers and criminals in her own family. There was no use in talking to Malika when she had an audience of people laughing at her stupid comments.

"Okay, okay, Malika! You're about to start up so let's just end it, okay? I don't wanna hear about no dead body!"

Malika laughed at Precious. "Oh, yeah, Presh, I forgot about how scary and sensitive you are. I'll just drop it then. Damn!"

Precious, Malika, and their other friends sat on the bench for a few more moments, talking about nothing special. They were all young girls trapped inside of grown women's bodies with their underdeveloped minds and superficial attitudes. Like so many teenage girls, they were growing up too fast. They didn't realize that there was more to adulthood than having casual sex and living life in the fast lane. Being an adult was about being responsible, and taking accountability for one's actions. That was something that neither one of them was mature enough to understand.

Although Precious's home life was much more stable than Malika's, she longed to be carefree without all the rules and regulations that her family imposed on her.

With her mother working long hours, a sister in college and an overbearing older brother, Precious longed for attention.

Precious was nothing but a sheltered and naïve little girl who was looking for love. Being that she had never known her father, she had a void that needed to be filled. She always wondered what it felt like to be loved by a man and Precious was willing to find that out any way that she could.

Chapter 5

Split Personality

Later that night, Poet and Mekhi were hanging out with a group of friends. On the weekends, they would congregate on Rockaway Avenue under the subway El and talk trash to each other while sipping on some Hennesy and Coke.

On this particular evening, Poet wasn't in the mood for trash talking and drinking. He listened intently as his cronies talked about the things they had done, even some of the crimes that they had allegedly committed. He chuckled to himself as they talked about what they would have done to this man and that one, not realizing that they were standing in the very presence of a certified killer.

But Poet wasn't trying to be some local street gangster. He was fortunate enough to have only had a couple of fist fights in the neighborhood that he grew up in. He had even carried a gun for many years but never had to use it until he killed the rapist.

Poet thought that the so-called gangsters people idolized were the same chumps who killed people they knew just to get a reputation. Poet couldn't see himself senselessly pumping bullets into some random dude from around the way just for recreation. What sense did that make? In doing that he would only end up with major beef or an asshole full of time in jail. Finally coming to terms with the murder, Poet felt that he killed someone who deserved to die and he was justified in taking that man's life. Plus, killing someone he didn't know or no one cared about just made it even easier to deal with.

In the month that had passed, Poet went from being regretful to feeling quite heroic. There was no time for self-pity. He also decided that it was time to take matters into his own hands and serve the criminals who corroded his neighborhood with some "hood justice." This was where justice was served on the street with the perp looking down the barrel of a gun and not inside of somebody's courtroom. The only punishment for their crimes would be death.

"Yo, Poet, what the hell is up with you?" Mekhi said, alarming his daydreaming friend. "You've been off the radar all day! Are you a'ight?"

Poet took off his fitted baseball cap and wiped the sweat from his forehead.

"Yeah, yeah, I'm good. I was just thinkin' about somethin', that's all," he replied.

"Well, that thinkin' about somethin' better be about some broad or money!" Mekhi shouted, causing everyone to burst out with laughter. "You're startin' to scare the shit outta me with all of this thinkin'! What am I supposed to think about all this daydreamin' that you're doin', huh? You got somethin' you need to tell your boy?"

Poet became annoyed with Mekhi and began to rub the peach fuzz on his chin. "I'm good, Khi. Just carry on with your conversation and stop worryin' about me. I said that I was okay."

All of Poet's friends gave him a strange look and continued conversing with each other. They all had known each other for most of their lives but Mekhi was the closest to Poet. He knew when something was going on with his friend. He just didn't understand why Poet wasn't talking to him about it.

After leaving their friends for the night, Mekhi and Poet walked home together. Once they were alone, Mekhi continued to pick Poet's brain about his thoughts. The only thing that it did was make Poet clam up even more.

"Hey, man," Mekhi began. "I thought that we were brothers. Somethin' is botherin' you and it seems like you don't want to talk to me about it. But you've been worryin' me with all this quiet storm shit. This zonin' out mess has been goin' on for like the last couple of days."

Poet looked at Mekhi and flinched as the wind hit his face. "It ain't nothin' against you if that's what you're thinkin', Khi. I'm just tryin' to look at life from a different perspective, that's all."

Mekhi laughed and breathed a sigh of relief. "I hear that!" he replied with a laugh. "Listen to you. Gettin' all educated on me and whatnot. Talkin' about some 'perspective on life' shit!"

Poet smiled. "You act like I'm stupid or somethin'!"

Mekhi playfully slap boxed Poet. "You are stupid!" replied Mekhi, catching Poet in the face with a soft slap to the right cheek.

Poet laughed and hit him back. Mekhi was happy that he was able to lighten the mood. When they arrived at his building, they gave each other a bear hug and went their separate ways.

As Poet walked through the Brownsville Houses courtyard, he caught a glimpse his sister Precious standing outside with some of her friends, including

Malika. She was one of the friends he couldn't stand.
He always thought that Malika was bad news and he
didn't like his sister being around her. Also, Malika
had one of the biggest mouths in the projects and Poet
made sure that he kept his little sister out of his business for fear that she would run back and tell her blab-
bermouth friend.

"What's up, Poet?" the obnoxious Malika shouted at
him, running over to Poet like he was some kind of rap
star. She held out her hand for a pound.

"What's up, Malika?" Poet replied, with a blank look
on his face. He ignored her hand and walked right
over to Precious. "Why are you out here at this time of
night?" he asked Precious, while looking at his watch.
It was almost 12:00 A.M. and seeing her outside with
Malika had set him off.

Precious looked at him up and down. "Because
Mommy said I could be out here!" she retorted and
turned her back to him.

Poet grabbed her arm. "Man, get your ass upstairs
before I embarrass you in front of your friends!" Precious refused to move. "Did you hear what I said?"

She puffed out her pretty mouth. "Damn, I heard
you! Why are you makin' me go upstairs so early? It's a
Saturday night!"

Poet shrugged his shoulders. "I don't give a fuck
about no Saturday night! Get up them stairs! Don't you
know a girl your age was raped in this buildin' a few
weeks ago?"

"So what? Dang! You're always tryin' to act like
you're somebody's daddy!"

"I am your fuckin' daddy, okay? Now get upstairs!"

Precious reluctantly walked away from her friends
after saying good night. It wasn't like anyone was going
to make fun of her because they knew the deal when

they saw Poet. In the back of their pubescent minds, they secretly wished they had someone to care enough about them to pull them off that bench in the court-yard.

Poet and Precious made their way upstairs in silence. He was about to go to work and he didn't need her to be outside running her mouth to their mother about his whereabouts.

"Mommy!" Precious shouted. "Your son makes me so sick! He made me come upstairs all early!" she yelled as she burst through the door.

Cheryl immediately walked out of the kitchen. "Child, please! It was almost time for you to come upstairs anyway! It's almost twelve o'clock in the morning!" she replied.

Precious walked into her bedroom and slammed the door.

"Slam a door in this house again and I'm gonna tear your behind up, little girl!" Cheryl loudly exclaimed. "You don't pay no kinda rent in here for you to be slamming any of my doors! You're not grown!" Cheryl looked at Poet and smiled. She kissed her only son on the cheek. "Hey, my Prince. Are you okay, baby?" she asked.

"Yeah, I'm good, Ma. I'm about to go to work," said Poet.

"Oh, you gotta go to work tonight, huh?" she asked.

Poet looked in the bathroom mirror. "Yeah, Ma, I'm out. You need any money?"

Cheryl stood in the doorway of the bathroom with a look of admiration on her face. She was so proud of her son for stepping up to the plate to help her out.

"Nah, baby, I'm good. Just be careful and call me later, okay?"

Poet kissed his mother one more time. "Okay, Ma. Love you."

"Love you too, Prince Poet."

Poet had been hustling drugs ever since he was sixteen years old because money was desperately needed in their household. He wasn't exactly proud of what he was doing and he felt bad about lying to his mother. But his father's refusal to be there for his family and financially support his own children was the reason that Poet was hustling in the first place.

James Washington's irresponsibility pissed him off so bad that there was no time to think about how devastated his mother would be if she found out the truth about what his job really was. But watching her work so hard to provide them with a roof over their heads, food, and the clothes on their backs had forced Poet to make some illegal moves.

Five minutes later, Poet walked down Rockaway Avenue, making his way to the drug house that he worked in. The "spot," as they called it, was a two-bedroom apartment belonging to Sha-Sha, a local base head, who let them use her place in return for a couple of hits on a crack pipe and a few extra dollars in her pocket. Section Eight paid most of the rent so she didn't have to pay much. Once her four kids were taken away from her by Administration of Children Services, it was definitely downhill from there. The only thing that was important to Sha-Sha was getting that next hit on the crack pipe.

A man named Bone was the ringleader of their operation. A hustler by nature, Bone had grown up in foster homes most of his life. Poverty had forced him to be on his own since he was nine years old. He was taken under the wing of some older hustlers who in turn taught him how to thrive in the business. So at the tender age of thirteen, Bone began his occupation as a drug dealer. Since then, he had become his own boss. If anyone wanted to get any drug money in Brownsville, they looked for Bone because he was the main connection.

Ironically, Bone was a reserved family man and was never really the flashy type. Bone felt that being that way was a lot less problematic than being some big-time baller who was always in the limelight. While so many of his counterparts chose to drive around in a Mercedes-Benz or a Range Rover, he kept it real simple. Having luxury cars and truck jewelry wasn't important to him. He felt that the flamboyant types of dealers were targets for the police and stick-up kids. Fortunately for him, Bone never felt the need to be a superstar like so many other dealers who thrived off the attention.

Bone had always kept it real with himself. He knew that illegal money was temporary and at any time everything that he owned could be gone with the blink of an eye. That's why he always chose to live within his means.

Bone imposed those same types of rules on whoever worked for him. He insisted that they stay out of trouble; he didn't need to bring any more heat to his operation. As far as he knew, everyone had complied with his demands so far.

As Poet headed toward the spot, he looked at the time and realized that he was going to be a few minutes late. He pulled out his cell phone and dialed Bone's number. After several rings, Bone finally picked up the phone.

"What up, Bone? It's me, Po. I'll be there in, like, five minutes," Poet told him.

"No, doubt, I'm here," Bone replied. "I done already started on that package for you. I gotta go meet up with my cousins from Uptown so me and . . . and . . . and . . . um, what's his name?"

"Jeff?" Poet volunteered. Jeff was one of Bone's partners.

"Damn, that's right, Jeff. Jeff is ridin' with me up there. I gotta get them this product. So just come through. I'm at the crib waitin' on you," Bone said, referring to Sha-Sha's apartment.

"A'ight, Bone. I'm there," Poet replied.

While on his way to Bone's spot, Poet walked past the abandoned building on Chester Street for the first time since he had murdered the rapist. He felt a pain shooting in his chest as the memory of that day haunted him.

Not having heard anything about the murder thus far, Poet had an urge to walk inside of the building where the crime occurred but Poet knew better. He knew that he didn't have any business being near the building. It was not the route that he would normally take. But curiosity got the best of him and he couldn't help but wonder if the body was where he had left it. He wondered how bad it had decomposed and how it smelled. It was only after seriously thinking about how much of a risk he was taking if someone just happened to see him coming out of the building that he stopped in his tracks. Poet couldn't take any chances on being connected to the murder.

When Poet finally arrived at the Bristol Street apartment, Bone cracked the door for him to slide in. The apartment was dark because every shade in the house was pulled down over the windows. It was very clean, thanks to them because Sha-Sha wasn't about to clean it. She was too busy with her drug habit.

Poet dropped his North Face knapsack in an armchair in the living room. He slowly walked into the kitchen where Bone was preparing a concoction of crack cocaine. The kitchen was a mess and baking powder was scattered all over the place. Bone ran some cold water in the pot and Poet watched as the hardened, cooked-up cocaine slid out of the pot resembling a small pie. Poet looked at the other "pies" that were neatly stacked up on the kitchen table.

"Damn, Bone!" Poet exclaimed while looking around the small kitchen and the mess Bone had made. "Looks like you were puttin' in a lot of work today."

"They're pretty, aren't they?" Bone asked, admiring his work. "I've been doin' this all day and now I'm tired as hell." Bone finished the last pie and placed it on the table. "Po, bag this stuff up for me, man. Just do these few and hold off on the other joints. Before you go home, go to the Ave and drop this stuff with Preme. He's gonna give you some money for me. It should be like two grand. I want you to take that money and put in your pocket. That's your pay for all your trouble."

Bone put on his jacket and continued with some more instructions for Poet, who was one of his most loyal workers. He liked Poet and saw a lot of hustler potential in the young man.

"I'll be back in like an hour. Pack like three of them kilos for me. I have to go and pick up Jeff by Howard Houses and when I call you, meet me outside with that. You know I don't like goin' near none of them projects with none of my product on me. The block is hot," he added, referring to the police activity in the area.

"Yeah, I know, Bone. I got you, man. I'll have it all wrapped up and ready to go before you get over here."

"My man," Bone said. "That's what I like to hear."

As soon as Bone walked out the door, Poet put on a pair of latex gloves. Poet wrapped up the work for Bone and placed it inside of a duffel bag. Then he sat at the kitchen table and pulled the Gem Star single-edge razors out of his pants pocket. He used the razors to chip away at the cooked-up cocaine. He then put the crack rocks into some small sandwich Baggies and twisted the bags up. Long gone were the plastic vials that the drug used to be stored in.

Twenty minutes later, Poet heard a knock on the door. He removed his brand new gun from the pocket of his Levi jeans. He crept toward the door, making sure that it wasn't anyone suspicious. His heart fluttered, hoping that it wasn't the day that the cops or some thieves would try to force their way into the drug spot. He breathed a sigh of relief when he saw that it was only Mekhi.

"What's good, Po?" Mekhi said as he walked in. "I see that you started without me. I know I'm late."

Poet returned to the kitchen table. "Yeah, you're late, punk. Where have you been?"

"I was at this girl's house, man; some chick I met the other day. You know the one I was tellin' you about? She lives up the hill near Rockaway Avenue."

Poet stopped what he was doing to look at his friend. "Man, didn't you tell me that that girl is like eighteen years old and still in high school? What can she do for you? You have all these older chicks tryin' to get at you and you settle for some teenage broad?"

Mekhi laughed and sat on the opposite end of the table. "Truthfully, I don't have time for older women, Po. We don't have anything in common and all they wanna do is spend my little bit of money. Older women are lookin' for someone to take care of them and how am I gonna do that when I still live with my grandmother?"

Poet smiled. "Well, I got to have me an older chick. I can't mess with these youngsters. My mind is too advanced and my fuck game is too official for these little chickadees out here," he said while stroking the hairs on his chin. "I'll have these young bitches out here tryin' to kill one another over me!" They both laughed.

"Well, I like younger girls," said Mekhi, meaning every bit of what he said. "You can mold them and make them into who you want them to be."

Poet shook his head. "You are crazy, Khi, but whatever floats your boat. Just don't get any of them chickadees pregnant."

Mekhi puffed his chest out. "Nah, man, I keep my Magnum supply on point. I'm not tryin' to have any babies right now!"

Poet and Mekhi continued to package and measure the drugs for the next hour, packing more plastic Baggies full of crack. When Bone called Poet, he ran outside to hand him the duffel bag with the kilos.

Hours later, they managed to finish up everything. After locking up the spot, they made their way to Preme and he handed Poet the $2,000. Mekhi and Poet then caught up with a few of their other friends and hung out for an hour or two. When everyone finally parted ways, it was five-thirty in the morning.

An exhausted Poet stopped at the corner of his block to give Mekhi a pound. All he wanted to do was go upstairs, take a hot shower, and go to bed.

"A'ight, Khi. I'll see you tomorrow, man."

"No doubt. I'll be at the spot early. Bone has some money he has to give me," Mekhi said while yawning loudly.

As Poet made his way toward his building, he noticed two men in the middle of his block tussling with each other. It was early in the morning so no one else was on that block but the three of them. As he got closer, Poet realized that one of the men was elderly. The younger man was getting the best of the older gentleman. Everything was happening so fast and before Poet could rush over to assist, he saw the younger man hit the older man with a gun butt to the forehead. The senior citizen instantly dropped to the ground and the man ran off into the darkness.

"Gimme back my money, sucker!" yelled the old man, who was trying to get off the ground. He looked to be in his late sixties, with a salt-and-pepper beard and a receding hairline. "That motherfucker done stole my whole paycheck!" the man shouted to no one in particular.

"Yo!" Poet called out to the mysterious thief, but it was too late. The rogue had managed to get away.

Poet quickly ran up to the older man. He recognized the old man as Mr. Leroy, who lived in the building across from him. Mr. Leroy was a quiet family man who kept to himself, doted on his many grandchildren, and was a well-respected old-timer in the neighborhood. He would give someone the shirt off his back if he had to.

"Mr. Leroy! Mr. Leroy! What happened?" Poet asked, bending down on one knee to help him sit up.

"Here I was walkin' from the twenty-four-hour check cashin' place from cashin' my Social Security check and John-John done took it upon himself to pull a gun out on me! He done took all of my got-damn money from the check I just cashed! I'll be hot damned!" Mr. Leroy yelled.

The culprit was John-John, a petty thief from the neighborhood, who would steal the underwear off someone's backside if they stood too close to him. Poet figured that John-John must have reached an all-time low by robbing and beating up Mr. Leroy.

Poet helped the man off the ground. It was then that he noticed the huge gash over Mr. Leroy's right eye. The older man was unsteady on his feet so Poet leaned

him against a parked car. He gave Mr. Leroy a bandanna from his pocket and told him to apply pressure
to the gash to stop the bleeding. Then Poet reached
in his other pocket and handed the man $500 of the
$2,000 that he was carrying. Mr. Leroy didn't want to
accept the money but Poet insisted.

Mr. Leroy reluctantly took the money from Poet.
"Boy, where did you get this kinda money? I hope you
ain't dealin' none of them crack rocks! My daughter,
Joyce, got hooked on them crack rocks! Don't you
know that them thangs is killin' our black folks?"

Poet understood what Mr. Leroy was saying but he
was mum about where money came from.

"Nah, Mr. Leroy. I don't deal any drugs," Poet lied.
"I have a job. Now please just take this money. Maybe
that will help you out until you get your next check." He
inspected the gash on Mr. Leroy's forehead. "Do you
wanna call the police?"

Mr. Leroy held his head down. Even though he was
an older man, he knew that there was a code of the
streets that he felt he had to abide by. If he called the
cops and pursued the situation, his family would never
be able to live there in peace. They had nowhere else to
go and he had grandchildren who lived in Brownsville
as well. He wouldn't want to put himself or his family at risk because he had "snitched" to the cops about
what happened to him.

"Now, Poet, you know damn well I ain't callin' no
cops! I might as well just let life get a hold of that John-
John. God don't like ugly and you don't have no good
luck by robbin' and stealin' the way he do! Somebody
gonna get that boy but it ain't gonna be me! I'm too old
for this bullshit."

Poet smiled and patted Mr. Leroy on the back. He
understood how the older man felt when it came to

making a complaint to the cops. But Poet was glad that
Mr. Leroy wasn't getting the police involved. Little did
he know, Poet was going to make sure John-John paid
for what he did.

"Don't worry about it, Mr. Leroy. John-John is gonna
be a'ight. Maybe you should go to Brookdale emergency
room and get that knot on your head checked out."

He placed his hand on Poet's shoulder to steady
himself. "No, baby boy, that's okay. Mr. Leroy is gonna
go upstairs and just be happy that the fool didn't kill
me. Thank you, young man, for what you did. You stay
outta trouble. God bless you."

Mr. Leroy walked away, still holding the handkerchief to his head. Poet stood still for a few moments, as
he watched the senior limp into his building. Mr. Leroy
was like a grandfather to many of the neighborhood
children and Poet was pretty sure that he had looked
out for John-John a time or two. Thinking about what
had just happened to the man; Poet felt his chest
tighten as he thought about what he was going to do
next. Once he got upstairs to his house, he had already
decided that John-John was definitely going to be his
next victim.

Later that afternoon, Precious was walking down
busy Rockaway Avenue on her way from the store. She
was listening to her iPod when Mekhi just happened to
walk up from behind, startling her. She turned around
and smiled as she stared at the flecks of green in his
beautiful eyes.

"What's up, missy?" Mekhi greeted. "Are you on your
way home?"

Precious smirked. "No, I'm off to your house!" she
said flirtatiously.

Mekhi chuckled. He thought that Precious was something else for a girl her age. She always had something witty to say to him.

"Baby girl, you ain't ready to come to my house. Trust me, once you walk through the door, you're not gonna want to leave."

"You don't know what I'll want to do," she replied, flashing that killer smile of hers. "Shoot, you just might not want me to leave!"

Mekhi tilted his head to the side and took in her beauty. Her high cheekbones, her mocha complexion, and the two braided plaits that fell to her shoulders gave her the look of an Indian squaw.

Mekhi waved her off. "Please, Presh, stop actin' like you're a big girl. You know good and damn well that you're still the big V," he said, glaring at Precious's crotch through her tight jeans.

Precious put the grocery bags that she was carrying on the ground and put both of her hands on her hips.

"How do you know that I'm the big V, Mekhi? You don't know what I could do and how good I can do it."

"You know how I know that you're still a virgin?" he asked.

Precious crossed her arms and tapped her foot. "I'm waitin'," she replied.

Mekhi shook his head. "Because you're nothin' but a big tease. I see how you're always tryin' to flirt with me and you haven't made no real attempt to get with me yet. Guess you're waitin' for me to come at you first, huh?" Mekhi said, walking around her and taking a quick glance at her plump derriere.

Precious blushed. She had never known Mekhi to talk to her like that but his straightforwardness excited her.

Precious uncrossed her arms and rolled her eyes at him. "Well, Mekhi, since you're such an expert on virgins, why don't you do somethin' about this virgin right here?"

Before Mekhi could answer her question, he looked up and saw Poet crossing the street. He was walking toward them.

"What's up, Khi? Hey, Presh. Comin' from the supermarket, huh?" he asked his sister, giving Mekhi a pound and looking at her with a frown on his face.

Mekhi and Precious tried to hide their disappointment, hoping that Poet wouldn't pick up on their awkwardness.

Precious sighed. "Yeah, I was on my way home. I just stopped to talk to Mekhi for a minute before I went in the house."

Poet looked at her. "Okay, good for you. Now see you later," he announced, waving her off.

Precious sucked her teeth, picked up the shopping bags, and continued walking down the block. Mekhi did everything in his power to keep from staring at Precious's firm derriere as she walked away from them.

"What were y'all talkin' about?" Poet asked. He trusted his friend but he didn't trust Precious.

Mekhi swallowed hard. He couldn't let Poet find out about his affinity for Precious. "She was just talkin' to me about school and her friends. Nothin' special. You know, Precious has always been like my little sister."

Poet stared at his friend. He hoped that Mekhi wasn't getting any ideas about his so-called "little sister."

"Yeah, okay. I'm just makin' sure. You know I'm hard on her because she's the youngest and you see how she looks. Precious doesn't look like your average sixteen-year old girl. Plus, she's ready to get that butt tapped but I ain't havin' that."

Yeah, and I'm gonna be the one to tap it, Mekhi thought.

Chapter 6

The Dirty Work

That morning, Shareef Oates walked into the Seventy-third Precinct dressed up in one of his many tailor-made suits. One of the requirements when working as a homicide detective was the business attire, and his neat appearance was something that gave him the edge over most detectives who worked in the department. The individuals he questioned on a daily basis respected it as well. How could someone take a detective seriously with a coffee stain on his shirt or an unkempt look about himself? Shareef was on top of his game in his career and he wanted to make sure that he always looked the part.

"Hey, Oates!" Lewis called out.

He was sitting at the tattered desk that they occupied every day. Oates walked over to Lewis and gave him a pound.

"What's up, Lew?" he said, admiring Lewis's pin-striped suit. "Nice threads, bruh."

Lewis looked at himself. "Thanks, man. You know I gotta keep it fresh. Some of these detectives cannot dress! You know we can't be a part of that shit right there," he said, admiring Oates's attire as well.

Oates smiled. "Yeah, you're right. Some of these cats like walking around here looking like fucking Columbo, all wrinkled and shit!" Oates replied. They both laughed loudly. "But I gotta give my man Columbo his props. Even though he wasn't much of a dresser, he knew his detective work."

"True, true," Lewis said, pausing for a moment. "Damn, it was something I had to tell you. What is it?" Lewis paused again, while staring at some paperwork. "Oh, yeah, this is what I had to tell you. This was on my desk first thing this morning. Looks like the body that we discovered the other day came back with some positive fingerprints."

"Positive fingerprints? Why am I not surprised?" Oates replied.

"Yeah, man. This guy was a real loser, too."

Lewis shuffled the papers around and handed some over to Oates so that he could inspect them for himself.

"Okay, the name of the dead bastard was Jerrod Timmons. Notorious felon and sex offender, unregistered sex offender, I might add. Homeless vagabond and crackhead extraordinaire. He did a few years in the joint for sexual abuse, rape in the second degree, sodomy, attempted robbery, I mean, why the fuck was this motherfucker still walking the streets?" Lewis asked.

Oates shrugged his shoulders while looking over Timmons's rap sheet. He stared at the picture and noticed the scar on his cheek.

"Damn, somebody gave him a nasty cut across his face, too. From the looks of this rap sheet, he probably deserved the shit!"

Lewis sighed and shook his head. "You ain't never lied, O."

"Hey, fellas," said a young detective by the name of Detective Vincent Patrone.

He was assigned to the sex crimes unit. Lewis and Oates greeted Patrone with a fist bump. The three men had a lot of respect for each other and even hung out with each other sometimes.

"What's up, Vinny Vin!" exclaimed Oates. "What's good with you?"

Patrone sat in an unoccupied chair and pulled it up to their desks. He had some paperwork in his hands, too.

"I have something for youse guys," Patrone announced. "Remember the fifteen-year-old girl, Erika Majors? She was the teenage girl that was raped in the staircase in Langston Hughes Houses a few weeks ago?" Lewis and Oates nodded their heads. "Well, guess what? We swept that crime scene and, lo and behold, we found a Magnum condom wrapper on the next staircase landing one flight down from where the girl was raped. Come to find out they had the fingerprints and DNA from your guy on it." Patrone looked at the paperwork in his hand. "Mr. Jerrod Timmons."

Lewis and Oates looked at each other. "You gotta be kiddin' me, Vinny," Lewis exclaimed.

Patrone handed Lewis the paperwork. The two homicide detectives looked at the paperwork in amazement.

"It's right here in black and white," Oates stated. He handed the paperwork back to Patrone. "I knew that this shit was gonna be a big case."

Patrone stood up. "When I questioned Erika, she gave me an accurate description of the rapist. One of the things that stood out to her was this huge scar on the right side of this creep's face. The dead man had this same scar in the same place. Looks like the murder of this guy, Timmons, could be a possible revenge killing on our hands."

"Well, the time of death, according to the pathology report, Timmons was killed the exact day that the rape occurred," Lewis stated. "The rape occurred between five-thirty and six A.M. and the killing was between six-fifteen and six forty-five A.M."

The three detectives sat around for another thirty minutes to talk about the new discovery.

When Patrone went back to his office, Oates leaned back in the rickety chair and closed his eyes.

"This shit is crazy, Lew. Where did Timmons go after the rape and who did he run into?"

Lewis shook his head. "You know what I think? Maybe Timmons went to cop some drugs after he committed the rape then maybe he tried to rob some dealer and they put a few in him."

Oates disagreed. "I don't think that Timmons was copping drugs, man. He wouldn't have had any time to do that. We all know the dealers are usually heading back to the house at that time of morning, especially after hustling all night. I believe that somebody followed his black ass and gave him the business after he raped that girl."

Lewis nodded his head in agreement. "That sounds about right. I'm telling you, O, you're the bomb, man."

Oates laughed. "I know I am. You know I'm the brains of this operation!"

Lewis waved him off. "Yeah, you are! But don't get too bigheaded. We haven't solved this case yet."

Oates put his palm on his forehead. "I know," he sighed. "I know."

It was eleven o'clock in the morning when Poet's cell phone rang loudly, waking him up from a nap. He shifted around the comforter to retrieve the phone. He answered it without looking at the caller ID.

"Hello?" he answered.

"What's up, Poet? I haven't seen you in a minute. Where have you been, mister?" said the female on the phone.

Poet sat up in his bed. He recognized the voice. It was Rakiyah, a friend with benefits who wanted to be more than a sex partner to him. She wanted a relationship and Poet was not ready to do that with her or any other woman for that matter. He glanced at his cell phone and saw that she had called him private. Poet sucked his teeth. If he had known that it was a private call, he would have never answered the phone. He hadn't been in the mood for any female company lately.

"Why are you callin' my phone private? You know I don't answer any private calls," he whispered.

"Well, you answered it this time! And plus, I didn't know what else to do, Poet! You haven't called me in the last couple of weeks and I was just wonderin' what was goin' on with you! You used to speak to me every day!"

Poet yawned. Considering all of the things that he had been through, he didn't have time for Rakiyah's complaining.

"Raki, look, I've been goin' through some things, man. I haven't had the time to be lollygaggin' on the phone with anybody."

Rakiyah paused. "You know what, Poet?" she said with an attitude. "I'm tired of bein' the one chasin' your young ass! I'm a grown-ass woman! If you wanna spend half of your life laid up in your momma's house, then go ahead. And I'm not gonna be sweatin' you, tryin' to get you to pay me some attention. I know plenty of dudes who would jump at the—" she said.

Poet stopped her midsentence. "Yeah, I know, I know there are plenty of dudes that would jump at the opportunity to be with you! Well, I'm gonna stop you right there. First of all, I never said that I was your man! When you started talkin' about me movin' in with you, I was buggin' out because at that time we had only been dealin' with each other for like two months! That was a turn-off! You don't know me from a can of paint but yet you want me to move in with you and your daughter? I could be a murderer, for all you know!"

Rakiyah laughed. "Please, Poet! If I don't know anything else, I know that you ain't no killer! I mean, what the hell, you live with your momma and your little sisters and you claim to have some little bullshit night job cleanin' office buildings! So let's stop it, okay? You're not killin' nobody!"

Poet shook his head in annoyance. It was obvious that Rakiyah cared too much about what she wanted to really digest what he was trying to say to her. She was so preoccupied with having him as her man. What she didn't realize was that she could very well be involved with someone who was dangerous.

As Rakiyah continued her rant, Poet put his phone on speaker while he straightened up his room. Every word that she uttered went in one ear and out the other. He finally picked up the phone again after five minutes of her ranting and raving.

Poet had too much on his mind to listen to Rakiyah's nagging. "Can you please just shut the hell up?" he screamed into the phone. "I'm gonna come over there today, a'ight? Damn!" He couldn't see her face but he knew that she was smiling. "Are you at home right now?"

Rakiyah calmed down instantly. "Yeah, I'm at home and I'm here by myself. Fallon is at my mother's house," she said, referring to her daughter.

"Well, I'm gettin' in the shower. Come and pick me up in about an hour. Okay?"

Rakiyah laughed. She was ready for him. "Yeah, whatever! I'm not comin' anywhere!"

Poet sucked his teeth. "Raki, don't play with me, girl. Just be here in an hour."

"Yeah, whatever," she replied.

Rakiyah hung up the phone and Poet shook his head as he ran the water for a shower. He had been on edge since the killing and maybe a nice piece of ass was what he needed to get his head right.

After the hour had passed, Poet looked at the caller ID on his ringing cell phone and smiled. After seeing Rakiyah's car double-parked in front of his building, something in his mind clicked. Why would he want to cut off an independent, self-sufficient woman who was obviously ready to do anything that he asked her to do? Poet figured that he might as well hold on to Rakiyah for a little while longer because from the looks of things, she would be more of an asset to him than a liability.

Poet tucked his gun inside of the waistband of his jeans. He planned on handling his business with Rakiyah, then after their sexual romp he would get the keys to her car to come back to Brownsville. He had more important business to tend to.

Once he was downstairs, Poet climbed into the passenger side of Rakiyah's late-model Toyota Corolla. She was smiling from ear to ear.

"You better had come to pick me up!" Poet said, playfully.

He kissed her on the lips and put his hand between her legs. He knew that Rakiyah loved his attention and that was all he needed to do to shut her up.

Rakiyah giggled and pushed his hand away. "Whatever, Poet!" she said, sounding like a teenage girl instead of the adult woman she was.

Poet settled into his seat and reached for the *Daily News* from the back seat. He skimmed through the news articles when he suddenly got stuck on one in particular. As he read it, he realized that they had an article about the rape in his building and the murder of the rapist. Poet felt his chest tighten up. Rakiyah looked at him strangely.

"Poet, are you all right?" she asked, taking her eyes off the road to glance at him. "Why are you so quiet all of sudden? You look a little pale in the face."

"Nah, it ain't nothin'," he replied, forgetting that he wasn't alone. "I'm good. Just readin' the paper."

Poet continued to read the article. The body had finally been found. The man was identified as a sex offender by the name of Jerrod Timmons.

"What are you readin', Poet?" Rakiyah asked, trying to peek over his shoulder as her car sat idling at a stoplight.

"Nothin' special," Poet replied. He thought it was strange that he had not heard anything about the killing from anyone in the neighborhood, and now here it was in the paper.

They continued the rest of their ride to Rakiyah's East New York residence in silence. Poet glared out the passenger window, wondering if the cops were on to the killer yet. His heart was beating so fast, he felt as if it were about to come out of his chest. Yet and still, the irresistible urge to make John-John pay for his thievery was stronger than ever. But this time, revenge wasn't the only thing on Poet's mind—murder had become his fetish.

Chapter 7

On The Low

Three hours later, Mekhi arose from his bed, waking up with a terrible headache. He looked at the clock. It was two o'clock on a Sunday afternoon to be exact. The nights that were being spent in Bone's stash house were killing him. He was never one to put in the hard work when it came to the hustle game but he loved the money, which was his main motivation for doing it.

Through his cracked window, he could hear the sounds of the ghetto: the police and ambulance sirens, people arguing directly under his window, and children outside playing. He closed the window and pulled down the shades. He wasn't in the mood for the noise. Then he slowly dragged himself to the bathroom.

No one was in the house that afternoon and he was happy about that. His grandmother, Miss Addie, had always kept a houseful of grandchildren. Mekhi had lived with her since he was eleven years when his mother, Dana, realized that she was fed up with the hostile environment that they lived in.

Growing up, Mekhi knew that his mother was nothing like some of the mothers of his close friends. Their mothers were ghetto fabulous with their colored hair weaves and acrylic nails. Mekhi was embarrassed by Dana's bohemian dressing, her thick natural hair, and her proper English. Dana was an artist and she was always very eccentric. She tried to force her son to live the same type of lifestyle but Mekhi resisted. He was not interested in sitting in someone's theater with his mother's buppie friends and their children. Learning about other cultures was not important to him.

The day that his mother decided to leave Brownsville behind, Mekhi cried his heart out for Dana. Although he was resentful of his mother's strange lifestyle, Mekhi was happy when she allowed him to stay with her mother.

The family thought that Dana had lost her everlasting mind when she wanted to take her only child on a cross-country excursion with her. Only Mekhi's grandmother was not having it. She insisted that her grandchild remain in Brooklyn with her and tried to talk her oldest daughter out of moving away. A few months later, before Dana ran off with some Caucasian artist, she pleaded with her son to come with her. Mekhi refused to leave Brooklyn and his beloved grandmother.

The last time he talked to his mother was five years before. She told him that she was living somewhere in Nevada. Dana even asked him if he would consider moving there with her. Of course, Mekhi refused. What his mother did and how she lived was not his concern.

Even though Dana had been separated from him for some years, Mekhi noticed that he had a lot of his mother's peculiar ways. He fought his artistic side tooth and nail because it reminded him so much of her. But at times he just couldn't resist his creativity. He even had several paintings hidden in his room; beautiful pieces that he was afraid to reveal to anyone because his own talent mystified him.

Returning to his bedroom, Mekhi climbed back into bed. Just as he was about to doze off again, he was startled by a small pebble hitting his window. He hopped out of the bed to see what was going on.

To his surprise, it was Precious standing outside. "Hey, Mekhi," she said with a wide grin on her face.

"Hey, what's up, Presh?" he asked with a stunned look on his face. "What are you doin' outside of my window?"

"Can I come upstairs?"

Precious's eyes widened at the sight of Mekhi's bare chest.

Mekhi was hesitant. "I dunno about that, Presh. What do you wanna come up here for?"

Her attitude changed. "You can find out once I get up there. Are you gonna let me come upstairs or what? "

Mekhi looked around to see if anyone saw them talking to each other in front of his window.

"A'ight. Come on up. Ain't nobody home anyway."

Precious smiled and walked into the building. She nervously walked up the stairs to Mekhi's second-floor apartment. When she arrived on his floor, he was standing there with the door wide open. There wasn't much to say; they both knew why she was there.

"Are you sure ready to do this, Precious?" he asked. "Remember, I'm not of them little boys that you be runnin' around the way with. I'm a grown man and I'm your brother's best friend. So don't leave here and start talkin' our business to any of your friends. We don't need nothin' to get back to your brother."

Precious shook her head and took off her jacket. She swallowed hard and looked at him with a serious glare.

"I'm ready for this, Mekhi. I've been ready for a while now. The question is are you ready?" she asked.

Mekhi looked down at his swollen penis, and then he looked at her. It was protruding through his boxers and Precious was staring at it. He was bigger than what she had ever seen before.

He took her face in his hands and began kissing her passionately. "I've been ready, girl. You just don't know."

They kissed for a few minutes, and then Mekhi picked Precious up and carried her in the back to his bedroom, locking the door behind him. He lay on top of her and began removing her clothing, piece by piece. Precious's heart was beating a mile a minute, knowing that there was no reason for her to be there.

Mekhi reached the Magnum condom that was in the top drawer of his nightstand and put it on. Precious lay there with her legs open and her eyes closed, clueless as to what to do next.

Mekhi pushed his penis inside Precious's virgin pussy slowly as she put her hands over her mouth to keep from screaming. When he began to kiss her again, she had totally forgotten about the pain. He continued to enter her, not forcing it at all and going at her pace. Precious was a little uncomfortable at first but after looking into Mekhi's beautiful green eyes, she knew that she was falling in love.

Meanwhile, he instructed her on how to make love to him.

"Move your hips a little bit, Presh, don't be scared, baby," he whispered.

"But it hurts," she whined.

"I'm sorry, baby, I'm so sorry. I don't wanna hurt you," he replied while kissing her on the neck.

After a few minutes, it began feeling real good to Precious. Mekhi told her to wrap her legs around him. When she did this, he submerged himself inside of her sugar walls and ground even harder than before. Suddenly, Precious began to have an orgasm. Never experiencing that feeling before, she thought she was about to have a heart attack. Mekhi smiled as he watched her eyes roll into the back of head. When he finally came, he collapsed on top of her. They stayed in the mission-ary position for a short time after, shocked that they had actually had sex with each other.

"Mekhi, I, I didn't know that it was gonna feel like that," Precious whispered. She couldn't even open her eyes. "It hurt so bad and felt so good at the same time."

Mekhi rolled off of Precious and onto his back. He took off the condom and flinched at the remnants of Precious's virgin blood on the latex. He wrapped it in a tissue and threw it in the garbage pail that was next to his bed.

"Damn. I feel bad, though. You're my man's little sister. I knew you all your life."

Precious sat up and wiped her vagina with a dark towel. "Mekhi, don't spoil the mood. I'll be sixteen next week and I'm very mature for my age. My brother don't have to know shit about what we're doin' with each other. I'm not sayin' anything. Are you?" she asked, poking out her lips.

Mekhi sighed. "I'm not sayin' nothin'! But I'm gonna say this. We can't stop doin' this, Presh. I've been checkin' you out for a minute and I don't wanna lose this."

Precious laughed. "Who said I was goin' to stop?"

Mekhi sighed again. One thing he did know, he had to keep their interlude a secret. He silently prayed that Precious would keep her mouth shut.

"Well, Poet can't find out, Presh, which means don't be tellin' your girlfriends about what we're doin' with each other, especially Malika, with her big-ass mouth!" Mekhi warned.

Precious sucked her teeth. "Are you crazy? I wouldn't tell anyone about me and you. My brother would have a fit. My mother would kill me! My friends, who all have the biggest crush on you and my brother, would be hatin' on me so much they would definitely try to put it out there! I don't want that to happen."

Mekhi turned over and begin kissing Precious. He felt himself rising to the occasion once again and they began making love for a second time.

Later that evening, at Rakiyah's apartment, with R. Kelly's "Your Body's Callin'" playing in the background, Poet watched in awe as his dick went in and out of Rakiyah's wet pussy. He closed his eyes, relishing the moment, as she moaned softly in his ear. He continued to stroke her slowly, while she squeezed his muscular ass. Rakiyah tightened her pussy around Poet's rod. His body began to shake as she continued to stroke upward. She wanted Poet to cum inside of her.

Poet felt himself about to ejaculate and immediately pulled out. His potent sperm spewed all over Rakiyah's ample breasts. She immediately sat up with her arms spread out.

"Poooeet!" she yelled. "Why do you always have to cum on me and not in me?"

Poet fell back on the queen-sized bed, exhausted from their session. "Why don't you ever just shut the hell up, Rakiyah? This is not the time! Damn!"

"Why would you shoot your cum all on me, Poet? Why do you be disrespectin' me like this?" she asked, looking down at the semen on her chest. "Disgustin'!"

She climbed out of bed with an attitude and scurried to the bathroom to wash up. Poet closed his eyes for a brief second, trying to capture a moment for himself. He had too many other things on his mind to concern himself with Rakiyah's foolishness. At the rate he was going, having a baby or being in a relationship with anyone was definitely out of the question.

Rakiyah came out of the bathroom with a warm washcloth and wiped off his penis. After a few minutes of listening to Rakiyah's mouth, Poet managed to pull himself out of bed and get dressed.

Rakiyah stopped nagging when she saw that Poet was putting his clothes on. "Where are you goin' now?"

He looked at her. "Man, I've been here all day! Do you honestly think I'm gonna sit around here and listen to your shit all night? You haven't done nothin' but complain since you fuckin' called me!"

Rakiyah sat on the bed and sighed. "I'm sorry, Po . . . I just . . . I just wanna be with you and whenever we get a chance to finally spend time together, I just don't know what else to do but argue. I'm just so frustrated."

"When we spend time together, why don't you make the best of it? Every time I come around, here you go with the beefin'. My thing is, I'm goin' through a lot right now, a lot of shit that I can't talk about and to tell you the truth, I don't need to be around no complainin' ass, whiny broad. If you don't cut it out, I'm gonna cut your ass off. So you need to take me the way I am or leave me alone."

Poet walked over to Rakiyah and pulled her naked body close to him. After his speech, he realized that he may never be the man Rakiyah deserved. Poet had a skeleton in his closet that could possibly come back to haunt him. She didn't need to be involved with someone like him.

"Listen," Poet whispered in her ear. "Just let me hold the keys to your car. I have to make a quick run. I'm back over here when I'm done, okay?"

Rakiyah wiped the tears off of her face and walked over to the nightstand. She gave Poet her car keys and climbed back into her bed.

Five minutes later, Poet was dressed and in the car. He was headed back toward his neighborhood. About fifteen minutes later, Poet found himself driving down Junius Street, looking for John-John. It was almost 8:00 P.M. and he knew that in a few hours he was going to have to head to Sha-Sha's crib, so he didn't have long to carry out his deed.

The number three train roared loudly on the elevated tracks above the dark street. Poet pulled Rakiyah's car over into a parking spot on Livonia Avenue, got out, and locked the door. He figured that he would fare better if he looked for John-John on foot.

As Poet walked toward Van Dyke Houses, he found exactly who he was searching for. It was John-John, who was standing nearby the building that he lived in. He had on an iPod that he'd probably stolen from somebody—everyone who knew John-John also knew that the man paid for nothing. He was rapping so loudly with the headphones in his ear that he didn't hear or even see Poet sneaking up behind him with his gun drawn. Poet wasn't going to give John-John the opportunity to see him coming. He pulled out the gun and put it to the nape of John-John's skinny neck, immediately pulling the trigger. The rogue fell forward on his face so hard, Poet could have sworn that he heard his skull crack on the pavement. John-John's blood was all over Poet's hands and brain matter was splattered on the upturned cuff of his dark denim jeans and the colorful Nike sneakers that were on his feet.

Poet stood by a moment and watched as John-John's body jerked violently. He had a smile on his face as he shot John-John in the head one more time while he was on the ground. A car alarm went off in the distance, prompting Poet to run through the dark streets, leaving John-John's lifeless body lying in a pool of blood on the sidewalk. After he was a few feet away from the body, Poet began walking briskly through the projects. He shoved the gun into his jeans pocket and decided that he would come back for Rakiyah's car later. He didn't want to take a chance on anyone seeing him pull off in it.

When Poet finally arrived at Mekhi's building, he couldn't believe his luck. Poet was happy that he didn't run into anyone before he made it to a safe place. Now he knew that he had to get it together before going upstairs to Mekhi's house. He didn't want to arouse anyone's suspicions.

Poet stepped into the staircase of the building and took off his navy blue jacket. He wiped John-John's blood off his face, hands, and sneakers with it. Then he calmly picked the brain matter off the hem of his dark denim jeans and uncuffed them. After making sure that he was cleaned up, Poet threw the bloodied jacket down the garbage chute.

Still amped up from the murder, Poet gave himself about ten minutes before he knocked on the door. Much to his dismay, Mekhi's grandmother, Miss Addie, opened it, greeted Poet a kiss on the cheek, and invited him inside.

"Hey, Poet, baby!" she said with a smile. "How are you feelin'?"

Poet watched as Miss Addie, who was a short, big-boned woman, waddle in front of him. "Mekhi is in his bedroom. You hear how loud he's playin' that music, right?"

Poet laughed. "Yes, I do!" He watched as Miss Addie fell back onto the couch. "How are you feelin' today, Miss Addie?" he asked.

Miss Addie slid back onto the sofa. She was watching Law & Order on the fifty-inch big screen television that her children had purchased for her last Christmas.

"I'm doin' pretty good, baby. My pressure is under control because I've been tryin' to eat right. Lord knows I miss me some fried chicken but I've been okay. How are my girls?" she asked, referring to Poet's mother and his sisters.

"They're fine, Miss Addie. They're fine." Poet paused for a moment. "Okay, Miss Addie, I'm gonna go in the room with Khi now. Good night."

Miss Addie's eyes were fixed on the television set. "Okay, baby. If you want somethin' to eat, help yourself."

"I'm good, Miss Addie. Thank you, though."

Poet knocked on Mekhi's door and the music was instantly turned down. Mekhi didn't open the door, thinking that it was just his grandmother.

"Yo, Khi, open the door," Poet ordered.

Mekhi swung the door open. When Poet stepped inside of his room, the first thing that he saw was the beautiful portrait of a woman. He knew that it was his friend's work.

Poet sat on the edge of Mekhi's bed. He tilted his head to the side while looking at the portrait. "Yo, Khi, who is that picture of? That girl looks a lot like Precious," Poet said.

Mekhi didn't look at him. "This female I know. You don't know her," he hesitantly replied. "But it's not finished yet."

"Word? It looks good though." Poet frowned. "It's funny how my little sister looks so much like the person that you painted, right?"

Mekhi looked at the picture and decided to finish it later. Little did Poet know, it was a picture of Precious. He felt even guiltier now that Poet was standing in his bedroom. His heart skipped a beat, thinking about the indecency that had occurred in his bedroom earlier that day with Poet's little sister.

Poet turned around and his eyes went straight to the condom wrappers on the nightstand by Mekhi's bed.

"Yeah! My boy was gettin' busy up in here!" he said excitedly.

Mekhi walked to his window and looked outside. He tried to change the subject. "Damn, what's up with all the cop cars? Somethin' must have happened."

Poet had mentally drowned out the sounds of police sirens. He knew exactly what happened.

"What else is new? So who was the female you had sex with, the same female in the picture?" Poet asked, ignoring Mekhi's comment about the police.

Mekhi swallowed nervously while putting the canvas and easel away in his closet.

"You don't know her, she's not from around here," Mekhi lied. He diverted his attention from Poet's watchful eye.

Poet shook his head. "Damn, we're keepin' secrets from each other now?" he asked, even though he was holding back some vital information from Mekhi as well. "You know we always tell each other everything."

Mekhi looked at Poet. "Well, you might not meet this one. She doesn't want anybody to know about her. She's a married woman," Mekhi said, telling another lie.

Poet put his hand over his mouth. "For real? She must be an older woman if she's married and all that! How old is she?"

Mekhi continued to lie with a smile on his face. "She's thirty years old with one kid and she's a cool chick," Mekhi began, wiping his sweaty hands on his T-shirt. "She's pretty and she's mad funny and easy to talk to."

Poet pointed at him and laughed. "See? I told you, man. Older chicks are the shit. Does she have any money?"

"Well, yeah, I guess she does. She works for some law firm in Manhattan and she says that her husband is borin' her to death. She told me that she needed a young thug like me in her life!" Mekhi exclaimed.

"Damn! Where did you meet her?" Poet asked, a little envious of his friend.

"I was in the city meetin' my Aunt Sharon at her job when I saw her comin' out of Starbucks." Mekhi threw some Nike boots on his feet. "But forget about all of that. What's up for tonight? Are we gonna go to Bone's spot or what?"

"Hell, yeah! I definitely need some money. After we finish baggin' the rest of that work, maybe we can roll out to a club or somethin'."

Mekhi looked at Poet and grinned. "C'mon now, you know damn well you're not gettin' into a club in Manhattan! You're under twenty-one and I'm not goin' to no teenybopper spot with their juice bars!" Mekhi announced with a laugh.

Poet was annoyed. "Fuck you, man!" he replied as Mekhi continued to laugh. "Well, I got Rakiyah's car. We could find somethin' to get into."

Mekhi's eyebrows shot up. "Word, you got Raki's car? That's what's up!"

After Mekhi got himself together, the friends made their way to Rakiyah's parked car. Poet was still hesitant to tell Mekhi what he had done.

As they got closer to the car, they noticed the large group of spectators that had gathered at the corner of Junius Street and Livonia Avenue.

"Damn, I wonder what happened over there? Somebody must have got killed," Mekhi said, stretching his neck to see what was going on. "Wanna go over there and see what's goin' on?"

Poet shook his head and waved his hand at the crowd of onlookers. "Aw, man, we don't need to go over there. Let's just be out," he replied.

Someone walked away from the crowd and Mekhi stopped the man. "Yo, what happened over there?" he inquired, as Poet walked off.

"Oh, yeah, you know that thievin' ass John-John?" the guy asked. Mekhi nodded his head. "Well, somebody done finally caught up to him and killed his ass! Looks like he done robbed the wrong somebody this time!" The man quickly walked away.

Mekhi looked down the block and saw that cops were still coming from everywhere. Poet was already waiting in the car when he climbed into the passenger seat.

"Damn, somebody killed John-John!" Mekhi said. "That's somethin'! That dude done got away with shit for years and nothing ever happened to him. Shoot, I used to think that John-John was one of the luckiest bastards ever. He did so much shit to so many people and yet he was still walkin' around like it was nothin'. I guess people out here ain't playin' no more, huh?"

"Oh, well, God don't like ugly. John-John has been a thief all his life and he had it comin' to him. Guess today was his judgment day," Poet casually replied without a bit of remorse.

Poet immediately pulled off, careful not to go anywhere near the crime scene. Mekhi sighed loudly as they drove away. He would have never guessed that John-John's killer was sitting right in the driver's seat of the car that they were in.

Chapter 8

Chance Meeting

Oates was awakened by the sounds of dogs barking in the yard of the house behind him. He swung his legs over the side of the bed and realized that his head was pounding him from lack of sleep. As he reached for the Advil bottle tucked away in the drawer of his nightstand, he smiled, thinking about how much fun he had at the party the night before.

Oates and Lewis pulled into a parking space not too far from the place they were going to party. It was the night that they were looking forward to. Both men had their own reasons for coming to the party of the year.

Lewis was a married man but that union was on its last leg. After about a year of living in different households, both he and his wife decided to part ways. Oates, who had been divorced for the last eight years, was looking to settle down with someone. He was hoping to meet someone decent at the party.

The Twenty-fifth Precinct always threw some great events. Every year, law enforcement personnel, uniformed and civilian, anticipated attending those events. The liquor was abundant and so were the men and women, who were gainfully employed by some of the most important agencies in New York City. Whether you wanted to meet that someone special or just have a good time, the Twenty-fifth Precinct events were definitely the places to go.

Oates and Lewis walked in the Armory, which was already packed and jumping with patrons. As they walked through the crowd, they were treated like celebrities by their colleagues and women alike, who knew all about the Seventy-third Precinct "Supreme Team." They were known for working on some of the most notorious homicide cases in the city and their work was commended throughout the five boroughs. They were there for five minutes when Lewis made a beeline for the bar. He was happy that he was able to drink because Oates was going to be the designated driver for the night.

"Man, I'm gonna walk over there to that bar to get me some of that truth serum," Lewis said, referring to alcohol. "You know I need my medicine!"

Oates laughed. "Well, you go right ahead, young man! I'm goin' to get my dance on. This music is the business!" he replied, doing a two-step to the old-school music that the deejay was playing.

After Lewis got his drinks from the open bar, the partners went their separate ways. As Oates made his way through the crowd, he ran into a few of his old cronies and some NYPD civilian employees he hadn't seen in years.

"Hey, Mr. Shareef Oates!" shouted an attractive woman, who obviously knew Oates well enough to call out his whole name. "I haven't seen your black ass in these parts in a minute!"

Oates laughed at her and gave the pretty woman a hug. "Hey, Brigitte! I haven't seen you around in a while either! What's up?"

Brigitte smiled at him while she nursed her third Thug Passion drink. "Nothin', boy! What's up with you? I heard that you and your boy, Lewis, are doing y'all thing over there in Brownsville!"

Oates shook his head. "Yeah, yeah, we're trying to anyway. How's One Police Plaza?" he asked, referring to the police headquarters where Brigitte worked.

She sighed. "It's cool but you know I miss the precincts. It ain't no action where I'm at. I miss the different people that I use to see while working in the precincts. It's so damn boring in Police Plaza!"

Oates smiled again. "I can imagine. But it's good that you went to headquarters, Brigitte. It's always room for growth there."

"Yeah, you're right. By the way, I was promoted to senior police administrative aide!"

"For real? That's good, sweetheart! I'm proud of you!"

Brigitte flung her long hair over her shoulder. "Thanks, babe." Brigitte invited her other girlfriends over to meet Oates. "These are my friends, Shareef. They're police administrative aides too. Shareef, this is Cheryl Washington and this is Zahariah Dixon. Ladies, this is Shareef Oates. Detective Shareef Oates," she said, while winking at the both of the ladies.

Oates politely shook their hands. "How are y'all ladies doing this evening?" he asked.

They each shook his hand and greeted him with a smile. As he was checking out Brigitte's friends he realized that they were some really nice-looking women, as well.

"Oh, yeah," Brigitte began. "By the way, Cheryl lives in Brownsville. She doesn't live too far from where you're stationed," she said, nudging him in the ribs with her elbow.

Oates looked at Cheryl. She looked very sexy in her outfit and obviously had some great fashion sense, with her cute mini-dress and four-inch heels on. Her hair was in big curls that dropped to her shoulders and her makeup was perfect, too. He thought that she was very attractive. Oates figured that she may have been around the same age as him even though she looked younger.

"Now how do you know that I wanted Detective Oates to know my business, Brigitte?" exclaimed Cheryl in a joking manner. "You know she loves to tell people's business, Mr. Oates!"

He laughed. "Call me Shareef, Mrs. Washington."

"And you can call me Cheryl."

Brigitte and Zahariah conveniently slid off and left the two standing there alone. Cheryl looked around for her friends.

"Now where did they go?" she asked herself. She looked back at Oates. "Well, they went off somewhere. They'll be back, I guess."

Oates smiled at Cheryl. He sensed her awkwardness with him. "You're fine, I don't bite, sweetie," he said. "Would you like to dance?"

Cheryl blushed and took Oates's hand. He led her onto the dance floor and ended up being with her until it was time for everyone to leave. After meeting her, Oates was not interested in meeting anyone else.

The party went on until four in the morning. By the end of the night, he had exchanged numbers with Cheryl. Oates would have loved to have driven her home but he remembered that he had Lewis with him.

"Would you mind calling me when you get home?" Oates asked. "I just wanna make sure that you get inside your apartment safely."

Cheryl smiled. Her beautiful pixie face glowed in the street light. "Sure, Shareef. I will call you."

"If you don't mind me asking, how old are you?" Oates inquired.

"Well," Cheryl sighed. "I'm going to be thirty-eight years old in July and I have three children. My son is almost twenty-one, I have a daughter who is eighteen, and another daughter who will be sixteen next week."

Oates nodded his head. "Oh, okay. You have grown-ups. I have a nineteen-year-old daughter myself. She's in her sophomore year in college."

"Wow, good for her! You have only one daughter, huh? That must be nice." Cheryl paused. "Can I ask you something?" Oates nodded his head. "Do you have a problem with dating a woman that lives in the projects?" she asked with a flirtatious look on her face.

Oates shook his head. He had a good time with Cheryl and he didn't need her crushing his hopes of getting with her. Oates figured that Cheryl was probably a little intimidated by the fact that he was a detective. He had to let her know that she didn't need to feel like that around him.

Oates held her hand. "Cheryl, you're a very attractive woman and I don't care anything about where you live! I don't care that you have three children. Shit, I wasn't born with a silver spoon in my mouth so who am I to judge you? You just seem like you're a nice person and I wanna get to know you better. If you let me, I want to take you out in the near future."

She smiled. "Okay," she whispered shyly.

Oates continued, "And it's not like you have small children. I mean, you can hang out, can't you?" Cheryl nodded her head. "Okay. If it's any consolation, I'm thirty-nine years old and I'm not into playing games. In other words, I'm a grown-ass man in every sense of the word. You'll see."

Cheryl smiled seductively and looked Oates up and down. "I can see that you're a grown-ass man and I will definitely call you when I get home, okay?"

Oates gave Cheryl a warm hug and watched as she sashayed to Brigitte's car. She waved back at him as they pulled off. When Oates walked to his truck, Lewis was asleep in the passenger seat with his mouth wide open. He laughed at his partner as he started up his vehicle and pulled off.

Oates shuffled off to the kitchen to get some water to take with his aspirin. Thinking about Cheryl had stopped the pounding in his head but he took the Advil anyway. After that, he went to his bedroom and climbed back into bed. He wanted to get some rest before they called him in for a new assignment. Working at the Seventy-third Precinct, anything could happen in the blink of an eye.

Chapter 9

Can't Change The Past

It was eight o'clock Monday morning when Precious was awakened from a deep slumber and it was the beginning of spring break from school. Precious was thankful that she had no statewide tests to take until later on in the week. Her body was aching and sore, stemming from the aftereffects of having sexual intercourse for the very first time.

She had to admit that although the sex with Mekhi was sort of spontaneous, it had been very special for her, or so she thought. It was everything that she hoped it would be and more. She had been thinking about Mekhi from the moment that she left his house the afternoon before and did everything in her power to keep from running back and forth to his apartment.

Precious didn't want to be too overzealous, afraid that it would only turn Mekhi off. Not only would that show her immaturity, it would only fuel curiosity among her peers and her family. But so far, Precious didn't have any regrets about what happened between the two of them.

"What's wrong with you? Why are you movin' all slow like you're in pain or somethin'?" Porsha asked.

Precious sucked her teeth. "What are you talkin' about, Porsha?" Precious retorted. "Why are you watchin' me anyway? Don't you have some of your own business to tend to?"

Porsha rolled her eyes at her. "I was just askin' you out of concern. You don't have to get all nasty with me. It just looks like you're in pain, that's all."

"Don't worry about me, Porsha. I'm okay, a'ight?" She got up from the bed to walk to the closet.

Porsha shrugged her shoulders. "It looks like you done went and had you some sex. I mean, look at you. You're even walkin' differently!" She giggled.

Precious turned around and looked at Porsha strangely. "What do you know about somebody havin' some sex? You don't know what you're talkin' about!"

Porsha slid into her jeans. "Trust me, I know, girl. I'm not a virgin my damn self."

Precious eyes widened with curiosity. "You're not a virgin? When did this happen?"

Porsha smiled. "It's been about a year now."

"Damn. Ain't this about a bitch? Miss Innocent isn't virgin."

Porsha shushed her. "First of all, I'm not any kind of innocent. I'm just a private person. And do not be tellin' anybody my business, neither. Nobody knows about this. Not even Mommy," she said, nervously glancing at the bedroom door. "And I'm on the Pill."

"You're on the Pill? Where did you get birth control pills from?" Precious whispered.

"From the Planned Parenthood clinic. Where else would I get the Pill from? I am not stupid! I got my birth control pills because even though I use condoms, I am not tryin' to get pregnant. Condoms do break. You think I wanna end up like Mommy with three kids and no man? Hell no! I gotta have myself together before I have me some babies."

Precious shook her head. She was surprised that Porsha had shared that information with her. They always had separate friends and lives. Now they had something in common. She still wasn't comfortable enough to reveal her secret to Porsha, though.

Precious smiled. "Well, Porsha, thanks for keepin' it real with me. I haven't tried to do anything yet but when I do, I'll let you know. Trust me, I'm gonna need some advice."

Porsha opened the bedroom door. She was on her way to a morning class at her college and she didn't want to be late.

"Well, if you are doin' your thing, remember to protect yourself. Make him wear that condom. It's a lot of STDs out there."

Precious nodded her head. "I will definitely do that."

Precious heard the apartment door close and she lay back on the bed. She was in no mood to do anything that day but be with Mekhi. She thought about his sweet lips and how much she wanted to kiss them. Instead of sitting around the house all day, she decided that she was going to do just that. Precious found the energy to get out of bed and get dressed.

About twenty minutes later, Mekhi turned over in his bed when he suddenly heard a familiar tap on his window. He thought that he was imagining things and when he heard it again, he climbed out of his bed and walked over to the window. Mekhi pulled back the curtain. Precious was standing outside. Looking at the clock, he saw that it was eight forty-five in the morning. He sighed and reluctantly opened his bedroom window. He knew that if Precious continued to come to his house unannounced, they were going to get caught.

"Girl, what are you doin' here so early in the morning? Don't you have to go to school or somethin'?" Mekhi said. "You must want somebody to catch you sneakin' over here!"

Precious sulked. "I couldn't help myself—I just wanted to see you, Mekhi," she replied.

Mekhi gave the signal for her to come upstairs. When she walked in his house, she draped her arms around his shoulders. He calmly pushed her off.

"Yo, Presh, you can't be comin' over here like this," he announced. "The pop-up nonsense ain't cool."

"Yeah, but now we can spend the whole day together," she replied.

Mekhi looked at Precious with the dead serious look on his face. "I don't want you to get into any trouble because I damn sure ain't tryin' to have no problems when I wanna see you."

Precious crossed her arms. "Do you know what I had to go through to get over here? Luckily, my mother is at work and Poet is still sleepin'. I don't have any school this week because its spring break and Poet doesn't even know that I left the house."

Mekhi ran his fingers through Precious's long hair. "Look, Presh, if you don't stop poppin' up over here, we're gonna get caught. At least call me first. We can't take any chances if we want to continue to see each other, right?"

Precious leaned against the wall. She didn't want to leave but Mekhi was making her feel bad about coming over unannounced.

"A'ight, I'll go back home this time," she said, walking out the door.

Having second thoughts about her leaving, Mekhi decided to pull her back inside the house and into his bedroom.

Meanwhile, Poet finally managed to drag himself out of bed. He was exhausted and had plans on staying in bed for the most of the day until it was time to go to Bone's spot later that night. After sitting around for a few minutes, Poet managed to get up and wash his face. After doing that, he lazily shuffled into the kitchen. He pulled some eggs and bacon out of the refrigerator to prepare breakfast for himself.

While eating his meal, his latest victim, John-John, came to mind. As long as he could remember, John-John had been single-handedly terrorizing their neighborhood for years, beginning his thieving spree by taking pedal bikes from children back in the early nineties. Poet figured that now that John-John was dead, it wasn't like the rotten scoundrel would be missed. Even the man's own mother couldn't stand the sight of her thieving offspring.

When he witnessed John-John robbing Mr. Leroy, all he envisioned was his own mother becoming a victim of the thief's wrath. Poet knew that he couldn't allow that to happen so John-John had to go.

As Poet ate his breakfast, he thought about how he killed John-John. When he committed his first murder, he was awakened by cold sweats and nightmares. But now he was the hunter and they were the prey.

Walking to his room, he heard the phone ring and ran to the living room to answer it.

"Hello?" Poet answered.

"Um, good afternoon, is this Cheryl Washington's cell phone number?" the male voice asked.

Poet moved the phone away from his ear and looked at the receiver. "No, it's her house number and she's not here. Who's this?" he asked, surprised to hear a man's voice on the other end of the phone.

"I'm Shareef Oates. I apologize for calling so early in the morning—I thought that this was her cell phone number. Do you know if she went to work this morning?"

"Wait a minute, bruh. Before you start askin' me a million questions, how do you know Cheryl Washington?"

"Excuse me?"

"I'm askin' you how you know my mother."

There was a slight pause. "Oh, so this is her son. How are you doing?"

"Yeah, I'm her son. The name's Poet. Anyway, how do you know my moms?"

"I know her from the job. Is there some kind of problem?" Oates asked as if he was confused with Poet's attitude.

"You know her from the job, huh?" Poet repeated.

"You heard me," Oates sarcastically replied.

"Are you like some NYPD clerical worker or somethin'?"

Oates sighed. He didn't have time for Poet, who was obviously a real smart ass. But he couldn't get mad at the young man for wanting to know who was calling his mother. He probably would have done the same thing, but in a roundabout and more respectful manner.

"No, I'm not and now you're asking me a million questions!" Oates replied, in a tone that let Poet know that he was talking to an adult. "I'm no clerical worker for the NYPD. I just happen to be a detective, Homicide Detective Shareef Oates of the Seventy-third Precinct at your service. Anything else you need to ask me?"

Poet calmed down a little. "Word? Homicide detective? I hear that." There was an awkward silence between the both of them. "Well, she's not here, my man. I'll tell her that you called."

"Well, thank you, um, what's your name again?"

"Poet."

"Thanks again, Poet."

"No doubt. One." Poet hung up the phone.

*A detective? Since when did my mother start talkin'
to detectives?* Poet thought.

The phone call from a Detective Shareef Oates had
Poet feeling uneasy. He didn't know what to think.
Was it a personal phone call or was Detective Oates
really calling his mother to inquire about him? Did the
cops find something out? Either way, Poet was going
to make sure that he didn't forget the detective's name.
Poet made a mental note to ask his mother some questions about the mysterious phone call from Detective
Oates when she arrived home from work that evening.

Chapter 10

The Complete Package

Oates hung up the phone and sat at his desk. He was thinking about Cheryl's son, Poet. It sounded like he was a real prize.

Maybe Poet needs to be doing something more constructive than screening his mother's phone calls, Oates thought.

He was still exhausted from the party he attended Saturday night. Not in the mood to do anything, Oates shuffled some of the papers on his desk and leaned back in his seat.

Lewis walked up to him with a cup of French vanilla coffee from DunkinDonuts and put it on Oates's desk. Oates took a large sip of his coffee and closed his eyes.

"What's up, homeboy?" Lewis asked. "I am beat but I'm glad that I didn't have a hangover yesterday."

Oates chuckled. "The way that you were throwing those drinks back the other night, I'm surprised you still don't have one." They both took another sip of their coffee. "You heard about that other body that was found over on Junius this weekend, right?" Oates asked.

Lewis sighed. "Yeah, man, I heard about John Moxley, also known as John-John, thirty-two years old and a professional thief. I heard about it. We can't take that case, man. We got too much on our plate as it is."

Oates huffed. "Hmmph. We're not taking that case."

All of a sudden, Sergeant Hayes walked over to their desks. "Good morning, gentlemen. I got some good news and some bad news."

"Oh, boy!" Lewis exclaimed. "I have a feeling it's all bad news. What is it?"

Sarge laughed. "The good news is that you guys are the best on the squad. The bad news is that you got the John Moxley case as well. I know it seems like a lot but I was told by my supervisor to choose the detectives that I wanted to handle the case. I chose you two because you guys are some of the best detectives on the squad."

Both Oates and Lewis threw their hands in the air. "Aw, damn!" Oates exclaimed. "C'mon, Sarge! We got a case overload already."

"Well, I'm sorry, fellas, but that's what it is. So you might as well get started on this."

Lewis and Oates watched their supervisor walk away. When he was out of sight, they began ranting and raving.

"Damn, I need a fucking vacation!" stated Oates. "This shit is really starting to get on my nerves, man!"

Lewis shook his head and leaned back in his chair. "We have to wrap these cases up, man. No more partyin' and playin' around anymore. We gotta get on the ball so that we can relax."

"Relax? Shit! I just met somebody really nice at that party the other night and now I'm not gonna be able to see her because I'm gonna be spending most of my time at work!"

"I gotta meet this feline, man. I can't remember much from the party."

Oates laughed. "Yeah, you were drunk as hell. Anyway, she's a nice-looking woman and she has, like, three kids of her own."

Lewis sat up. "Whoa! Three kids? Damn! Are you ready for that, O?" he asked with a look of concern on his face.

"Man, calm down! Her kids are practically grown. They're twenty-one, eighteen, and her youngest is sixteen. I can't beat that."

Lewis chuckled. "Oh, okay, so she doesn't have any babies. Anybody out of the house yet?"

"Well, when I accidently called Cheryl's house phone this morning, her son, the twenty-one-year-old, instantly started interrogating me. I almost told his nosey ass to go take the got damn police test!"

Lewis laughed. "Well, you know how that is. You know how boys are over their mothers, man."

"That's why I couldn't get mad at the whippersnapper. But I'm also not gonna be dealing with the questionnaire every time I call her house."

"It sounds like you got some serious plans for this one. That's cool. Where does she live?"

"She lives in Brownsville, right in Langston Hughes projects."

Lewis put his hand to his mouth. "Damn! I mean, how are you going to see her when she's living in this rough-ass neighborhood; the same neighborhood that just happens to be in our jurisdiction?"

"She seems like a nice lady and, hey, she's a single mother. She probably can't afford to live anywhere else on her salary. She's been holding it down by herself for the last sixteen years, she said."

"Was she married before?" Lewis asked.

Oates shook his head. "Yeah, she was married before."

"So what's up with this son of hers? He better be pulling his own weight."

"Well, she claims he helps her out with the finances. He has some night job doing janitorial work. I just hope that he has a legit job and not out in these streets doing some illegal bullshit."

"I have to ask. Don't you feel like this relationship with this woman is a conflict of interest? Let's just say if, God forbid, her son is into some illegal shit and you just happen to find out about it. What would you do then?"

Oates was beginning to get annoyed with all the what-ifs.

"Man, listen, Cheryl and I just met each other. We haven't even had a full conversation yet. I can't consume my personal life and worry about conflicts of interest because if I worried about that, I wouldn't be with nobody. I'm just going to see where this thing goes."

Lewis shrugged his shoulders. "Just be careful. You never know what's going on in these people lives, especially with their children. These people don't tell you everything."

The telephone at Oates's desk rang once and he picked it up immediately. It was a man on the phone wanting to talk to him about John-John, the deceased thief. Oates gave Lewis a look. They both hoped that the phone call would help crack the murder case.

"Detective Oates, how may I help you?" he said when he answered the phone.

"Good mornin', Detective Oates, my name is Leroy Pugh and I live in the Brownsville Houses. I knew the dead man and I just wanna say that John-John robbed me and I prayed for that boy, yes, I did. But I never once wanted him to die. I ain't the most religious man in the world but I do believe in the Lord and I had to ease my conscience and call you to let you know that!" Mr. Leroy exclaimed.

Oates frowned. "Um, Mr. Pugh, I appreciate you calling me but why did you wait until now? When he robbed you, why didn't you make a police report?"

"I was scared to, Detective Oates. I know it ain't right but I feel like if I would have made the police report, that boy would have been alive to this day. Oh, Lord, I shoulda just called the police!"

"Okay, Mr. Pugh, what happened the night that you were robbed?" Oates asked. He put Mr. Leroy on speakerphone so that Lewis could hear too.

"Well, I got up early that mornin' on the third around five-thirty or so to cash my little Social Security check, figurin' that if I cashed it early, nobody would be around to see me do it. You know, these sorry-ass Negroes always askin' for a piece of change. So I made my way to the twenty-four-hour check cashin' place on Rockaway and Linden Boulevard. When I got back home, I got out my car and all of a sudden I see John-John walkin' up to me. I didn't pay the boy no mind 'cause he's from the neighborhood and he went to school with my baby daughter, Jackie. Anyhow, he walked right up to me and pulled out this pistol, a black pistol, I think it was black."

"Okay, Mr. Pugh. When he pulled out the gun, did he say anything to you?" Oates asked.

"Well, he said, 'Give it up, old man, before I blow your fuckin' wig off!' I think I was more shocked that he talked to me sideways than I was at the fact he was robbin' me!"

"What happened next?"

"Well, me and this robbin' fool started strugglin' and he started riflin' through my pockets and took my money, which was like over a thousand dollars. I was goin' at it with the fool until he clocked me in the head with the butt of his pistol. I felt dizzy and fell out for a moment or two."

"Well, did he get away at this time?"

"Yeah, um, he ran away with my damn money and a young man from the neighborhood ran right over and helped me to my feet. He made sure I got to my buildin' safe and he even gave me five hundred dollars of his own money to replace the money that the robbin' fool stole from me. I tried givin' it back to him but he wouldn't let me do it."

Lewis and Oates were curious about the young man who had obviously saved Mr. Pugh's life. "Who was the young man that helped you? What was his name?"

"Oh, yeah, that young man that helped me, his name is Poet. Real odd name. He probably the only black man in America with a name like that but he's a very nice young man. He lives in the buildings across the street from me and I've known him since he was a little chap runnin' around these parts."

Oates put his hand on his chin.

Poet. Poet Washington, he thought. *Wow.*

After talking to Mr. Pugh and getting his information, Oates hung up the phone and looked at his partner.

Lewis was confused. "What's up, O?"

"Poet is Cheryl's son. I can't believe this," Oates stated. "Why is he a witness to this robbery and where did he get five hundred dollars to just give away to some old man?"

"Didn't his mother tell you that he had a night job?" Lewis asked.

"Yeah, she did, but Mr. Pugh claimed that he was robbed around five-thirty that morning. I'm wondering what his work hours are. Now that Poet is a potential witness in this case leading up to Moxley's murder, he has to be interviewed."

Lewis shook his head. He felt bad for Oates because he seemed like he really liked Cheryl. But he had told him so. Now it was a conflict of interest for real.

"Damn, O. Let's hope that this Poet fella isn't a suspect. You know, retribution for the robbery of Leroy Pugh wouldn't be too far-fetched."

Lewis sighed and Oates just shook his head.

Later on that night, while in his living room watching television, Oates thought about Cheryl again. He felt the nervous butterflies rumbling in his stomach and sucked his teeth. He was beginning to think that meeting her was more than just some coincidence.

Oates was pissed that Mr. Pugh had even brought Poet's name up, making the younger man a potential witness to a robbery. He almost wished that he could make it an open-and-shut case for his own selfish reasons. But unfortunately with the deceased's criminal background, there were too many suspects to do that. John Moxley had made a career out of thievery for too many years and his killer could have been anybody, including Poet Washington. How could he tell the woman he was going to be dating that her son was a witness to a robbery and possibly a potential suspect in a murder case?

Oates's vibrating cell phone interrupted his thoughts. He took a look at the caller ID, saw Cheryl's phone number, and sighed.

"Hey, sweetie," he said. "How are you doing this evening?"

"I'm good. How are you?" she asked. "Were you resting because you can just call me tomorrow—" she said.

Oates cut her off. "No, sweetheart, it's cool. I was just lying here on my couch, chilling out and watchin' TV. What are you doing?"

"I'm in my bedroom, with the door closed, doing the same thing that you're doing. This is what I do most of the time. Go to work and come home. My kids are old enough to take care of themselves. As a matter of fact, they cook *me* dinner."

Oates laughed. "Man, you got it good!" He paused for a moment. "Oh, yeah, I accidently called your house phone this morning and had the pleasure of speaking to your son. Sounds like a really nice young man."

Cheryl laughed. "Now, you know you are lying through your teeth! Poet is a mess! He called me at work and began asking me a thousand and one questions and I told his butt off. He didn't disrespect you, did he? Don't make me have to check him!"

"No, no!" Oates said with a laugh. "He just seemed to be a little too curious, even though I can't get mad at him about that. I guess he just wanted to know who was calling his mother. Trust me, I won't be calling your home phone anytime soon. I have your cell phone number memorized now!" Cheryl laughed loudly. "But on a serious note, maybe one day I'll get a chance to meet Mr. Poet."

Cheryl sighed. "Well, I hope that you can meet him too and talk some sense into him. Lord knows I worry about him so much. I just pray that he's not getting into any trouble out here. I take great pride in the way I raised my children. I just hope they incorporate my good values into their everyday lives. Let's face it, they're not babies anymore."

Based on the way Cheryl spoke about her children, he knew that if Poet was in the street doing some shady dealings, they were purely his own decision.

There was a silent pause. "You know, Shareef, sometimes I feel like I could have been a better mother to my kids. Although I work hard, I was so busy trying to get myself together that I feel that I may have neglected them in the process. I know that they love me but it's been really hard having a full-time job, making ends meet, and trying to give each of them the individual attention that they needed. It just feels as if it's not enough of me to go around."

Cheryl continued, "I'm older now and I've been by myself for too long. Now I feel that I'm ready for some male companionship. But trying to maintain a relationship with someone is just as hard! I mean, once I tell some men that I have three kids with no active father in their lives, they're usually on the first thing smoking!"

Oates smiled. "Look, Cheryl, don't feel like that. If a man is interested in being with you, you and your children are supposed to be one complete package, no matter how old they are. Your kids are a very important part of your life, just like my daughter is an important part of mine. How is your son handling his father not being in his life?"

"Well, so far, so good. It was hard for him for a while and I saw where he was displaying some kind of hostility when his father first left. He used to get into a lot of trouble in school but since he's gotten older, he's been much better. He has this notion that he's the man of the house and trust me, he takes that title extremely serious."

"So has he ever been arrested or got into any trouble with the law?"

"Never," replied Cheryl. "I know that he's out there doing the right thing. I just know he is."

Cheryl sounded as if she had a lot of faith in her son but, unfortunately, Oates's instincts were telling him something different. Although he had never laid eyes on Poet, he could tell that something wasn't right with the young man. He was going to make sure that he kept a close eye on Poet Washington.

Chapter 11

To the Grave

Everything had been pretty quiet for the past week and Poet had managed to play it cool. He was careful not to sway from his usual activities but was still mum about the murders.

On the other hand, Mekhi was beginning to avoid Poet. Unlike his best friend, Mekhi had a conscience, a conscience that was bothering him. He felt bad about lying up with his best friend's little sister but he just couldn't help himself. It had become harder and harder for him to control himself whenever Precious was around him.

Because she was underage and supposed to be like family to Mekhi, their relationship had to be a secret. It would be too scandalous if it ever came out. The Washingtons would never trust him again and their strong ties with Mekhi would become undone.

Poet had picked up on Mekhi's standoffish attitude and felt that he was to blame for it. He knew that they used to tell each other everything and Poet didn't feel right about having to hide something so serious from his right-hand man. His boy would never judge him and, of course, Poet knew that Mekhi would take the secret to the grave. They were two of a kind. So after wrestling with the idea for a few days, Poet decided that he would tell Mekhi about the murders. He didn't want to push his friend away any longer.

Poet called Mekhi on his phone and he picked up on the first ring.

"What's up, Khi?" yelled Poet. Mekhi held the phone away from his ear, with a smile on his face. "Where are you at?"

Mekhi laughed. "I'm in the house," he replied, relieved that he could go one more day without Poet finding out about him and Precious.

"Well, come outside. Let's go get some liquor!" Poet exclaimed.

"Bet."

Mekhi put on some sneakers and a hooded sweatshirt. He kissed his grandmother, who was on the couch, as usual, and watching her *Law & Order* reruns.

When Mekhi walked outside, Poet was waiting in front of the building in a rental car. It was a black late-model Nissan Maxima.

"Damn, Po!" Mekhi announced, hopping in on the passenger side of the vehicle. "Who rented you this car?"

"Rakiyah did. You know I got her in a smash!"

Mekhi laughed. "This is hot! Why didn't you just take her car?"

"Nah, man, I don't like drivin' her whip. Havin' her car will give her a valid reason to blow up my phone and Rakiyah's a pain in the ass." They both agreed.

Shortly after, they made a pit stop at the liquor store and bought some Hennessy and Hpnotiq. Then they purchased some Poland Spring bottled waters, poured the water out of them and put the concoction of liquors into the bottles.

After they completed that mission, Poet suggested that they go for a drive.

"You wanna know somethin'?" Poet began as he took a drive down St. John's Place. "I consider you a blood brother, you know that, right?"

Mekhi laughed nervously. "Yeah, Po. That's real talk."

Poet took a swig of his drink. "Ever since we were little kids, we always said that we shouldn't keep secrets from each other. Well, I've been hidin' some real heavy shit from you. I noticed that you've been avoidin' me lately and I assumed that you probably feel like I'm on some funny style shit with you."

"Yeah, I was thinkin' that you were actin' a little funny and whatnot."

Poet placed his bottle in the holder and lit a cigarette. "It was nothin' against you. It's just that I just been havin' a lot on my mind lately."

Mekhi took a big gulp of the liquor. He was hoping that Poet had not found out about him and Precious, but he had to play it cool.

"Now, Po, you can talk to me about anything, bruh! You know that. You know how we get down. We may hang out with some of these cats but we're not as close to them as we are to each other."

Poet shook his head in agreement but did not crack a smile. "No doubt," he said, flicking cigarette ashes out of the open driver's side window.

"So what's up then? What's been botherin' you, man?"

"A lot of things, man. I just don't like how these cats move nowadays. You don't know who to trust, dudes are just violatin' people like crazy, and I feel like I have to be one of the people that does somethin' about the shit."

Mekhi took a deep breath. "Does somethin' like what?"

"Just take matters into my own hands, you know what I'm sayin'? And I'm goin' to continue to take matters into my own hands, if necessary. I don't want nobody fuckin' with me or my family."

"Look, Po, I don't know what you're talkin' about but I didn't mean—" Mekhi began, but Poet cut him off.

"What I'm tryin' to say is that I killed somebody, Khi."

Mekhi spit out his drink. He wiped the liquor off the dashboard with the sleeve of his hooded sweatshirt.

"You did what? When? Killed who? I mean, why?" Mekhi asked, with a shocked look on his face. He was surprised yet relieved that Poet didn't mention anything about him and Precious.

Poet laughed at his friend's anxiousness. "Yo, Khi, relax, man! It's not that serious, bruh!"

Mekhi looked at Poet strangely. "What do you mean, it's not that serious? You just told me that you killed somebody! Who did you kill, Po? When did this happen?"

"Well, remember a few weeks ago, the mornin' that I came home pissy drunk after Ham's house party? Man, I walked in my buildin' and this dude comes runnin' out of the staircase and damn near runs me over. After waitin' for the elevator, I decided to walk upstairs to the crib, right, and I get to the fifth floor and there was this little girl, lyin' there on the dirty-ass staircase floor, with no fuckin' clothes on!"

"Are you talkin' about the girl that got raped in your building?" Mekhi asked with an astonished look on his face.

"Yes, the girl that I'm talkin' about is the one that got raped in my buildin' a few weeks ago!"

Mekhi nodded his head. "You never really talked about what happened but I want to know—what happened?"

"Man, Khi, the girl was fucked up. The person that raped her gave her a black eye, she was all bruised up and she was bleedin' from between her legs. I asked her what happened and who had done that to her. When she described the rapist to me, I realized that it was the same motherfucker that almost knocked me down in the lobby! I covered her up with my jacket then I ran and knocked on Miss Ida's door and asked her to call 911 for the girl. After I made sure that she was okay, I ran back outside to the store for some smokes. My nerves were bad, and at the same time, I was hopin' that the dude in question was still around the way somewhere."

Mekhi shook his head. "C'mon, Po. You know that dude was long gone! He raped shorty and was outta there! He would have been a fool to stick around!"

"I said the same thing. But somethin' in me was ragin', know what I mean? I knew that if I ever saw this dude again, I was gonna beat the brakes off his ass! So now I'm tight, right, my high is blown, and this little girl's bloody face is stuck in my mind when all of sudden, who do I see? I see the same guy that the girl had described to me, walkin' past the bodega on Rockaway. He was on the other side of the street so I followed this dude, right, and as soon as he turned that first corner, I caught up to him, dragged his raggedy ass into an abandoned buildin' down the block and pushed his fuckin' wig back! I just left him lyin' there in all his blood with his head blown off."

After hearing the details of what happened that day, Mekhi was dumbfounded. "I don't know what to say."

Everything that Poet was telling him sounded so surreal. As Poet went on to give him even more details about the murder, Mekhi began to feel more and more uncomfortable. Now he knew that if Poet found out about him and Precious, he may be just as good as dead too.

Poet laughed loudly, getting more hyper by the minute. He felt relieved to finally tell his best friend about the murders.

"And that's not the only one I put a bullet in. On my way home from the spot one night, I saw Mr. Leroy gettin' robbed. This cat pistol-whipped Mr. Leroy and got him for his whole Social Security check! When I went to help him, the dude ran away."

"That's beat, man! Who would do that shit to cool-ass Mr. Leroy? That old man don't never bother anybody!"

"Well, John-John was the one that robbed him. Remember the night we passed by that crowd and we found out that John-John had got bodied?" Poet asked, referring to John-John's murder. Mekhi nodded his head. "Well, that was my work," Poet bragged, puffing out his chest.

Mekhi put his hand to his mouth. "So that's why you didn't wanna go over and take a look at the body that night? The night you had Raki's car and . . . John-John was . . . What the hell, Po? You didn't kill one person, you killed two people!"

"It's like I can't help it now, Khi. It feels like I have to get at these grimy-ass motherfuckers now. They're the motherfuckers out here preyin' on innocent people! The foul shit that some people do to other people just bothers me!"

Mekhi continued to stare at Poet. He couldn't believe that the man he loved like a brother, the person he had known all his life, was now a full-fledged murderer. And of course, he was putting his own life in danger by sleeping with his murderous friend's little sister.

"I don't know what to say, Po." They both were quiet. "You know that what you're doin' ain't right, don't you? You can't run around and kill every bad person in the world! Don't you think that killin' them would make you just as bad as them?"

Poet stopped at a red light and looked at Mekhi. His friend had a worried look on his face. Poet knew that Mekhi was not built for murder and his own ego was at an all-time high. Not only was he no longer afraid to kill anyone but Poet was convinced that the world needed more people like him.

"Well, I'm gonna be the one to take some of these low-budget motherfuckers out of their misery! All I keep thinkin' about is what if my sisters and mother were to be raped or get robbed? The police ain't doin' nothin' so murder is my only option! I'm not about to let my family become no victims out here!"

Mekhi shook his head and laughed in disbelief. "Man, you have really lost your damn mind! Even though what you're sayin' sounds good, the reality is you can't stop shit like that from happenin'! We, as people, just have to be careful at all times and 'hope' that shit like that don't happen to us." Mekhi replied after he took a swig of his drink. "But I do want to know somethin': how did it feel to pull that trigger? I mean, did you get some kind of rush from killin' these dudes?"

The light turned green and Poet continued to drive. "The first time I did it, I felt some regret. I was scared. I felt guilty. But after I really thought about why I had done it, it didn't have an effect on me at all. To me, by killin' these bastards, I was just savin' another life. The point is this: now that the rapist is dead, is he rapin' anybody else?"

Mekhi shook his head as Poet talked on. "And look at John-John. He's not gonna be able to rob no more Mr. Leroys or anybody else, is he? What about the time he took your bike back in the days, do you remember how hurt you were?"

Mekhi frowned. Poet did have a valid point. "Word, I was kinda tight when he took my Mongoose! That bike was a classic!"

"There you go. I rest my case."

"But seriously, Po, aren't you scared of the cops catchin' up to you?"

Poet shrugged his shoulders. He didn't give a damn about the cops. If they were doing their jobs the right way, he wouldn't have to do their dirty work.

"Man, do you think that one time gives a shit about those losers? Plus, the cops ain't lookin' out for us. That's why sometimes we have to take matters into our own hands. Bottom line is I would kill somebody if I have to just to protect my family. Like I said before, the police are not doin' it!"

As they drove throughout Brooklyn, the seriousness of what Poet had done finally hit Mekhi. From the expression on Poet's face alone, Mekhi knew that his friend meant business. He realized that sneaking around with Precious might have been a crucial mistake; a mistake that may just cost him his life. Unfortunately, he loved Precious that much to risk it all for her.

Chapter 12

Precious Moments

While Poet and Mekhi were hanging out, Porsha and Precious were at home getting ready for bed. Precious was throwing things around on her bed so that she could lie down when Porsha noticed her attitude.

"Girl, what is wrong with you?" Porsha asked as she wrapped her hair in the mirror.

Precious sucked in some air. "I dunno, Porsha, I've just been kinda tired lately, that's all," she replied.

Porsha plopped down on her bed. "You have somethin' you want to talk about?"

Precious fixed the scarf on her own head. "No, I don't."

"Look, Precious, if you got somethin' that you need to get off your chest, you need to go ahead and do it. I know that we haven't always seen eye to eye but you are my only sister and my younger sister, at that. The least you can do is talk to me because I know you damn sure ain't tryin to tell Mommy nothin'!"

Precious sighed loudly. Porsha was right. She had been trying to maintain her composure but it was getting harder and harder to do that. She was beginning to have deep feelings for Mekhi and she really didn't know how to handle those emotions. It was very difficult to not being able to tell anyone about her first love. She figured that she might as well talk to Porsha about the situation since she was no longer a virgin herself.

"Okay, I'm not a virgin anymore. I lost my virginity a few days ago."

Porsha chuckled. "Are you serious? Was that the day that I noticed that you were in pain?"

"Yes, that was the day," she admitted. "It hurt at first but now it seems like I want to have sex with this person all the time. I can't help myself. I'm feelin' him so much, Porsha! Is that normal?"

Porsha smiled. "Yeah, girl, that's normal. But let me ask you somethin'. Did you use protection?"

"He used a condom each time," Precious replied.

"Now I'm waitin' for you to tell me who this guy is," Porsha asked as she fluffed out her pillow and lay down.

Precious was hesitant. "You have to promise me that you won't tell anybody, Porsha. I'm so serious. You can't tell anybody. I'm so trustin' you right now."

Porsha held up her right hand. "I won't tell a soul," she replied anxiously. "Okay, now who is the guy?"

"Okay." Precious hesitated. "It was, um . . . Mekhi."

Porsha's jaw dropped and she sat up in her bed. "You mean Mekhi Porter? Our friend Mekhi? Poet's friend Mekhi?"

"Yes, Porsha, that Mekhi."

"The same Mekhi who's like a brother to us?"

Precious held her head down. "Yes."

There was an uncomfortable silence between the sisters.

Porsha lay back down. "Wow," she said. "Mekhi is fine, though. I used to check him out myself but I'm a little too old for Mekhi's taste. He likes them young thangs, like you." They both giggled. "But, seriously, Presh, you have to be careful. He knows that he's not even supposed to be messin' with you. He's too old for you. If Mommy finds out, she would have a fit and Mekhi's ass will be under the jail, if Poet doesn't try to kill him first!"

Precious shook her head. "But Mekhi is only five years older than me and I will be sixteen tomorrow!" she whined.

Porsha walked over and sat down beside Precious. "Presh, Mekhi is twenty-one years old. Technically, he's an adult. At his age, he knows that he shouldn't be dealin' with a girl your age. But if you really like him, which I knew that you always did, your secret is safe with me. Just remember to stay on your P's and Q's."

"Thanks, Porsha. I appreciate the advice."

The two sisters hugged each other. With that conversation, they had created a bond that would probably last for the rest of their lives. What they didn't realize was that after everything was said and done, they would have no other choice but to rely on each other for emotional support.

It was following night when friends and family gathered at the apartment for Precious's sweet sixteen birthday affair. It was 10:30 P.M. and the party of forty guests was in full swing. Poet supplied the sounds from his laptop, which was connected to a large speaker in the living room. The music turned the simple get-together into an all-out bash.

Poet and some of his neighborhood friends were lined up in the kitchen savoring the delicacies that Cheryl had prepared for the event. Precious and Malika were in the middle of the spacious living room, showing off their dance skills. Considering everything that was probably going on in their lives, everyone seemed to be having a good time.

Meanwhile, a somber Mekhi stood against the wall, watching Precious's every move. He was zeroing in on the tight-fitting dress that she was wearing. It left little to the imagination. After taking pictures and making her grand entrance, Precious's four-inch platform stillettos were thrown to the side. Her long hair was flowing, courtesy of her Dominican hairstylist, and Precious looked much older than her sixteen years.

Unfortunately for Mekhi, he was not having a good time. He was unable to take his eyes off Precious. He watched as she moved among her crowd of friends, bothered by the way that she interacted with her male associates. Although their relationship was a secret, the plan was for them to act as if everything were normal, especially when they were around Poet. Now, for some reason, he felt as if Precious was avoiding him.

Poet walked over to Mekhi, interrupting his thoughts.

"Hey, Khi," Poet said. "Why you not dancin', man?" Poet asked him over the loud music.

Mekhi sighed. "I'm good, son. I'm just standin' here, takin' everything in, that's all," Mekhi replied, catching a glimpse of Precious whispering in a male friend's ear.

He couldn't let Poet know that he was suffering from the green-eyed monster. Mekhi looked again and Precious was rubbing her behind on one of her male associates' groin area. He felt his chest tighten with jealousy.

"Wow! My baby sister is sixteen!" Poet exclaimed, admiring how pretty Precious looked. "Damn, I remember holdin' that little girl in my arms! Don't you, Khi?" he asked. "Now look at her!"

Mekhi nodded his head while Poet beamed with pride. Poet then branched off and walked toward Porsha and her friends.

Mekhi smirked. "Yeah, I remember holdin' her in my arms too," he said to himself, only he was thinking about how he had just made love to her a few days before her birthday.

Precious finally made her way over to him. "What's up, Mekhi?" she whispered in his ear.

"What's up?" he replied with an attitude. "It's about time you came over here. It seems like you done danced with every young cat in the party, except me."

Mekhi couldn't believe that he was acting like a fool over a sixteen-year-old girl. He just couldn't control his feelings.

Precious laughed, which irritated Mekhi even more. "Are you jealous, Khi? I thought that we were supposed to be keepin' our relationship a secret?" she asked, sounding more mature than her sixteen years.

"Yeah, we are, but that doesn't mean that we have to disrespect each other, does it? Do you see me flirtin' with other females in front of you?"

Precious rolled her eyes at him. "C'mon, Mekhi, it's my birthday party and you should be happy that I'm havin' a good time. Why are you stressin'?"

"Because you're lettin' these young dudes get all in your face while I'm standin' right here."

Precious shook her head. She grabbed Mekhi's hand. "Mekhi, none of them boys can't do the things that you do to me. It's all about us, okay? You don't have nothin' to worry about."

He sighed and kissed her on the cheek. "You're right. I'm sorry for actin' so jealous. It's just that you look gorgeous. I never saw you lookin' like this before."

"Thank you, Mekhi."

They both stood there looking at each other as the partygoers mingled around them.

"You know what? I'm gonna chill out. Go and have a good time with your friends," he said.

An hour later, Precious' mother asked Poet to turn the music down and told everyone to gather around the beautiful red velvet cake.

Precious stood at the center of the round glass table while everyone stood around singing Stevie Wonder's version of "Happy Birthday." Someone told her to make a wish. Precious closed her eyes, made a wish, and blew out the lit number sixteen candle on the large sheet cake. Her family and other guests happily cheered and Cheryl hugged her youngest daughter. While the cake was being cut, Poet turned the music back on.

The party continued until Cheryl finally dismissed everyone at 1:30 A.M. The attendees said good-bye to each other and filed out into the hallway. When the last guest walked out, Cheryl hugged her daughters. She took some aspirin for her headache and went straight to bed.

Meanwhile, Poet and Porsha left the apartment to walk their friends and other family members downstairs. Precious and Mekhi stayed behind to put away the rest of the food from the party.

"So you had a good time, huh?" Mekhi asked as he put a bowl of potato salad in the refrigerator.

Precious smiled as she brushed her hair off of her shoulders. "Of course I did. Mommy surprised me—I didn't even know that she was plannin' a party for me."

Mekhi shrugged his shoulders. "Yeah, it was nice. Looks like you really enjoyed dancin' with all those dudes, too."

Precious looked at Mekhi strangely. "What's wrong with you, Khi? Why are you actin' so jealous all of a sudden?"

"Yo, Precious, don't play with me, okay? You're mine, you hear me? I've been wantin' to get with you for years. Now that I finally have you to myself, I'm not tryin' to let you go," he said.

"You know I had to play it off! What was I supposed to do? Be in your face all night?" she replied with a confused look on her face.

Mekhi grabbed Precious by the collar of her dress and pulled her close to him.

"You didn't have to be in my face all night but that doesn't mean that you can mess with any other guy."

The adolescent Precious was flattered by his actions and she kissed Mekhi on the lips.

"Look, Presh, I really love you. You're like the best thing that has ever happened to me. You just don't know," he said, holding her face in his hands.

Precious blushed. "And I love you too, Khi. I just want you to believe that."

He nodded his head and kissed her again.

Suddenly, the sound of the key in the door interrupted them and they quickly moved away from each other. Poet and Porsha were laughing as they stepped inside of the apartment.

Poet walked into the kitchen. "Hey, Khi, are you ready to bounce?" he asked, clueless to what had just transpired between his little sister and best friend.

Porsha looked at Precious with a smirk on her face. Precious caught her expression and shushed her.

"Um, yeah, I'm ready. I was just helpin' Presh put away this food. We're outta here," Mekhi responded.

His heart was beating a mile a minute and his erection had gone down. As soon as the men walked out the door, Porsha gave Precious a look.

"Girl, what the hell was y'all doin' in here?" she whispered. "Don't you know that Mommy is right in the bedroom?"

Precious smiled. "Please, Porsha. Mommy is out of it. She took a Tylenol PM for a headache and went straight to bed. She's probably counting her last sheep right now."

Porsha took off her jacket and threw it on the sofa. "Just be careful and don't start gettin' too loose with him. This situation is gonna be real fucked up if it gets out."

"Guess what? Mekhi told me that he loves me tonight."

Porsha just shook her head. "I'm gonna tell you again to just be careful, Presh."

Precious started shaking her butt. "I'm sixteen now! You know I got this!"

"Well, it's goin' to be a not-so-sweet sixteen if you and him don't get a grip."

When Porsha left her alone, Precious danced around the living room. She was on cloud nine just thinking about what Mekhi said. It was the first time in her life a man had ever said that he loved her. Forbidden love or not, she was going to enjoy every minute of Mekhi's love and affection. Ruining the friendship between Poet and Mekhi was the last thing on her mind.

Chapter 13

Paper Chase

An hour after Precious's party was over, Poet and Mekhi were at the spot packing up some product for Bone when he walked into the kitchen. He had a look on his face that meant business.

"Poet, I gotta talk to you, man," Bone announced. "It's about somethin' very important."

"No doubt, Bone, what's up?" Poet inquired with a concerned look on his face.

Bone beckoned the young hustler toward the back of the apartment where the bedrooms were. Poet was slightly nervous because Bone was so low-key; one never knew what he had up his sleeve when he needed to talk to them.

Did he find out about the killings? Poet thought.

Bone closed the bedroom door and Poet sat on one of the bunk beds, which were once occupied by Sha-Sha's children.

"Listen, Po, I decided to let you hold down this spot for me," Bone said.

Poet's face lit up like he had hit the lotto. "Word, Bone?" He hopped off the bed and gave Bone a pound. "That's what's up! But why me, though?"

Bone leaned on the door of the bedroom. "Because I feel that you're a loyal motherfucker, somebody that I can trust. You've been down with me since you were sixteen years old and I've never had a problem with you, no miscounts, no stealin' my shit, it's been nothin'," Bone said. "Plus, you got that know-how when it comes to this game. A lot of cats don't have that at your age. Let's take your boy, Khi. He ain't built for this shit and the only reason he's doin' it is because you're doin' this."

Poet had to agree with Bone on that one. Mekhi didn't really have a knack for hustling. If anything, he was more of an artist. It was obvious that he didn't have the confidence or motivation to do anything with his talent or to even get a job. Because of his slacker ways, Poet knew that Mekhi had no other choice but to hustle drugs if he wanted to have some money in his pocket.

"Yeah, you might be right about that, Bone, but Khi is a'ight. He's just doin' what he has to do to make him some paper."

"Yeah, he's a good dude but you are the one that takes care of my business and I appreciate that shit. To show you how much, I got somethin' for you."

Bone pulled out some car keys. Poet was surprised. "Oh, shit! Yo, Bone, are you serious, man?"

Bone smiled. "Hell yeah, I'm serious! This white boy owed me some money and shit and his people have a car dealership. Instead of payin' me my money, I told him to give me a car and he did that. I really didn't need another car so I decided to let you have it. It's a 2007 Toyota Camry. I was able to get some temporary plates on it for the next sixty days but you're gonna have to get it registered and get some insurance on it."

For a brief second, Poet thought about what his mother was going to say. By the time Bone handed him the keys to the car, he had already figured out a good lie to tell her.

"Good lookin' out!" Poet exclaimed happily.

Bone smiled. "No doubt, shorty! Just keep doin' what you do for me. It's gonna be more responsibility but you're gonna be makin' more money, as well. I'm willin' to give you $1,500 a week to hold this spot down for me. Make sure all of my products are good. Keep in contact with connects on this end. Make sure Sha-Sha's ass stays outta here so she won't be stealin' nothin' from me. Can you handle that?"

Poet nodded his head.

Bone smiled. "Cool." His look turned serious. "But listen, man, its rules to this shit, real talk. You gotta keep your nose clean. I take my business very serious and I don't need nothin' or nobody bringin' no heat to me or my business. Fuck up my paper and that's your ass! *Comprende,* amigo?"

"Man, I got you," Poet promised and gave Bone another pound. After making sure that everything was on point, Bone finally got into his car and headed home.

Poet held the car keys in his hand and smiled proudly. Poet walked into the living room and looked out the window at the steel-grey 2007 Toyota Camry that was parked in front of the building. It was a nice late-model vehicle, nothing too luxurious. When he walked back into the kitchen, he had a big smile on his face. Mekhi was already at the kitchen table bagging up some cooked-up crack cocaine.

"What the hell are you so happy about?" Mekhi asked while chopping a large piece of crack rock with a single-edge razor.

Poet pulled out the keys to the Toyota Camry. "I got me a car, man! Bone just gave me a car!"

"Word?" Mekhi said, happy for his friend. Poet jiggled the car keys in the air.

"That's what's up but what made him do that?" asked Mekhi.

"I'm gonna be takin' over this spot for him. I'm responsible for it from now on. Bone is gonna give me a nice amount of money a week to run this shit for him."

Mekhi looked at Poet and shook his head. "Damn, Po, are you ready for that? Holdin' down this spot is goin' to be a lot of responsibility. You're gonna have to chill out with those things that you told me about the other night," he said, referring to the murders that Poet had confessed to committing.

Poet sighed as he plopped down in a chair. "Don't even remind me about all that. I'm tryin' to act like all none of that shit ever happened. So from this day on, I don't wanna bring it up anymore."

Mekhi readily agreed. "Oh, you don't have to worry about me sayin' shit about none of that. I'm gonna act like you never told me a thing." They slapped each other five.

While Mekhi had his art, for Poet, the only escape from the ghetto was money. The look on his mother's face was priceless every time he gave her some cash to help out with the bills around the house. Although Poet hated to admit it, the hustling worked for him. He even managed put some money away for a rainy day.

Both men were extremely quiet as Poet prepared some more cocaine to cook up. Mekhi had found love with Precious and Poet was making more money to help support his family. In their own minds, it seemed as if things were looking up for the two friends, but unfortunately their happiness was going to be short-lived.

Chapter 14

The Boiling Point

The next day, it was a sunny Saturday morning and Mekhi was hanging out at Poet's house. He was anxious to take a spin in Poet's new car.

"Are your sisters up, Po?" Mekhi asked the second after he walked in Poet's door. He was hoping that he would see Precious, even if it was only for a minute.

Poet looked at Mekhi with a frown on his face. "Yeah, they're awake. Why?" Poet asked.

"I was just askin' because it's so quiet in here, that's all. They're usually arguin' or playin' some loud-ass music in their bedroom."

"It's still early but give them time. They'll be at their usual bullshit in a minute," Poet said with a laugh.

When Poet walked into the kitchen, Mekhi walked toward the back to the bathroom. As soon as he reached for the bathroom knob, Precious walked out of her bedroom, wearing a tight T-shirt and some boy shorts. Her perky behind looked like two small basketballs.

"Damn," Mekhi mumbled to himself, looking over his shoulder to see if Poet had come out of the kitchen.

Precious stood in front of Mekhi with her round ass and full B-cup breasts to match. She had her hair wrapped in large hairpins and some loose pieces of hair cascaded over her shoulders. Mekhi was relieved when he heard Poet in the kitchen talking on his cell phone.

He figured that the coast was clear at least for a little while.

"You look good, Presh," he said while licking his lips.

Precious smiled. "You do too," she replied. Precious rubbed her hand across Mekhi's rod. "Go into the bathroom and let me kiss it one time."

Mekhi frowned. "Are you crazy, girl?" he whispered. "Your brother's in the kitchen and ain't your mother and sister here?"

"Forget about them. My mother is in her bedroom, still knocked out," Precious said as she proceeded to unzip his pants.

"Yo, Khi!" Poet yelled from the front. "I'm goin' downstairs to wait for Rakiyah. She gotta gimme somethin'. Make yourself comfortable. I'll be back!"

They heard the door slam and quickly went into the bathroom together.

"We gotta make it quick!" Mekhi said, his breathing becoming heavier by the minute.

Precious locked the bathroom door behind them and squatted in front of him. She hurriedly took his penis out and put it into her mouth. Mekhi was in heaven, as he watched her head go up and down on his joint. While Precious sucked him off like a professional, he tried to suppress his moans. She slobbered and slurped on Mekhi's erection, like she was licking an oversized Popsicle.

As young and sexually inexperienced as Precious was when it came to vaginal sex, she was a pro when it came to oral. Mekhi was relishing the moment. He didn't even know that Precious knew how to give blow jobs.

Precious pleasured Mekhi for five minutes. Unable to control himself, he took his penis out of her mouth and ejaculated on the bathroom floor. Precious quickly cleaned up the mess as Mekhi stood there for a few moments, trying to get his head together. She snuck out of the bathroom and, after a few more minutes had passed, Mekhi adjusted his clothing and threw some water on his face. By the time he walked out of the bathroom, Poet was back upstairs. Mekhi played it cool by acting like he had been watching television the entire time.

"Is everything a'ight?" Mekhi asked with his eyes glued to the TV.

He was barely able to look Poet in the eye. He nervously picked up the remote and began skimming through the channels of the wide-screen television.

"Yeah, everything is good," Poet answered, oblivious to what had just occurred between Mekhi and his baby sister. "Raki is gonna do the insurance and registration for my car so I'm real good now," he announced happily.

Mekhi shook his head, still weak from the fellatio that Precious had performed on him.

"Oh, okay, that's what's up," Mekhi replied lazily. "When are you gonna tell your moms about the car?"

Poet hesitated. "I don't know, man. Honestly, I really don't wanna tell her shit!"

"Well, don't tell her, then. You know Miss Cheryl's gonna want to know all the particulars."

Suddenly, Precious walked out into the living room and plopped on the couch next to Mekhi, wearing the same boy shorts and T-shirt that had him mesmerized earlier. Mekhi's heart skipped a beat as Poet looked at his sister like she was crazy.

"Yo! Go back in the fuckin' room and put some clothes on!" Poet yelled, with his nose turned up at her attire. "You don't have no business comin' in here lookin' like that!"

Precious looked at Mekhi, whose green eyes appeared to be bulging out of his head. "Oh please, Poet, it's just you and Mekhi and besides, this is my house too!" Precious retorted. "I can go wherever I want to up in here!"

Poet walked toward Precious and Mekhi got up and took a step in between them. "C'mon, Po, just leave her alone. Just let her chill in here for a minute."

To calm himself down, Poet walked in the back toward his bedroom. Mekhi looked at Precious, who wore a smug expression on her face.

"Why are you in here?" Mekhi whispered. "What are you tryin' to do?" he asked.

Precious leaned on his shoulder. "Sit with my boo," she cooed, while rubbing his muscular chest. "I love you so much, Mekhi."

She kissed him on the lips. Mekhi jumped up off the sofa and looked toward Poet's open bedroom door. He heard Poet in the back fussing to himself and sweat began to form under his armpits.

"Yo, you need to stop playin' like this, Presh," Mekhi stated, continuing to talk in a whisper.

Precious laughed. "He ain't thinkin' about us! Why are you so scared of him anyway?"

Suddenly, Cheryl walked into the living room with her head tied up in a scarf and her robe on. She was awakened by all the noise. Precious straightened up and Mekhi froze.

"How you doin', Miss Cheryl?" he asked.

"Hello, Mekhi, I'm fine and you?" Cheryl replied, looking at her daughter in a disapproving manner.

"I'm fine."

Mekhi walked out of the living room, leaving Precious alone with her mother.

"Stand up, Precious, let me see what you have on."

Precious slowly stood up. Her mother looked at her attire with disgust.

"If you don't get in that room and put some clothes on, I will stomp a mudhole in your ass! You know better than to be walking around like that in front of your brother's grown-ass friend! Now do what I say before I go off on you in here!" Cheryl said, pointing to Precious's bedroom.

Poet and Mekhi walked out of the bedroom and Precious was standing by her door with a devious look on her face.

"Bye, Poet! Bye, Khi!" Precious announced with a wave and a smile before going into her room.

Mekhi waved and Poet walked past her. Mekhi turned around to see Precious blowing a kiss at him. They both kissed Cheryl on her cheek before they walked out the door.

Once they were in the hallway, Poet began talking about Precious.

"That little bitch, excuse me for callin' my sister that, but she's gonna make me smack the shit outta her! She's just too damn grown!" Poet yelled out as they ran down the staircase. "And she was flirtin' with you, man! All of that was for you!"

Mekhi attempted to smooth things over. "Man, just leave it alone. I don't pay Precious no mind. She just does shit to get under your skin. She's a little sister. That's what they do."

"Yeah, but I think she has a crush on you, Khi and you're like family to us. I mean, you knew her since she was a baby!"

Mekhi's heart skipped a beat. "Yeah, you're right but I don't think she has a crush on me. Precious is like a little sister to me. She's harmless."

"Easy for you to say. You don't have to live with her annoyin' ass. If you did, you would probably feel the same way I do!"

When they arrived at Poet's car, there were five men sitting on the hood and the trunk of his new car. Poet glared at the hoodlums and pressed the alarm button. When they still didn't move, Mekhi knew that there was about to be a showdown, especially after he saw who it was. It was Pumpkin and some of his most loyal soldiers, an assorted group of flunkies who did everything he told them to do.

Terrence "Pumpkin" Watts was a notorious Bloods leader that lived in Brownsville for many years. He had been bad news ever since anyone could remember and was apparently just miserable for no reason. People feared him, though, knowing that he had a terrible temper and a huge following of hungry, young wannabe gangsters that would give their lives just to prove themselves to him. Pumpkin was also very cunning, to say the least. He was so charismatic that it would be easy for him to convince someone to do what he wanted them to do, without succumbing to physical violence. His charisma mixed with a disregard for human life was combustible.

Pumpkin's Gangster Killer Bloods set in Brownsville was tighter than tight, thanks to his callousness. He was suspected of conspiring to commit several murders but because of the people's unwillingness to testify against the thug, nothing ever materialized and he was still on the streets. Unfortunately, Pumpkin didn't realize his gangbanging days were about to be over. He didn't know that the path he was about to cross was that of a killer.

"Um, my man, could you excuse me? This is my car that you and your flunkies are sittin' on!" Poet announced in a condescending tone.

Mekhi stood nearby with his hand over his mouth. It felt as if he was going to go to the bathroom on himself.

Pumpkin stood up. He was a few inches shorter than Poet but much stockier.

"Yo, who are you talkin' to?" Pumpkin asked, pointing his finger a few inches away from Poet's face. "'Cause I ain't none of your mans!" he added, looking at the frightened Mekhi with an angry look on his face. "And none of my comrades ain't no fuckin' flunkies, bitch-made motherfucker!"

His soldiers stood around Pumpkin, eager to put in work.

"Yo, Pee, you want me to eat his food?" a short, slim man with bad acne asked Pumpkin. He pulled a large box cutter out of his pocket.

Poet laughed. He wasn't scared of any of them. "I'm talkin' to you!" he said to Pumpkin.

The way that Poet was reacting to Pumpkin's intimidating behavior, Mekhi knew then that his friend had finally gone off the deep end when he said that.

Mekhi stepped in between the two men. Pumpkin's eyes had turned the same color as the red Yankees hat that he wore on his head.

Suddenly, Mekhi interrupted the standoff between the two men. "Yo, Pumpkin, look! It ain't nothin', Blood! He's just tryin' to get in his whip, that's all!" he said.

Pumpkin looked at Poet from head to toe. "Yo, bitch, you better act like you know who you're fuckin' with! I'm gonna see you, though!" Pumpkin said with a smirk on his face as he walked away.

Pumpkin didn't want to seem like a punk because he walked away from Poet. The only reason he hadn't beat Poet down within inches of his life was because he knew that the younger man was well protected by Bone and Preme. Bone had allowed Pumpkin to hustle and get a little money around the way and he didn't want to risk his connections by taking out one of Bone's most loyal cronies.

Poet waved him off. "Whatever! All I want is for you and your little guard dogs to stay the fuck off my car!"

Pumpkin stopped and turned around. "Yo, Khi, you better get your boy! You better run down my mother-fuckin' resume to this pussy ass dude!"

After the heated exchange with Pumpkin, Mekhi and Poet finally got into the car. Once they pulled off, Mekhi looked at Poet like he was some crazed lunatic.

"Yo, Po, man, what was all that about?" Mekhi asked. "We both know that Pumpkin is a certified nutcase! Them little flunkies he got runnin' around with him will kill your ass, too. All he gotta do is just say the word and you're toe-tagged!"

"Fuck Pumpkin!" Poet shouted. He was unfazed by what had just transpired between them. "I ain't never like his ass anyway and he ain't never liked me! Fake wannabe gangster! The only thing he does is walk around the hood fuckin' with people all the time. Maybe he'll be the next dude I put on my hit list."

Mekhi shook his head in amazement. "Yo, you gotta be kiddin' me! I know you're not tryin' to kill that dude!"

Poet smirked. He already knew what he was going to do. There was no need to let Mekhi in on his plans. He would just try to talk him out of taking care of Pumpkin.

"You know what, Khi? Forget I even said anything about that, okay?" Poet said, rolling his eyes. "Like I said before, fuck a Pumpkin!"

***

Later on that night, at around 12:30 A.M., Pumpkin
walked out of a bodega with one of his many female
suitors. While he was far from being a poster boy
like Tyson Beckford, he was attractive enough for the
women to be physically attracted to him. Unsurpris-
ingly, Pumpkin had a penchant for being abusive
toward women, so as soon as they stepped out of the
store, he pushed the woman outside and onto the sidewalk. He was still upset over the run-in with Poet so he
was going to teach somebody a lesson tonight.

"Bitch, I will fuckin' beat the shit outta you! Don't
you ever disrespect Damu, you worthless ho!" he
screamed while slapping the woman in her face several
times. People stopped and watched but did not dare
step in to help the crying female.

"Pumpkin, I didn't sleep with him! I promise you,
I didn't! I didn't even know that he was a Crab!" the
woman said, referring to a Crip gang member.

Slap! Slap! The sounds of Pumpkin's right hand
connecting with her face echoed from down the block.
Pumpkin looked possessed as he gave the female a
merciless beating. Dizzy with pain, she tried to get up
and fell to the ground again. This time he began kicking
her. She balled up into the fetal position, as his Timber-
land boots made contact with her abdomen.

"Fuckin' stupid bitch! Runnin' around messin' with
these Crabs!" he said. "When you fuck with me, you're
supposed to represent Blood, you nasty ho!"

Pumpkin looked up and saw a police car down the
block. Regaining some common sense, he calmly
walked away from the crying girl, abandoning her battered body in the middle of the sidewalk. His flunkies,
who were standing nearby, also walked in different
directions, leaving Pumpkin to walk through the dark

streets of Brownsville alone. They didn't want to draw any attention from the patrolling officers.

After beating up the girl, Pumpkin decided that it wasn't the ego boost that he needed. Now he had to go home to his baby mother and terrorize her. Someone would have to pay for the humiliation that he experienced earlier that day. He didn't like to be punked in front of his comrades and, after some careful consideration, Pumpkin decided that Poet needed to get exactly what he deserved.

As Pumpkin walked down Lott Avenue toward his place of residence, he was unaware of the shadow lurking in the dark directly across the street. Normally, one of his soldiers would have walked with him, making sure he got home safely. But it was okay because he had not a care in the world, never giving a thought to the pummeling that he had just allocated to the young woman. Pumpkin's lack of respect for women, and for people in general, had just bought him a one-way ticket to an impending death.

As Pumpkin walked through the abandoned parking lot near his building, Poet walked directly up to him. In his hand, he held a 9 mm with an extended modified clip and was pointing it directly in the face of the fearless Pumpkin.

Pumpkin held his hands up. "Wow, son," he began, as the corners of his mouth turned upward to form a disturbing smile. "So you got to me first, huh?"

Poet held the gun steadily in his hand just in case Pumpkin tried to grab it. "Yeah, motherfucker, I got to you first but I ain't got too much time for conversation. How you wanna die, bullet in the head or a body shot?"

Pumpkin laughed. "Oh, so you think I'm goin' out like a fuckin' sucker, huh?"

Poet looked around him. "Well, I don't see none of your flunkies around so I guess so!"

Suddenly, Pumpkin lunged at Poet and tried to grab the gun away from his grasp. With the adrenaline flowing and youthful aggression on their side, they began fighting for their lives. Pumpkin sent a powerful blow to Poet's chin, which temporarily dazed him. With the weapon still in his hand, Poet struck Pumpkin in the head with the side of the gun. Pumpkin grabbed the side of his head and began falling backward, losing his footing on the gravel that was strewn throughout the parking lot.

As Pumpkin was going down, Poet immediately began letting off rounds from the 9 mm. He was unmoved as he watched Pumpkin's body jerk from the impact of the bullets. Pumpkin finally slammed into the building adjacent to the parking lot and slid down the brick wall. Even though it was pitch black outside, Poet stood there and watched Pumpkin take his last breath. All that could be seen were the whites of Pumpkin's eyes, which were still open from the shock of being shot. Blood dripped from his forehead and down to his chin. Poet heard someone yell in the distance and he ran away as fast as his feet could carry him.

In an attempt to catch his breath, Poet ducked into a nearby building, which just happened to be empty. His heart was beating rapidly and he was sweating bullets. Poet was finally able to understand why he was committing such sadistic acts.

It was the pent-up anger that Poet had felt for so many years after his father left the family. His issues with abandonment were surfacing and it seemed as if there was nothing that he could do to stop his destructive behavior. He was disappointed in himself because after all of the years of trying to stay on track, he was messing up terribly. The "good" deed that he had performed by removing the rapist had turned into premeditated murder when he killed the thieving John-John, and now Pumpkin was the next victim in line.

Poet began experiencing an onset of different emotions, like anger, denial, and guilt, along with the realization that the previous encounter with the notorious Pumpkin could have cost him his life. Poet knew that he was living a lie and, unfortunately, after his actions that night, he had revealed that he was not a vigilante or a superhero; he was a murderer.

Never having to experience a brush with death before, Poet dropped the gun and fell to the floor of the abandoned building. He covered his face and began to weep loudly, not caring who heard him.

A half hour passed quickly and Poet attempted to get himself together. He peeked out the doorway to make sure no one was around. Then Poet heard some police sirens nearby. Sitting in the building was not safe. He picked up the gun from the floor and wrapped it in a bandanna that he had found in his pocket. Poet thought about getting rid of it but he couldn't afford to get rid of another gun.

Poet walked out of the building and strolled down the deserted block. His knees were about to buckle and he had to wait awhile before he headed home. He tucked the gun under his arm and hurriedly called Mekhi on his cell phone. Mekhi picked up the phone immediately.

"What up, Po?" he yelled into the phone. "Where are you at? I saw your car parked in front of your buildin'."

Poet was breathing heavily. "Yo, Khi, I . . . I . . ." Poet stammered.

"Yo, Po, are you a'ight? You okay?" Mekhi shouted.

"I killed him, son. I just killed Pumpkin." There was silence on the other end of the phone.

"You did what?"

"You heard me, man! I fuckin' killed Pumpkin, man. I just killed him a few minutes ago."

"What the hell . . . Po, why the hell are you doin' this? I mean, I know why but—," Khi began while trying to make sense of what Poet was telling him.

"Look, Khi, I need you to meet me, okay? I can't walk no farther. Feels like I can't make it . . . I need you, man."

"Where are you at?"

"I'm on"—Poet paused as he looked at the street sign—"I'm on Newport near Rockaway, man."

"I'm on my way."

As Mekhi walked down Rockaway, he was visibly upset. His friend had taken this killing spree over the limit and now he was being dragged into it. The killings were becoming more frequent and, at any given moment, everything was going to come to a brutal end. He loved Poet like a brother but it was only going to get worse if he didn't get help.

As Mekhi walked up the block, he was taken aback by the stillness of the night. It made him very nervous as he approached the location where he was to meet Poet. He turned the corner and heard a hissing noise coming from the side of a building. It was Poet, who was standing in the dark, looking like a madman. When he stepped out of the shadows, Mekhi noticed the wrapped-up gun that was casually tucked under his arm.

"Po, why do you still have that gun on you, man?" he asked in amazement, assuming that it was the weapon that Poet had used to kill Pumpkin.

Poet laughed and looked at the gun like it was the first time he had seen it.

"Oh, yeah. The gun. I'm keepin' this," he replied.

"You know got-damn well you can't keep that gun! What if the police run up on you and you have that dirty-ass gun on you? Then what? This gun has bodies on it! You gotta get rid of it!" Mekhi reached for the gun. "C'mon, Po, give it up! I can't let you walk around with this shit!"

Poet backed up from his reach. Mekhi could see the crazed look in his eyes under the streetlight.

"It's my gun and I'm keepin' it!" Poet yelled, holding the gun close to his body.

Mekhi attempted to calm Poet down. "Okay, okay. Why can't I hold it for you?"

Poet shook his head. "I don't want you to hold it, man. I might have to use this shit again."

Mekhi eased up. "Okay, look, you can't go home tonight. Come to my crib and stay the night, okay?"

Poet nodded his head in agreement. He knew that he couldn't go home in the mental state that he was in. As they walked back toward the projects, Poet kept holding on to the gun for dear life. Meanwhile, Mekhi picked up the phone and made a secret phone call to Precious.

"Hello?" answered Precious.

"Hey," Mekhi began, while walking next to the exhausted Poet. "Don't come to my house tomorrow mornin'. My man, Poet, is spendin' the night. We'll hang out some other time."

Precious sucked her teeth. "Kiss my ass, Mekhi," she replied with an attitude.

"I'll call you tomorrow," he said, but she had already hung the phone up on him.

Poet looked at Mekhi. He was a little paranoid. "Yo, man, who was that?"

"Just some chick I was supposed to see tomorrow mornin'."

Poet, who seemed to be getting back to his old self as the moments passed, looked at Mekhi with a smile on his face.

"Anybody I know?"

"Nah, you don't know this chick," Mekhi casually replied and wiped some sweat from his brow.

Mekhi looked at his phone and deleted his last outgoing call. Then the friends walked the rest of the way home in silence.

Chapter 15

The Heat is On

It was a sunny Sunday morning and Oates and Lewis were driving around their sector in the unmarked squad car. They had just gotten wind of another murder that had occurred earlier that morning. The deceased had been identified as Terrence Watts, better known as Pumpkin, an infamous Blood leader. They hated to see another black man become a fatality but Pumpkin was a completely different topic.

"Damn, it took somebody this long to kill that motherfucker?" Lewis asked, while Oates drove the vehicle.

Oates shook his head. "Man, you're heartless!" he stated. "Pumpkin was somebody's child, you know."

Lewis looked out the passenger side window. "I don't give a fuck about him being somebody's child. He was a disgusting human being and it's too bad we didn't kill his ass first!"

Oates shook his head. He held his head up. "God," he began. "I am not cosigning this idiot's thoughts or his opinions about that black man's death. Detective Lewis is very ignorant so please forgive him, for he knows not what he speaks!"

They both keeled over from laughter. "O, you are crazy! Anyway, I'm just glad we don't have that case. All that gang shit is a serious pain in the ass," Lewis said.

"Yeah, I know." The detectives passed the Langston Hughes projects and Oates thought about Cheryl. "Wonder what's up with my new friend?"

Lewis looked at his partner. "Are you talking about Cheryl, your project princess?"

Oates shook his head and chuckled. "Now why does she have to be a project princess? You're always trying to snap on somebody!"

Lewis laughed. "No, my brother, that's a compliment! I mean, she seems like a nice lady and you like her so she gets a pass. You know it's so many other names associated with the projects like project hood rat, project nympho . . ." he said, before bursting into laughter.

Oates chuckled again. "Okay, okay, bruh, I get the point! Damn! Why you gotta be so extra?"

Lewis shrugged his shoulders. "You know me, I just like to laugh and have a good time. That's why I'm getting a divorce now. My wife says that I don't take shit serious. I mean, how could she say that? Look at what I do for a living! It doesn't get any more serious than this shit here!"

Oates nodded his head in agreement as they pulled over to get some bottled water from a bodega on Blake Avenue. While walking in the store, Oates was greeted with loud salsa music and some young men arguing over beer.

"Yo, Poet, man, youse a grimy-ass dude, son!" a dark brown fellow shouted to the young man standing near the potato chip rack. "It's your turn to buy the beer, son!"

"What? I ain't never said that I was gonna buy any beer!" Poet lied, with a smirk on his face.

The chocolate-complexioned guy smiled. "Damn, you're a liar, son! Wait until I tell Khi this shit! You said you was gonna buy the beer, you cheap bastard!"

Poet laughed. "My beer buyin' days are over, kid! I supply the wheels now so y'all cats gotta buy the beer! Gas is expensive!"

The dark-skinned guy walked up to counter with two six packs of Corona while Oates was standing there paying for his water. When the guy walked out, Poet and Oates were standing at the counter alone.

"Let me have a Dutch, Paco!" Poet called out to the cashier behind the counter. Suddenly, he turned around and looked at Oates up and down. "Yo, you're the police, huh?" he asked.

Oates laughed. *So this must be the notorious Poet, Cheryl's little prince*, he thought. *What a prize.*

"Yeah, I'm a detective. Detective Oates. How are you doing, Poet?"

Oates held out his hand for him to shake it. Poet extended his hand as well.

"Oh, okay!" Poet exclaimed with a smile. "So you're the cat that called my moms the other day? What are you doin' on this side of town?"

Oates smirked. "I work in the Seventy-third Precinct." Poet stopped smiling. "What's up with you? Are you staying out of trouble?"

Even though he was slightly nervous about meeting the detective, Poet puffed his chest out.

"Who, me? Yeah, I am. I'm just chillin'." Poet paused and looked at Oates in his suit. "Nice suit. Guess that's the uniform for a homicide detective, huh?"

"Yeah, that's right." There was an awkward silence between them. "By the way, I need to ask you a few questions, Poet. When could you make it down to the station?"

Poet grabbed his change and the Dutch cigar from the counter.

"Make it down to the stationhouse? For what?" Poet asked with a hint of nervousness in his voice. He hoped Oates didn't notice.

"I've been meaning to talk to you about the robbery of Mr. Leroy Pugh. He said that you helped him out that night."

"Oh, I don't have to come down to the stationhouse for that. We could talk about that right here. Mr. Leroy got robbed. The guy ran off before I got to him and I just helped out an old friend, that's all. Why?"

Oates nodded his head. "So you didn't know who robbed Mr. Leroy?"

"No, I didn't. I couldn't see the thief because he had dark clothes on. Mr. Leroy mentioned a name but I didn't pay that any mind. I just wanted to make sure that he was okay."

"Okay, I see," said Oates. "Well, it was nice meeting you, Poet. I'm looking forward to meeting your sisters, too. Oh, and tell your mother that I'll call her later."

Poet's face looked flushed when he said that. "Yeah, I'll tell her. Later." He practically ran out of the store.

When Oates got back into the squad car, he pointed out Poet to Lewis.

"Hey, Lew, that's Poet, Cheryl's son."

Lewis squinted to get a better look at the young man, who was walking toward a steel-grey Camry and getting in on the driver's side.

"Hmmm, a late-model Toyota Camry with temporary plates. Is that his car?"

"Well, it isn't his mother's. She doesn't have a car. We gotta keep an eye on this guy, Lew. Remember that face."

Oates and Lewis didn't see Poet watching them like a hawk as they drove away.

***

"So I heard that you met my Poet today," Cheryl said to Oates. He called her as soon as he got home that evening.

"Yeah, I met him," Oates replied. There was silence on both ends.

"Oh, my goodness, I hope he wasn't rude to you or—" she began.

Oates cut her off. "Cheryl, stop worrying about that! It's okay. Actually, he was pretty good with the whole introduction thing. I was surprised."

Cheryl laughed. "Well, it's good to know that he wasn't acting like a fool. I wouldn't have had any of that."

"I know, sweetheart, I know. So what's up, when do you wanna hang out with me?"

"Well, hopefully soon. It's been pretty hectic this past week so I just was trying to relax. Did you have any plans?"

"Well, we can do some dinner, drinks. Anything you want."

"I don't know too many places to eat or drink. I don't go out much anymore."

"You mean that you're saving all that prettiness for the house? You're kidding me, right?"

Cheryl grinned. "You are so crazy! Wherever you want to take me is fine—as long as I get out of this house."

Oates smiled. "Well, you hang with me and you're gonna go places. I promise you that."

Cheryl sighed. "It's a relief to finally meet someone decent, I'll say that. I really appreciate you."

"No problem, miss. I appreciate you too." Oates yawned. "Look, sweetheart, I'm about to take me a shower and go to bed. I have some things I gotta do in the morning. So I'll speak to you tomorrow, okay?"

"No problem. You have a good night."
"You too."

The next day, Oates and Lewis sat at their desk and interviewed a few witnesses in their murder cases. They had a few leads, but at the end of it all they were still no closer to finding the killers than they were when they first started investigating. Both victims, Jerrod Timmons and John Moxley, had a long list of enemies and they didn't know where to start. The dead-end interrogations with the persons of interest were becoming monotonous. They knew that they had to step up their game and find some new leads.

Detective Patrone came over to their desks to talk about another case that had just opened.

"Do you guys have any leads on the Timmons case yet?" he asked.

Lewis shrugged his shoulders. "Nah, Vinny, we're still waiting for a fucking miracle over here," replied Lewis with a fake Italian accent.

Patrone laughed. "Yeah, we've been pretty busy too. Hey, you heard about the Watts case?"

Lewis and Oates looked at each other. "Nah, what's up?" asked Oates.

"Well, Hopewell and Mickens got a lead on that one. They said that your boy, Pumpkin—hell of a name for a tough guy—had a verbal altercation with this young buck from the neighborhood. Everyone in the hood is talking about it."

Oates crossed his arms. "But that's still not much to go on, Vin. This guy, Pumpkin, was a real asshole. I'm pretty sure that he had more enemies than our dead guys, you know, the rapist and the thief."

"Yeah, you're right," Vinny agreed. "But no one is going to actually admit to hating this guy, Pumpkin. They're scared to death of him. If anything, they're gonna try to put his killing on anybody just to get the heat off them. You know how many Crip gang members have already called Hopewell?"

"I can imagine," announced Lewis.

"Exactly. Well, the person that I heard he had the argument with on the day that he was murdered was some guy named Poet. Youse heard of him?"

"Poet?" Oates repeated. "So this is the guy Pumpkin had the argument with on the night he died, huh?"

"Yeah, so we've heard. Hopewell is looking to bring this guy in for questioning. Fortunately, he's never been arrested, but they got a printout of his driver's license picture from the DMV." Vinny put a picture of Poet from his driver's license on Oates's desk. "So, if you guys see him anywhere in the streets, you may need to bring him in for questioning. You gotta talk to Hopewell about the other details."

Vinny walked away and Oates looked at the picture on his desk. "Damn, Lew! This little motherfucker's name is coming up again! What did I tell you? I knew something was up with his ass! I was really trying to avoid questioning him about the Moxley case but I can't hold out anymore."

Lewis rubbed his goatee. "Ain't this about a bitch? Are you gonna tell his mother about the investigation?"

"Hell no! This is police business. I'm not gonna get her involved. Let him tell her. Cheryl and I got a date this week."

Lewis laughed. "Damn! You're still going to hang out with this woman and her son is being questioned for a murder? You're a trooper, my man!"

Oates plopped down in the seat and thought about what Lewis said. Talking to Cheryl about Poet couldn't hurt their union. Or could it?

Chapter 16

Lies, Lies, and More Lies

It was around 6:30 P.M. Sunday night. Poet got out of his parked car and anxiously looked over his shoulder. He was still unnerved after running into Detective Oates in the bodega. The streets were talking about Pumpkin's death and paranoia was getting the best of him. If Bone found out, Poet knew that his money well would be dried up real soon.

When Poet finally arrived at the spot, he put the key in the door and Bone swung the door open. He pulled Poet inside.

Poet looked confused. "What's good, Bone?" he asked.

Bone plopped down on the sofa and told Poet to sit down too. "Yo, Po, what's up with you?" Bone inquired. "Didn't I tell you to keep your nose clean?"

Poet frowned. "What are you talkin' about?"

"I'm talkin' about Pumpkin! Word in the hood is that you smoked him last night!"

Poet wasn't about to admit his guilt. "Who the fuck is goin' around sayin' that stupid shit?"

"Well, accordin' to the hood, you and Pumpkin got into it the other day because him and some of his comrades was sittin' on your fuckin' car. Y'all had some words and he threatened you or some shit like that and the next thing you know, the motherfucker ends up dead!"

Poet sucked his teeth. "Yo, Bone, this is my fuckin' word, I ain't do shit to Pumpkin! I wasn't even there when he got smoked. I don't know why 'the hood got my name in their mouths!"

"Listen, Po, you're my little man and everything but I run a business here and I ain't tryin' to take the heat for no bullshit out in the street! You wanna shoot and kill motherfuckers, you go right ahead, but gimme back my car keys and gimme the keys to this crib. I don't want none of that bullshit to come my way, do you understand me?"

Poet shook his head. "Bone, I ain't tryin' to put you out there like that and, word to mother, I ain't do shit to Pumpkin! It's about a million and one dudes that could have smoked Pumpkin!"

Bone stood up. He wasn't so sure that he could believe Poet, but he remained very calm. There was no sense in getting himself all worked up over something that hadn't been proven. This time, he was going to give Poet the benefit of the doubt.

"Well, this shit ain't even up for discussion anymore—I'm outta here. Khi called me and said that he was on his way. So y'all take care of my shit and don't—I repeat, don't—be havin' no broads in my spot, neither!" he said, lightening up the tension between them.

Poet laughed. "C'mon, Bone, do you think we would disrespect you like that? We don't mix the business with pleasure, son!"

Bone smiled. "Yeah, okay! I don't want no problems. I'm trustin' your ass!"

Poet waved Bone off. "You're good money, Bizzy Bone! Now go home to your wife and kids, man. We got this!"

Bone walked out of the apartment and Poet watched from the window as he got into his car. When he drove away, Poet breathed a sigh of relief and immediately called Mekhi on his cell phone.

"Yo, Khi, where are you at?" Poet asked.

"I'm leavin' the crib. Why?" Mekhi asked.

"Just wonderin' if you heard anything about that Pumpkin thing yet."

"Nah, I haven't. You heard anything?"

"Nah, but Bone asked me about it as soon as I walked in here. He was like he heard it from the hood. You haven't said anything to anybody, did you?"

Mekhi looked at the cell phone to see if he was hearing things. "What? Yo, Po, look, man, I'm on your team! You're actin' real paranoid right now."

"Whatever. Just hurry up. I'm not comfortable bein' in here by myself."

"A'ight, I'm there," Mekhi said before hanging up with Poet.

Mekhi turned around and kissed Precious on the lips. He massaged her butt then got up and began to put on his clothes.

"Where you goin', Khi?" she asked, still lying in the bed.

"I'm goin' to meet your brother," he replied.

Precious sulked. She reluctantly got up to put her clothes on too. "Damn, why are you always dissin' me for my brother? Forget about my brother. Stay with me today!"

Mekhi ignored Precious's temper tantrum. "Please, Presh, don't stress me out, please. Just put your clothes on so that we can break out. I have to meet Poet."

All of a sudden, Precious slapped him in the face. Mekhi froze in his tracks.

"What the fuck did you hit me for, man?" he asked. His face was still stinging from the slap.

"Because you're always puttin' my brother before me! You give him more attention than you give me when I'm the one that you're fuckin'!"

Mekhi continued to get dressed. "Yo, get the hell out of my house before I hurt you, Precious! Don't you ever put your fuckin' hands on me again!"

Precious grinned. She walked right up to him. "What are you gonna do if I do put my hands on you again? You can't kick my ass! I'm your best friend's sister, remember?"

"Well, touch me again and find out."

Precious dug her nails into his left arm. Mekhi slapped her so hard that she fell back against a wall with his paintings on it. One painting fell on her head and she began crying.

"You're a fuckin' sucker! I can't stand you!" she yelled.

Mekhi inspected his scratched-up arm and lifted her up by her collar. "I told you do not put your fuckin' hands on me again!" He pushed Precious and she fell again. "Now get your shit and get the fuck outta my house!"

The crying Precious quickly got herself together and gathered her things. She walked out of Mekhi's room without giving him any eye contact.

When he heard the door slam, Mekhi shook his head as he thought about what he had just done. Not only was he sleeping with Precious, he had resorted to putting his hands on her, too, and it would have been nothing for her to tell Poet what happened between them. After all, when he hit her, he had given Precious the ammunition to reveal their dirty little secret.

Mekhi's stomach felt queasy as he walked out of his building to meet up with Poet. He knew that Precious was too immature to handle their so-called "relationship" but the damage was already done. Now that things looked as if they were about to become unpleasant between him and Precious, it could be nothing but trouble.

Precious walked out of Mekhi's house with an attitude and a swollen face from the slap that she received from him. Frustrated with being pushed to the side for her brother, she had lashed out at Mekhi and she knew that she was wrong for that. But the truth was that Precious was no longer feeling the secrecy, and her feelings for Mekhi were getting out of control. Something had to give before she lost her mind.

It was still fairly early and Precious didn't see any of her friends at their usual hangout spot. She decided to walk to the corner store to grab a few things before going home. Her face was still pulsating on the side where Mekhi had slapped her and, of course, she was still pissed.

"Hey, Precious," said a young man who was standing in front of the store, smoking a cigarette. He greeted her with a smile and put his cigarette out with his foot.

"Oh, hey, Kody," Precious said. "What are you up to?"

"Nothin'. I was just hangin' out. I'm kind of bored, too. It ain't nothin' to do around here." Kody began checking her out from head to toe. "You're lookin' real good these days, Precious," he said, biting his bottom lip.

Precious blushed and checked herself out as if she didn't believe him. "Yeah? I do?"

Kody smiled. "Yeah, you do. And damn, your body is lookin' right, too." He locked eyes with Precious. "You know that I've been watchin' you for a minute, right?"

"How long is a minute?"

"For years. You know that you're that chick around here."

Precious giggled. "Is that right?"

Kody chuckled and imitated her voice. "Is that right? Yeah, that's right."

They both smiled at each other. Twenty-five-year-old Kody was a handsome young man who had a knack for having sex with young, impressionable teenage girls. Rumor had it that he was also pimping young girls.

His sexy bedroom eyes had Precious stuck for a moment and she kept smiling as he stared at her.

"So what's up? Do you wanna come and hang out with me at my house?"

Precious shrugged her shoulders. "I don't even know you like that, Kody, so why would I want to come with you to your house?" she asked while batting her eyes.

Kody laughed at the gesture. "You can come with me because you know me from around the way. It ain't like I'm some stranger. And not to mention, I done already told you that I've been checkin' you out for a minute. I been wantin' to talk to you for a while but it never was the right time. So come on and hang out with me, cutie. Let's have some fun."

Precious smiled at Kody. She didn't see why hanging out with him was a problem because, first of all, he wasn't really a stranger. He lived right in the neighborhood and she did see him all the time. Second of all, hanging with Kody would be the perfect revenge for the way that Mekhi was treating her. Precious was tired of playing second fiddle to Poet anyway. Her hand went to the swollen side of her face. She was going to make sure that Mekhi paid for hitting her and making her feel as if she didn't matter to him.

"All right, I'll hang out with you," Precious said with a smile. "But only for a little while."

Kody smirked. "And that's all the time we need." Precious and Kody took off for his house.

Kody lived with his father in a tidy home on Bristol Street that was located not too far from the housing projects that Precious lived in. When they walked inside the house, Precious knew that she was about to get more than she bargained for. Kody was much older than her and, of course, much more experienced than she was, making her fearful of him yet curious at the same time.

Suddenly she remembered Poet warning her and Porsha about Kody and his friends, and now being in his house had defied everything that Poet had told her about the man.

But of course, Precious didn't care. She enjoyed rebelling against Poet. She figured what her family didn't know wouldn't hurt them.

"So what have you been up to, Miss Precious?" Kody asked as he picked up the remote and turned on the television.

"Just hangin' out with my friends, goin' to school and stuff," she replied with a mischievous look on her face.

"So how old are you now, like, eighteen?" Kody asked.

"No, I'm . . ." she said before changing her mind. "I mean, yeah, somethin' like that."

Kody smiled. "What do you mean somethin' like that? Either you're eighteen or not."

"Oh, what I meant is that I will be eighteen, um, like next year some time."

Kody shook his head and chuckled. "You're somethin' else, Precious. For a minute I thought that you were younger. I always see you rollin' with Malika and all of them shorties from the PJ's. I figured that you were around their age."

"Oh, no! I'm the oldest of the crew."

Kody guzzled down his soda. "Let me ask you another question. Are you still a virgin?"

Precious frowned. "Hell no! What made you ask me that?"

"I dunno. You just don't seem like you're out there like some of these chicks. I think you're very sexy."

She blushed. "Well, my mother taught me better than that."

They stared at each other for a brief moment. "Do you mind if I kiss you, Precious?"

Precious smiled shyly and shrugged her shoulders. "I don't care."

Kody held Precious's face in his hands and he gave her a sweet, adoring kiss. When Kody went to undo the buttons on her shirt, Precious stopped him.

"I can't do this, Kody," she exclaimed. She stood up. "I just can't do it."

Kody walked over to Precious and pulled her closer to him. "I'm not gonna hurt you, baby. I just wanna make love to you, sweetie."

Kody continued to coax her. No one had ever spoken so sweetly to her, and all the fears that she had a minute before were pushed to the side.

"Take your clothes off for Daddy," he said softly. "Come on. Let me see that pretty body of yours."

The way he was talking to Precious made her feel sexy. She knew that Mekhi loved her but Kody was making feel like a real woman. But now that she was no longer a virgin, Precious felt as if she had matured sexually and she could handle Kody.

As if she was mesmerized by Kody's soft voice, Precious slowly removed her shirt then slid out of her tight stretch jeans. She stood in front of Kody with her panties and bra on waiting for his approval. Kody walked around her like she was on an auction block.

"Damn, look at that ass, baby," he said, tapping her butt cheek lightly and making it bounce. "Take that shit off."

Precious finally came out of her bra and panty set. Kody plopped on the couch in front of her.

"You are a bad ass little momma, you know that?" Kody said. "All the dudes that I know wanna fuck that pussy. We have discussions about how good that young, sweet pussy is."

"For real?" Precious giggled, impressed with the direct sexual remarks that Kody was making.

"Yeah, we do."

Kody opened his pants and kicked them off. He took off his shirt to reveal a well-toned physique.

Precious was beginning to feel tingly all over. Kody then pulled out his large penis and began jerking off to her nakedness. Precious didn't know what to do next.

"Kody, what do you want me to do? Do you want me to give you some head?"

Kody knew what he was doing. After all, he was a twenty-five-year-old man who had been around the block and back. He used to watch Precious rip and run around the neighborhood, practically flaunting herself to boys, and men too. Initially, he wanted to get with Porsha, who, of course, wouldn't give a local guy like him the time of day. But when he saw how her little sister, Precious, had developed overnight and that she seemed so much easier to get with, Porsha was just a passing phase for him.

"Just stand right there and watch me jerk this dick, baby," Kody said as he continued to pleasure himself.

Precious stood there for a few more moments with an uncomfortable look on her face.

Suddenly, Kody stood up and removed all of his clothing. He walked up to Precious and kissed her. Precious surrendered to what she thought were loving kisses. He told her to wrap her arms around his neck. Then Kody lifted Precious up and took her upstairs to his bedroom. There he laid her on the queen-sized bed. He spread her legs open and went down on her, using his expert tongue to sop up her juices. Precious, who had never experienced a man performing cunnilingus on her, began moaning loudly. Precious covered her eyes and did everything in her power to keep from crying tears of pleasure.

What is goin' on? she thought as she felt her body shudder from the multiple orgasms that she was having.

To make her have multiple orgasms, it was obvious Kody had more skills in the bedroom than Mekhi did. Precious felt immediate adoration toward him because of it.

When Kody finally penetrated her, her tightness felt so good to him. Because of that feeling, he was addicted to young pussy. He hadn't even bothered to put on a condom when he entered Precious. He wanted to feel everything. Precious was moaning like crazy as Kody slowly ground her walls. He sucked on her tender nipples as he pushed himself all the way inside of her, until she screamed out his name. Kody's dick had touched a spot, a spot that Precious never knew was there. She shook her head from side to side.

"What are you doin' to me?" she whispered as her body trembled. "Why do I feel like this?" Kody wrapped his arms around her frame. "That's your G-spot, baby. A man ain't never touched that spot before, huh?" he asked as he continued to stroke her insides.

"Oh, my goodness! No, nobody has ever made me feel like this before!"

Kody kept on going, not even bothering to put Precious in different sexual positions. He knew that she wasn't ready for that yet. For now, he just wanted to sex her young pussy. After about twenty minutes of being inside of her, Kody felt himself about to cum. But he needed to ask her the question.

"Yo, Presh, can I cum in you, baby?"

Precious was so caught up in the moment, she screamed yes. Kody ejaculated inside of her. He continued to pump rapidly, and eventually Precious came again as well.

After their interlude, they both lay sprawled across the bed. A smile of satisfaction came over Kody's face. He knew that Precious wasn't eighteen years old but that was fine with him. He wanted her and he had gotten what he wanted. That was all that mattered to him. If only her brother, Poet knew. . . .

Precious looked at the time and jumped up all of a sudden. "I have to go now, Kody. My mother is gonna be lookin' for me," she said.

"Your mother? You got a curfew? I thought you said that you were eighteen?" he asked with a smirk on his face.

Precious hesitated. "Um, well, I do still live in her house so I have to abide by her rules."

Kody shrugged his shoulders. He couldn't care less about Precious having to go home because he was sexually satisfied. Next time he saw her, she was going to be ready to do whatever he wanted her to.

"I hear that," Kody replied with a yawn. His flaccid penis was still dripping with her juices.

"Anyway, your clothes are downstairs. I'm tired. You can let yourself out. I'll lock the door later."

Kody then turned over and proceeded to close his eyes.

Precious stood there for a moment, feeling slighted by Kody's nonchalant attitude. But she didn't have time to gripe about it. She quickly ran downstairs, put her clothes on, and ran out the door. Once she was outside, she walked rapidly down the block toward the projects. She had to get home. She had had enough of the grown woman business for the night.

Chapter 17

Law and Order

Things were pretty quiet in "the 'Ville" for the next few days. With Pumpkin deceased, his Blood set was pretty much defunct now that the leader of the gang was gone. John-John, the thief, was dead and once again kids were comfortable with riding their bikes through the courtyards of the projects. Senior citizens could cash their Social Security checks without having to worry about being robbed. The rapist, Jerrod Timmons, who was basically nameless until his untimely death, was gone forever without fanfare. The women of Brownsville were left to breathe easy for the time being until the next up-and-coming pervert decided he wanted to attack. It was a harsh reality, but fortunately the sign of the times prepared the people of Brownsville for the worst.

Poet was taken in for questioning in the murder of Terrence "Pumpkin" Watts. Poet was able to maintain his composure in front of the detectives, staring them in the eyes when he answered their questions, and made sure that he didn't fidget or stumble over one word. After watching shows like *CSI, Law & Order,* and *The First 48,* Poet was able to keep a straight face.

Poet was unable to lie about the argument between him and Pumpkin because there had been too many witnesses. But he was able to provide the detectives with a solid alibi. He simply told them that he was at Mekhi's house on the night of the killing.

The interrogation went on between Poet and homicide detectives Hopewell and Mickens for at least three hours. There was no page left unturned and Poet couldn't wait for the whole process to be over. He wasn't nervous about being questioned by the detectives—he just didn't want to end up in jail.

"Well, Mr. Washington, we can see that you have never been arrested. What are you doing with yourself these days? Are you gainfully employed?"

"Look, Detective, I didn't kill Pumpkin, okay? Now why do you wanna question me about anything else?" Poet asked. "I done already told you where I was the night that he was killed. Why do you wanna know where I work and all that?"

Detective Hopewell looked at Mickens and smirked. "Yeah, you're a pretty clever guy, Poet. Just to let you know, this is still going to be an open case and you're a person of interest, so don't leave town."

When Poet walked out of the precinct after the extensive interrogation, he thought about the warning that Detective Hopewell had given him: "don't leave town." Poet smiled and mocked the burly detective as he walked to his car.

"Don't leave town," Poet said. "What the fuck is he talkin' about? Fuck him and fuck Pumpkin too."

Poet got into his car and pulled off. He didn't think that he should be questioned about anything, let alone a murder. Pumpkin, along with the others, was a nuisance to the community and they had to go. If anything, Poet felt that he should be getting rewarded for his outstanding work.

***

Meanwhile, Oates walked through the precinct, talking with his peers, when Lewis walked up to him.

"Yo, O, your boy Poet was just questioned by Hopewell. He walked out of here a few minutes before we walked in," Lewis said.

Oates looked around the precinct as if he was hoping to see Poet standing around. "You're kiddin' me. Where is he now?"

"He left. He just got into his car and left."

Oates sucked his teeth. "Man, this is bad. Where's Hopewell?"

"Him and Mickens are still in the interrogation room going over some paperwork. Maybe you need to go holler at them."

"No doubt." Oates paused for a second. "Lew, come walk with me, man."

Lewis obliged and they walked toward the small room with the one-way glass. Oates knocked on the door and Hopewell opened it, inviting the two detectives inside. They took their seats.

"Hey, what's up, O?" Hopewell greeted. "What's good?"

"Man, what's up with Poet Washington?" Oates asked, getting straight to the point.

Hopewell shook his head. "Man, that little bastard was lying through his teeth! I know for a fact that he smoked Pumpkin Watts!"

"But do you have any physical evidence of this, Hope?"

"Nah, not really but c'mon, O, this is a typical revenge killing, man! Pumpkin Watts' name has been splattered all over our desks for some time now and you know after some bullshit argument these two had the other day, Pumpkin was definitely coming

for Poet! We questioned a few of Pumpkin's so-called
cronies and they told us that killing Poet was already
confirmed before the man was murdered. Poet had dis-
respected a Blood leader. They would rather die themselves before they let some random motherfucker like
Poet disrespect them in front of their comrades and get
away with it."

Oates and Lewis nodded in agreement. Hopewell
had a point. "Damn, Hope," Oates said, putting his
head in his hands.

Hopewell frowned and pulled Oates to the side.
"What's up, O? Is this guy your family or something?"
he asked.

"He's not related to me or anything like that but his
mother is a real good friend of mine. I would hate to see
her go through the bullshit, if you know what I mean."

Hopewell smiled. Oates was ten years his junior and
he liked him as a detective and as a person. Unfortunately, Oates was getting emotionally involved with a
family member of a potential murder suspect and that
wasn't a good look. Emotions ran high and good police
work could be tainted because of someone's personal
involvement with a suspect.

Hopewell shrugged his shoulders. "Well, O, I don't
know what to tell you. We're still investigating and we're
still questioning some other people. It's a sixty percent
chance that this guy, Poet, is our fella. All the fingers are
pointing in his direction, O, but without any strong physical evidence, we can't book him off the word of some gang
members. Now there's one person that we didn't question
and that was his friend, Mekhi Porter. Poet's alibi in this
case relies heavily on Porter's confession. Poet claims that
he was at Porter's house during the hours that Pumpkin
was killed. We have to confirm that."

Oates sighed loudly. "So what about his job? This murder occurred on a weeknight, didn't it?"

Hopewell rubbed his chin. "Job?" Hopewell looked around to make sure his partner, Mickens, wasn't within earshot of their conversation. He was engrossed in a chat with Lewis about the Knicks game.

"Are you kidding me?" Hopewell said. "Poet Washington don't have no damn job, O! He's out there hustlin' for Bone. You know Bone, man. Bone has the Brownsville drug game on lock." Oates shook his head. "Well, Bone is Poet's boss. Poet thinks that we don't know this shit but we done already got the drop on his ass!"

"Wow. And he told his mother that he had a night job cleaning corporate buildings or some shit like that. You see how these children lie to their parents?" Oates angrily stated.

"Yep, now you see. Poet seems like he could have been a likeable guy but when you tell one lie, you gotta tell another, then another. Anyway, young buck, as far as his mother is concerned, I don't think that you should tell her anything. But you have to make that decision on your own. Who am I to tell you not to do somethin'? You're a grown man." Hopewell chuckled. "She must be fine, huh?"

Oates's face flushed with embarrassment. "Hell, yeah, she is fine as hell! Why do you think I'm so upset about her son? I don't want anything standing in the way of me getting with this woman."

Hopewell looked around again. He was the type of brother who always acted like he had the biggest secret in the world to tell you. "Well, between me and you, I think that you shouldn't stop seeing the woman. Whatever her son does out in the street is not a reflection of her as a mother. She sounds as if she's a good woman, you like her, y'all grown, so do you. Even though I don't believe that you should shit where you eat, but, hey what the fuck? You only live once, right?"

Oates sighed and gave Hopewell five. "Yeah, man. You're right. Her son isn't my problem. It's just that she's such a nice lady and I like her. She's a single mother, doing the best that she can, you know? I feel kinda bad for her."

"Well, I can see why you would feel bad for the woman. She's probably working hard, coming home and not really giving any thought to what her son is do-ing out in these streets because technically the moth-erfucker is a grown-ass man. I'm sure that she doesn't know about all the stuff that's going on. Trust me."

Oates and Lewis walked out of the room after con-versing with Hopewell and Mickens. As he sat at his desk, Oates' mood was melancholic. Lewis knew when to leave well enough alone.

"Hey, O, do you need something from the store?" Lewis asked.

"No, I'm okay," he replied, leaning back in his chair with his eyes closed.

He sighed as he grappled with the thought of telling Cheryl about her son. He had finally met someone who he could get into and now this bullshit was happen-ing. Unlike so many of his other relationships that he had let go because of minor problems, he was going to work this one out. Cheryl made him feel that it would be worth it.

Chapter 18

Bad News

The next night, Oates and Cheryl went out on their first date. After they had an intimate dinner at a Thai restaurant in Boerum Hill, Oates suggested that they take a nice walk on the Brooklyn promenade. Cheryl was looking radiant in her fitted jeans and a sheer lemon-yellow blouse. She was just the right weight for her five foot two frame, and her reddish brown hair blew in the soothing breeze that came off the East River.

Oates felt his heart beating rapidly as he took in her natural beauty. He hadn't felt that way about anyone in a long time. He wanted to kiss Cheryl but he told himself it was probably too soon for that type of affection. He preferred to just take it slow.

After walking for a few minutes, they both decided to sit down and watch the Manhattan skyline.

"Shareef, I must say that I'm really enjoying myself with you," she said with a smile.

"Me too, Cheryl. Me too." He paused. "And I have to admit that you look fabulous! I wouldn't believe that you were damn near forty years old with three children!"

Cheryl laughed loudly. "Yeah, babe, thirty-eight years old and I'm knocking on forty's door. I try to stay fit by eating healthy. I have never been a big woman but, hey, now that I'm getting up there in age, the pounds might start to pack on. My mother is a petite woman too, so I guess I have some good genes."

Oates checked her out. "I can see that." Cheryl blushed. They both looked across the water at the moonlight shining in the distance. The mood was definitely right— it was a romantic moment.

Unfortunately, that moment that Oates had waited for was about to be put on hold. He knew that Poet was Cheryl's pride and joy. He had even held back on questioning him about the Leroy Pugh robbery because he wanted to make sure that things were solidified between him and Cheryl first. But when the subject came up of Poet being a person of interest in Pumpkin's murder, Oates realized that the situation was getting out of control. Now it was up to him to tell Cheryl the ugly truth about her beloved son. "Cheryl, I know that this is our first date, but I have to talk to you about something very important."

Cheryl rolled her eyes up in her head. "Oh my goodness, you live with somebody, don't you? Are you married?"

Oates frowned. "Hell no to number one and a definite hell no to number two! I was ready to talk about something totally different." Cheryl looked relieved. "In order for us to build a solid friendship that could possibly turn into a committed relationship, we're going to have to trust each other and I really need you to trust me. I'm not trying to do anything to hurt you and I am definitely not trying to start out a relationship by keeping secrets from you."

Cheryl looked confused. She was unsure of what Oates was talking about, especially since this was their second time seeing each other in person.

Oates sighed. "Well, it's like this. You know that I'm a homicide detective and I love my work. My job means the world to me, I do it with pride, and I've learned over the years to not take my work home. That's why I always kept it separate from my personal life. So when certain things that are affiliated with my work hit close to home, it bothers me."

"I don't understand where you're going with this, Shareef," Cheryl said with a bewildered look on her face.

"Cheryl, your son, Poet, um, I don't know if he told you or not but he was brought into the precinct the other day for questioning."

Cheryl's eyes bulged out of her head. "He was what? What the hell for?" she exclaimed.

Oates regretted that he even brought it up, but he felt that it was his duty to tell her what was going on with her eldest child.

Oates sighed. "He's a person of interest in a murder case, the murder of Terrence Watts."

Cheryl seemed as if she was trying to remember something. "Terrence Watts? That name sounds familiar. Who is that?"

"You probably know him as Pumpkin."

Cheryl put her hand to her mouth. "Pumpkin? Oh, my God. They just recently found that young man dead on Lott Avenue."

"I know. Your son and Pumpkin allegedly had a run-in the same day Pumpkin was murdered. He was questioned about it and even though the investigation is still going on, his name came up. I'm so sorry, Cheryl."

Cheryl's bottom lip began to quiver. "Did he do it? I mean, do they have any evidence that he did this?"

Oates looked at the water. "That could be a long time coming. If they don't have any witnesses to actually identify him, then the detectives have to send any physical evidence that they got from the crime scene, like DNA or shell casings or bullets, to a lab for fingerprints, blood. That could take a month or so." There was an uncomfortable silence between them. "I'm sorry, Cheryl, but I just felt like I had to tell you, just in case anything comes up. I couldn't see myself smiling in your face knowing that I had some information as important as this and not tell you anything."

Cheryl looked down. "I understand. Trust me, I do. I can't, I can't even be upset right now. I respect the fact that you told me this when my son wasn't even man enough to come and tell me himself. I thought that we were closer than that."

Oates put his arm around Cheryl and pulled her closer to him. "Cheryl, you're a beautiful woman and I'm sure that you did a good job in raising your children. God forbid if—notice that I said if—he did do something like this, it would be no indication of bad parenting on your part."

She sighed. "Well, thank you, Shareef. I appreciate the compliment but I do blame myself for some things. I mean, Poet never had that father figure in his life. His father left us when I was pregnant with my youngest daughter. I felt so guilty about his father not being there for him now I think that I might have given him too much leeway. And the least I could have done was allowed myself the opportunity to meet a decent man, someone who could be a role model for Poet. I have dated a few men but things just didn't work out. They weren't right for me or my children."

Oates nodded his head. "Cheryl, you can't blame yourself. It's not your fault. You did what you had to do. Of course, you're human, we need some type of companionship and you had that. But in the interim, you also chose not to have just any man come into your home and be around your children who did not deserve to be there. I'm not mad at that. That just shows how unselfish you are and that you don't mind making sacrifices for your family."

"I guess so," she said with a sigh. They were both quiet for a moment. "I just hope that Poet didn't have anything to do with that murder. That would break my heart."

Cheryl leaned her head on Oates's chest and wiped a tear from her eye.

Chapter 19

A New Attitude

The day after Poet was questioned by the Seventy-third Precinct homicide detectives, he was in a bad mood. Pumpkin and his loyal cronies had been antagonizing people in the neighborhood for years. He was still amazed that anyone would even try to persecute him for the murder of Pumpkin Watts.

As Poet turned onto Rockaway Avenue to walk toward Pitkin Avenue, he ran into Kody Bradford. They had known each other for some years but would only speak to each other in passing. Poet was never a real fan of Kody, who was rumored to be pimping young girls. Even though they never had a run-in, Poet had no interest in trying to be any more than just civil to the man.

"What's up, Po," said Kody.

"What's up, Kody," Poet said.

"Nothin', man, I'm good and you?" asked Kody, giving him his signature sneaky, side-eyed look.

"I'm good," Poet said as he was walking away.

Then a smirk came over Kody's face. "Yo, Poet, I've been meanin' to ask you, how's your sisters doin'?"

Poet turned around. He frowned. "Come again?" he asked.

"How's your sisters? I haven't seen them around here in a minute."

Poet clenched his jaw. Why would Kody ask him about his sisters? He decided that he wasn't going to allow Kody to get him upset. He had enough problems.

"They're good. Porsha is in college and Precious, well, Precious is in the eleventh grade. She's just turned sixteen," Poet said sarcastically, just in case Kody had any ideas.

Kody turned up his lip and nodded his head. "Word? Little Precious is sixteen now? Damn, time sure does fly," he replied, rubbing his chin. He was getting a kick out of being facetious. "Word on the street is that you're doin' some big things out here, Po."

"Like what?" replied Poet, folding his arms. He was finished with the conversation but Kody seemed to want to keep talking to him for some reason. Poet was trying to find out why.

"It's a rumor goin' around about how you killed Pumpkin."

"Oh, yeah?" Poet said with a chuckle. "And there's a rumor goin' around about how you're fuckin' and pimpin' little girls."

Kody gave Poet a strange look. "Is that right?"

"Yeah, that's right."

The two men just stared each other down but no one said a word for a few seconds.

Kody chuckled loudly. "Damn, these some lyin' ass motherfuckers in the hood."

Poet had a serious look on his face. "Ain't they?"

"A'ight, Po, you got that one, homeboy. I'm outta here. Later."

Poet gave Kody a head nod and the peace sign. "Deuces."

When Poet finally made it upstairs, he knocked on the girls' bedroom door. When Precious saw that it was him at the door, she instantly caught an attitude.

"Yeah?" she asked.

Poet pushed past her and sat on Porsha's bed. "So what's up, Presh?"

Precious frowned. "What do you want? And why are you in my room?"

"I need to ask you somethin'."

Precious sucked her teeth. "Oh, boy. What is it now?"

"Kody asked about you and Porsha today and I was just curious as to why he was askin' about y'all two all of a sudden. He hasn't tried to talk to you, has he?"

Precious felt like her heart skipped a beat. "Oh, my goodness, Poet! Kody is grown. Plus, I don't mess with anyone in this neighborhood. All I do is go to school and come home," she lied.

Poet gave her a look. "That's your best bet. Please don't get nobody fuckin' killed out here. I'm tellin' you." Just as Precious was about to object Poet stopped her. "Do you hear me?" Poet asked.

"Yeah, I hear you, but—why are you always treatin' me like a kid?"

"Because you are a kid. You're my little sister. It's my duty to make sure that nothin' happens to you, Mommy, or Porsha because the man that supposed to be our father ain't around here to handle his business."

Precious looked away from her brother's intense stare. She didn't want him to see the guilty expression on her face.

"I don't mess with none of these guys around here, Poet."

"Well, I'm gonna warn you about Kody once again. I heard that him and his boys were pimpin' young girls. I wouldn't wanna have to hurt that dude for violatin' my family."

"Okay, okay, Poet. You got it."

When Poet walked out of the room, Precious fell back onto the twin bed. She looked up at the ceiling and sighed.

For the next two days, Poet was extremely cautious now that he knew that the cops were watching his every move. He didn't want to bring any heat to Bone, Mekhi, or to his family, as if his mother needed any more problems.

On the third day, Poet decided to stay at home. He called Bone and told him that he needed a break. Bone wasn't happy about it but he understood. Poet retreated to his bedroom for some much needed rest.

As he lay in his bed, listening to his iPod, his mother gently knocked on the door.

"Come in," he said. Cheryl walked in. She stood by the door for a few seconds, staring at him.

"What's up, Ma?" Poet asked, sitting upright in the bed and taking the headphones out of his ears.

"Poet, why didn't you tell me about the detectives questioning you the other day?" she asked, finally gathering up the nerve to ask him about it.

He sucked his teeth. "Your detective boyfriend told you that, didn't he?"

"It doesn't matter who told me, Poet. Why were you being questioned by the police?"

Poet sighed. "They think that I had somethin' to do with that Pumpkin killin'. I ain't did sh—I mean, nothin'.'"
Cheryl paced around the small room. "You know, Poet, I thought that you and I had a very good relationship; a relationship where we can talk about anything and we can be honest with each other. The bottom line is you are the child and I'm the parent. I'm in charge here and anytime you fuck up, it falls back on me. Now I'm trying

to understand why you were questioned by the police and you neglected to tell me that. This just doesn't sit too well with me. Are you in some kind of trouble?"

Poet looked around. "I said no, Ma! Damn!"

He was really starting to not like Oates.

Bitch-ass Oates, he thought as his mother stared him in the face, looking for an answer.

Cheryl was livid. "I just want to know when you were going to tell me about the interrogation, Poet!" she screamed. "It's fucked up and it's embarrassing for someone who lives outside of this house to come and tell me that my son is a suspect in a murder case!"

"Well, whoever told you that need to mind their damn business!" Poet shouted. "That questionin' shit wasn't about nothin' because I didn't do anything. That's why I didn't tell you about it!"

Cheryl screwed up her face. "You know what, Prince Poet Washington? If you want be out in these streets, running around like a maniac and killing folks and selling drugs, you can get the fuck out of my house! I don't want it around me; I don't want it around my daughters. That money that you have been giving me probably is nothing but dirty-ass drug money and I don't want it or need it!"

Poet frowned. "Ma, ain't nobody doin' nothin'—"

She cut him off. "Don't lie to me, Poet!" she yelled. "I'm not stupid! You're out there doing all kinds of shit! And now I'm hearin' that you're riding around in a brand new car?" Poet looked surprised when she said that. "Yeah, I know all about it! But I'm saying that to say this. If you get into any trouble, do not call me! I've raised you better than that!" Poet stood up and re-trieved his boots from the closet to leave. "That's right, get your shit and get out of my house! I can't bear to look at your lying face right now!"

Cheryl walked into her room and slammed the door. Poet was left alone in his bedroom with a confused expression on his face. Porsha and Precious came to the doorway and looked at him but were quiet. He could tell that they felt bad for him, but at that moment, he didn't need anyone's sympathy. He needed to get out of that house before he said some things that he would eventually regret.

Chapter 20

All Fall Down

A few minutes later, Poet was walking out of his building. He had to run to his vehicle because it was raining so hard. Once he started the car up, it took everything for him to gather up the strength to drive to Bone's spot.

He was emotionally exhausted from the argument with his mother and everything else that was going on in his life. Didn't she understand that everything that he did was for her and his sisters? Poet sold the drugs for the money to take care of his mother and sisters. He committed those murders because he was going to make sure that they didn't have to be subjected to anything if he could help it.

What was normally a five-minute drive from Poet's building to Sha-Sha's apartment took him like fifteen minutes because of the heavy rainstorm. Using his key to enter the apartment, he was met at the door by Sha-Sha. She looked like she had just been caught digging her hand in the cookie jar.

"What the fuck are you doin' in here, Sha-Sha?" Poet asked with a suspicious look on his face. Sha-Sha knew that she wasn't supposed to be there alone when there were drugs inside of the house.

The drug-addicted Sha-Sha had been banned from her own apartment when Bone decided to make it into one of his drug spots.

"Nothin', I just stopped by to get my . . ." she began, not knowing what else to say.

Poet stood in the doorway waiting for her answer. After thirty seconds had passed, Sha-Sha never found the words to support the lie that she was about to tell.

"How did you get in here?" he asked.

Sha-Sha shrugged her shoulders. She had spent the night there, after picking the lock the night before. She had ransacked the place until she found the drugs.

Poet stepped inside and grabbed her by the collar. He shook her violently and, not surprisingly, an eight ball of crack cocaine fell out of her shirt.

"Yo, what the . . . ?" Poet said, looking at the drugs on the floor. He slapped Sha-Sha so hard that she fell against the wall. Her nose began to bleed instantly. "You're stealin' from Bone now?"

"I just thought that I could—" she whined. Poet kicked her into the front door and she cried out in pain.

"You got the nerve to be stealin' from us when we take care of your black ass?" Poet said through clenched teeth.

Sha-Sha cowered in the corner, unsure of Poet's next move. Frustrated, he pulled out a gun and put it in her mouth.

"I should blow your fuckin' brains out right here, you fuckin' crackhead!" Poet snarled. "You wanna steal, huh? As a matter of fact, get the fuck up and come take a ride with me! I got somethin' for your ass!"

Poet began forcing Sha-Sha to her feet. He pushed the gun into the small of her back. "I'm so sorry, Poet! Please don't kill me! I'm so sorry!"

"Nah, fuck that! You'll have me on fucked-up terms with Bone because of your crackhead-ass! I got enough heat on me already so I'm gonna take care of this shit right now!"

Poet practically dragged Sha-Sha to his car in the heavy downpour of rain. He forced her to get in on the driver's side and she slid over to the passenger seat. Too scared to make a run for it, Sha-Sha watched as he locked the doors and pulled off. During the drive, Sha-Sha cried and cried. She knew that she was defenseless against the muscular Poet. Years of drug use had ravaged her body and she was so thin, Poet probably could have killed her with his bare hands.

Poet took off, heading toward East New York. Sha-Sha begged and pleaded with him as he sped down Flatlands toward Fountain Avenue. He parked near an abandoned street not too far from the Gateway Mall area. As the heavy rain splattered across the windshield, Sha-Sha shuddered with fear and continued to beg for her life.

"Please, Poet, don't hurt me! I just got desperate and nobody was there to give me nothin'. I just happened to find some shit and took it upon myself to take it," she said.

Poet was remorseless. "I ain't tryin' to hear you, Sha-Sha. I thought that we had an understandin'." He looked at her and smacked her in the back of the head. "Get out of my fuckin' car. Now!" he yelled.

Sha-Sha hesitated as she opened the car door. Poet leaned over from the driver's seat and pushed her out the door to the ground. He quickly got out and walked around the car. Poet pointed the gun at Sha-Sha. She tried to take off running but her feet got stuck in a pile of mud.

Poet raised the gun and shot at Sha-Sha in the back of her head. Blood splattered all over the ground. Sha-Sha went face first to the ground. As the rain washed away the gory mess, he shot her three more times, watching as the bullets entered her ninety-pound frame. Poet looked down at the bloody corpse and smiled. After a few seconds, he calmly got back into his car and drove away, leaving Sha-Sha's lifeless body in a muddy ditch.

As Poet headed back to the neighborhood, he began to get more and more agitated. But he wasn't consumed with the fact that he killed yet another person. He felt that he was justified when it came to taking care of the people who served no purpose in society. No one cared about them so why should he be the exception?

Poet's ringing cell phone startled him. On the caller ID, he saw that it was Bone's number. He really wasn't ready to speak to Bone yet but reluctantly answered the phone anyway.

"What's up, Bone?" Poet said.

"Yo, Po, what's up with Sha-Sha? News just got back to me that you left outta here whippin' her ass! What did she do?" he asked.

"I caught that bitch stealin' from you, Bone! I caught her walkin' out of the house with some of your drugs in her pocket!"

"What? She's not even supposed to be there unless she's with one of us! Anyway, where is she at now?" Bone asked.

"I don't know where she is, man, and I don't give a fuck about where she is. She bounced after I whipped her ass."

Bone looked at the phone. Lately he had become very suspicious of the way that Poet was acting. The rumors of Poet gunning down Pumpkin were disturbing. If Poet did do something to Sha-Sha, he didn't want to know anything about it.

"Oh, really? She bounced, huh?" Bone asked.

"Yeah, Bone, she broke out. I whipped her ass and she broke out. I'm on my way back over to the crib right now."

Bone cut him off. "Nah, son, you're good for the night. Go home and get some rest. I got this shit covered over here." If Sha-Sha didn't appear at the house in the next day or so, like she usually did when she needed a fix, Bone would already know that that was sign that she was dead. Bone was already preparing to clean out Sha-Sha's apartment and take his business elsewhere.

"Oh, I see. Okay, Bone. Call me if you need me," Poet said.

"Yeah, right," Bone replied with a hint of sarcasm, and hung up the phone.

Poet was confused with Bone's reaction. He had plans on finishing off some work at the spot and possibly staying there for a night or two. Poet sucked his teeth. He sighed, then reluctantly picked up the cell phone to call Rakiyah. He was in no mood for her nagging, but at that point he had no other choice because he couldn't go home just yet. He needed a place to lay his head until he was able to smooth things over with his mother.

The next morning, Precious walked outside of her building with a messenger bag slung across her body. As she got farther down the block, she was surprised when she spotted Malika standing at the corner of Rockaway Avenue talking to Kody. She couldn't help but wonder if she was the topic of discussion.

"What's up, Malika? What's up, Kody?" she said.

Kody nodded his head at her and Malika smiled. "What's up, Presh? You all ready to go to school like a good little girl, huh?" she asked.

"Yeah, I am, I guess," she replied with a sigh, looking at the Manhattan-bound number three train rumbling on the elevated train tracks in the distance. "I wish I could stay home today."

Malika smirked and so did Kody. "I was thinkin'," Malika began. "Did you wanna come to Kody's house with me? He's got a friend that he wants you to meet."

Precious frowned. "Friend for me?" she asked, with a confused look on her face.

"Yeah, a friend for you. You know Eric, right?"

Precious knew of Eric but that wasn't the problem. Why was she being hooked up with the friend and not Malika? Didn't she just have a sexual tryst with Kody the other day?

"I know of him," she replied. "But I was never officially introduced to him." Precious thought that Eric was really cute but he was no Kody. She couldn't believe that Kody was about to pass her off to his friend. That was clearly disrespectful but she was afraid to say no.

"So where's your big brother, Poet?" Kody asked mockingly.

Precious was still pissed off with the arrangement. "He's around, I guess. I ain't his fuckin' keeper."

Kody laughed loudly. He was getting a kick out of Precious's attitude. He knew that she was a little jealous.

"So are you gonna come with us or what, Precious?" Malika asked.

Precious shrugged her shoulders. "A'ight, I'll hang out with y'all," she replied.

They waited for Eric to meet them. He was a dark-skinned fellow with a set of beautiful white teeth. He was about six feet and in comparison to Precious's five feet two inches, he looked like a giant. But Precious wasn't feeling him. She was still trying to understand why Kody had pushed her to the side for Malika, who wasn't half as pretty as she was.

The four of them made their way to Kody's empty
house. They sat in the living room and the girls sipped
on wine coolers while they all got acquainted with each
other. The guys guzzled down some Corona beers.

"So, um, Precious, how old did you say you were?"
Kody asked, putting her on the spot.

"Um, I'm—" Precious began.

Malika cut her off. "We're both eighteen," she lied.

Kody nodded his head. "Hmm. Y'all eighteen, huh?"
He took a swig of his Corona and looked at Eric, who
sat on the loveseat with a smug expression on his face.

"So if y'all eighteen, that must mean that y'all are
some experienced bitches when it comes to pleasin' a
man," Kody challenged.

"Of course!" Malika announced. She knew that she
had no real experience with men. Truthfully speaking, not too many guys could tolerate Malika and her
mouth, let alone have sex with her.

"So what if a man gave y'all a few dollars to do what
he wanted, would y'all do it?" Kody asked, nudging
Eric on the arm.

"Pay us for sex?" asked Malika. "It depends on how
much he's payin' and what he looks like."

Precious shrugged her shoulders. "I don't know
about that," she said.

"Yo, Malika, take off your clothes for me," Kody ordered. "Let me see what you're workin' with and I will
let you know how much a man will pay for it."

Eager to please, Malika immediately began undress-
ing. She stood in the middle of the living room with
her bra and panties on while the men checked her out.
Kody wasn't impressed with Malika's body. He thought
that her titties were too small, her ass was too flat, and
she had no hips.

*A perverted, old white man would love her. She's
built like a boy,* Kody thought.

Kody had already told Eric about Precious's body and he couldn't wait to see her naked. Precious stood in the middle of the living room, acting timid.

Kody nudged Eric. "Yo, Presh! Stop actin' all shy and shit and get naked! Fuck is you waitin' for, ma?" he asked.

Precious stood up and slowly took off her clothes. At sixteen, her measurements were thirty-four–twenty-six–thirty-six.

"Damn!" said Eric. "Her body is official!" Kody agreed. "Turn around."

Malika looked at Precious's physical attributes and frowned. She never knew that her best friend had a body like that.

"Yo, Presh, kiss Malika for us," Eric demanded. A disgusted look came over Precious's face. "Go ahead. Kiss her."

"I'm not kissin' her," replied Precious. "I'm not gay."

"We don't give a fuck about all that," Kody said, standing in between the two. "Let me help y'all little young bitches out. I can see that y'all don't know what to do."

Kody began kissing Malika first. He stuck his tongue in her mouth and she reciprocated. They kissed for about thirty seconds. Then he kissed Precious. Even though she was uncomfortable with what was going on, she was enamored with his delicate kisses. At that point, she decided that she would do anything that Kody wanted her to do.

Kody was able to convince the girls to kiss each other and they did exactly as they were told from that point on. Kissing a girl wasn't as bad as Precious thought. After a few minutes, she began to get into it. They removed their bra and panties and Precious began feeling all over Malika's naked frame. Kody and Eric watched as the girls fell onto the couch and began grinding on each other. Kody smiled as he looked back at the video camera that was strategically placed on the windowsill. The girls didn't even realize that they were being taped.

Kody and Eric slapped each other five as they instructed the two teens to perform oral sex on each other. Kody guided them on how to pleasure each other by making them lick the clitoris and make love to the vagina with their tongues. After this went on for approximately twenty minutes, Kody pulled them apart and he began kissing Malika, sucking Precious' wet juices off her face. Then Eric walked over to Precious and put her hands on his erect penis.

Eric got undressed and climbed on top of her. Precious willingly opened her legs for him. He didn't have on a condom when he entered her. He began stroking her vagina, putting her into every position that he could think of.

"You like this dick, baby?" he asked, looking into her eyes.

"Yes, I do," she replied, feeling every stroke of his hard penis.

"Call me Daddy," Eric said as he watched his rod go in and out of her tight pussy.

"Daddy, Daddy," she panted.

"Good girl," he replied. "I like when my bitches talk to me while I'm fuckin' them." He smiled and kissed Precious on the forehead while he continued having sex with her on the couch.

Precious looked over to her right and watched Kody sex Malika. They were going at it and the only sounds that could be heard in the living room were the pleasurable moans of all parties involved.

When they first arrived at Kody's house, Precious had her reservations. All she could hear was her brother's voice warning her to stay away from the likes of

Kody. But it was too late. Sex made her feel complete. Precious was enjoying all of the attention that she was receiving from men, even if it was the wrong kind of attention.

After a half hour had passed, Eric and Precious were still going at it on the sofa. Kody came over and tapped Eric on the shoulder. He gave his friend the signal and Eric walked over to have sex with Malika. Kody began kissing Precious on her neck and began sexing her too. After a few minutes passed, Kody turned Precious around in the doggie style position.

Meanwhile, the tape in the hidden video camera was still rolling. Kody smiled into the camera as Precious enjoyed every minute of the sexual romp.

Poet sat in his car on the corner of Bristol and Sutter Avenues. Needing a moment to himself, he put his seat back and closed his eyes while he took in the sounds of some slow jams on the radio. He cracked his driver's side window open and let the spring breeze blow in his face. After a few minutes, he dozed off.

An hour later, Poet was awakened by the sounds of voices. The voices were coming from four people standing on the corner of Bristol, adjacent to where his car was parked. Poet sat up to see where the voices were coming from. When he looked up, he saw Malika and two guys. But nothing prepared him for who he saw standing with the three. It was none other than his little sister, Precious.

He tilted his head to the side and rubbed his eyes. He wanted to make sure that he wasn't seeing things. Kody slapped Precious on her butt and she giggled. Eric did the same thing and got the same response from her.

Upon seeing the two men disrespecting her like that, Poet felt a tear roll down his face. His biggest fear was that Precious had been turned into a whore by the same kind of men he had fought so hard to keep her away from.

Killing the two men in front of big-mouth Malika and his whorish little sister was not a good idea, so Poet had to compose himself. He assumed that the police were watching his every move and he didn't want to do anything too erratic. That would only bring more negative attention to him and he didn't need that. So far, everything he had done had been pretty low-key with the exception of the Pumpkin situation and he wanted to keep it that way.

Poet ducked when he saw that the girls were walking toward his car. He breathed a sigh of relief as they passed him by. They hadn't noticed him sitting there. He watched them until they disappeared from his sight, then Poet looked at the time. It was one thirty-five in the afternoon. Not only was Precious hanging around with Kody, the alleged pimp, and his boy Eric, but she had cut school to do it. This made him even angrier.

As his thirst for Kody's blood intensified, Poet looked at his gun again, only this time a sinister smile came across his face.

"Won't be needin' you this time, Nadia," Poet said, calling his gun by the nickname he had given it. "A bullet is gonna be too good for this motherfucker."

Chapter 21

No Turning Back

Later on that evening, Poet knocked on Mekhi's door. Mekhi opened the door and Poet followed him into his bedroom.

"What's up with Bone, Po?" Mekhi asked. "He called me earlier and told me that he didn't need us at the spot today."

Poet sucked his teeth. "Man, I don't know what's up with that cat. I got enough money to go into business for myself, man. I'm tired of relyin' on the next man for some paper."

"Well, he was tellin' me that Sha-Sha got caught stealin' or somethin'."

Poet shrugged his shoulders. "What he was tryin' to tell you is that I caught Sha-Sha stealin' drugs. She was comin' out of the crib with an eight ball and who knows what else she had on her."

"So what happened to her? Where is Sha-Sha now?"

Poet shrugged his shoulders again. "Where do you think she is, son?"

Mekhi blinked real fast. "I don't know."

"Man, you know where she is."

Mekhi covered his eyes with his hands. "You mean you done killed Sha-Sha too?" he asked. "Ah, man! You're really buggin' now!"

Poet began pacing the room. "What was I supposed to do? Didn't Bone leave me in charge?" Mekhi nodded his head in agreement. "Okay, so bein' that I was in charge, anything that went down in that crib was my responsibility, man. That bitch violated so I had to put her to rest, and you know what? I didn't give a fuck about doin' it. And besides, she was a crackhead anyway! Who's goin' to miss her?"

Mekhi tried to make sense of what Poet was saying to him. His best friend was standing in the middle of his bedroom telling him that he had committed yet another murder. He felt sick to his stomach.

"And if she was on drugs it wasn't your problem. These people that you have killed had families, people that loved them. And if they were that fucked up, maybe they wasn't worth you killin' them at all. Why would you risk your freedom for a bunch of nobodies, man? Now this is the fourth person that you told me that you did this to and you still don't get it. I gotta walk around with this burden on me."

"How do you think that I feel, Khi?" Poet asked, pounding on his chest.

Mekhi tilted his head to the side and looked at him. "That's the problem. I don't think that you're feelin' anything because when I look at you, I don't see nothin', no feelin', no remorse. I don't see a person who has any regrets about what he did."

Poet plopped down on Mekhi's bed. He put his face in his hands. "You know, Khi, maybe you're right. I don't give a fuck. I don't care about much of shit these days. I tried to step up and be a man, hold my mother and my little sisters down . . . Now my mother done flipped out on me, Precious is probably out there hoin' around by now . . . Shit is fucked up!"

Mekhi was curious about what Poet had to say about his youngest sibling.

"What happened with Precious?" Mekhi asked. He hadn't seen her in a few days and she had not called him since they had the fight. He had been wondering what was up with her.

Poet sighed loudly before he began the story. "Man, I was sittin' in the car near Bristol, right, and who do I see standin' there with Kody and Eric? Malika and Precious! Now we both know how those dudes get down. We've been hearin' about them pimpin' young girls for a minute now. These dudes, Eric and Kody, were smackin' her on the ass and everything like she was some tramp! It broke my heart to see my little sister with these cats and Malika's stank behind!"

Mekhi felt tense. "You actually saw them smackin' Precious on the ass?" he asked.

"Yeah, smackin' her on the ass, and I hate to say it but she looked like she was lovin' it. One of them lames done fucked my sister, man. I just know it."

Mekhi got up and walked over to the closet. He didn't want Poet to see the frustration on his face. He was really stressed out.

Kody and my Precious? Mekhi thought.

Poet continued talking. "I can't believe that shit! All this shit is comin' at me at the same time!"

Mekhi got himself together and turned around to face his friend. Thinking about Precious having sex with Kody had changed his mood. "Everything that's comin' at you is your own fault, Poet! You can't be runnin' around killin' people just for the fun of it!" he yelled.

Poet stood up. "You know what? Fuck you, Khi! You're supposed to be my man and now it seems like you're passin' judgment on me! You know why I did what I did to these people!"

Mekhi crossed his arms. "Nah, man, I don't know why but I'm sure you about to tell me!"

"Because I'm tired, Khi. I'm tired of the same shit, man. I'm tired of livin' in this fuckin' ghetto-ass neighborhood. I'm tired of not bein' shit or bein' able to contribute nothin' to society. I mean, look at you. You're talented, you can do somethin' other than be a fuckin' drug dealer. Me? I don't know what I wanna do with my life! And I can't end up like my pops, man. He was pussy, a sucker, a coward. He left my mother with two and half kids! I hate that dude!"

"Okay, so your father ain't shit! You don't have to be like him. Now you done went and fucked up your life. The police are closin' on you, Po! What are you goin' to do now?"

Poet paced back and forth. "Let's just change the subject, man. I'm gonna act like none of this ever happened. I'm gonna pretend that we didn't have this conversation."

"Well, it happened, man! Stop tryin' to brush shit under the rug now that the police is closin' in on your ass! No matter how much we don't talk about it, it's not gonna go away!"

The next morning, as Cheryl traveled to work, she thought about her son. She was worried sick over him and she really hadn't wanted him to leave the house the day of their argument. The words that she had spoken were said out of anger and disappointment. All she was trying to do was make him understand the seriousness of being questioned by the police about a crime, whether he did it or not.

But the way Poet acted when she asked him about it scared her. He didn't seem afraid or worried about anything. Her worst fear was that her son had actually committed the murder. Cheryl silently prayed that she had not raised some deranged killer.

After making it through most of the morning, it was twelve o'clock in the afternoon when her job phone rang. Cheryl worked in crime statistics at the Tenth Precinct in Manhattan's Chelsea area. She had a lot of paperwork to finish up and when she looked at the pile on her desk, lunch was not an option. She hoped the phone call wasn't more work for her.

"Tenth Precinct, Police Administrative Aide Washington, how may I help you?" she said, holding the phone on one shoulder while she typed on the computer keyboard.

"Hello, beautiful," said the male voice on the phone.

Considering everything that was going through her mind, Cheryl managed to smile. "Hello, Mr. Oates. How are you this afternoon?"

"Hmmm. I don't know. I was just about to head toward the Brooklyn Bridge when I thought about how I would love to take one gorgeous woman to lunch by the name of Cheryl. Do you know her?"

Cheryl laughed. "I don't know. Can't say that I know that wench but I sure wish that I was in her shoes. I would love to be in the company of a fine gentleman like yourself."

Suddenly her office door opened and Oates was standing in the doorway with a dozen yellow roses in his hand. He hung up his cell phone and laughed at the shocked look on Cheryl's face.

"Hello, baby. I thought I would surprise you with this today. Let's go get some lunch."

Cheryl took the roses out of his hands and gave him a sweet kiss on the lips. "Mmm, thank you, Shareef. You are the best, I swear, but how can I go to lunch with all this work? I have to hand in these statistics by next week!"

Oates waved his hand at the pile of papers. "Look, I asked your desk sergeant if it was okay to take my baby to lunch and that's what I'm gonna do." He held his arm out for her to grab it. Cheryl smiled and picked up her pocketbook. "Now let's go."

They walked downstairs and the cops who were downstairs gave them a standing ovation. Cheryl blushed and Oates smiled from ear to ear as they walked out of the precinct, hand in hand. Once they were outside, they were greeted with a bright, sunny day.

"I know this nice little bistro up the block," she said.

Oates stopped and kissed Cheryl on the lips. "Wherever your heart desires is where we will go. Did you want me to drive?"

Cheryl glanced at his truck. "Let's walk. It's gorgeous out here today."

They strolled down Eighth Avenue and passed Twenty-third Street. It was a quaint restaurant with outside seating. Cheryl and Oates sat outside, placed their order, and took in the sounds of the city. Once the waiter brought the food to their table, Cheryl inhaled the sweet smell of the delicious chow that they were about to devour.

"So how's everything with you, sweetheart?" Oates asked while watching as she ate her salad.

Cheryl took the napkin and wiped her mouth. "Everything is not okay, Shareef. Poet left my house the other day."

"Really? Why is that?"

"When I asked him about the interrogation, he was just as nonchalant about it. From the way he reacted when I asked him about it, it seemed like he had no intentions of telling me, either. If you didn't mention it, I wouldn't have ever known."

Oates shook his head. "Well, I'm glad I did. I owe you that much and Poet does too. I don't understand why he didn't tell you."

"Can I ask you an honest question?"

"Shoot," Oates said while eating his food.

"Is my son still being investigated for this murder? Is he really a suspect?"

Oates looked around and nervously shifted in his seat. "I'm not sure, Cheryl."

She waved her hand. "I know, I know. You can't tell me. I'm sorry for asking."

Oates put his hand on top of hers. "Listen, I'm going to help you as much as I can. But honestly, just because he is accused that doesn't necessarily mean that he actually killed Pumpkin. This guy, Pumpkin, was a no-torious gang leader and had a lot of enemies; there are a lot of suspects in this murder case. Poet isn't the only one, if that makes you feel a little better."

Cheryl sighed. "Well, I'm still worried about him. But for some strange reason, Poet isn't worried about himself. I don't know if that is a sign that he didn't do it or if he did it and has convinced himself that he's not guilty. Then to find out that he's out there selling drugs and stuff, and that he's riding around in this new car, it's like his whole life, this persona of being the perfect son, was just one big lie. I had to ask myself is this young man really my child? I always instilled good values in my children."

Oates shook his head. He didn't know what to say to Cheryl. "I don't know, Cheryl. I can't call it. I can understand your fears, though. I just wish that I could talk to Poet."

"I wish that you could too. But I don't want you to jeopardize your position for Poet. He's going to be twenty-one years old next month and, legally, he's going to be a adult. I did everything that I could for him, taught him right from wrong. If he wants to go out there and fuck up his life, then that's on him. He's just going to be a carbon copy of his father."

"It sounds like you're giving up on him, Cheryl."

"No, Shareef. I don't wanna give up on Poet. Poet is giving up on Poet. Plus, I don't have the energy to deal with his bullshit right now," she replied while she ate her main course meal. "I just don't. I have two daughters that depend on me and Poet is not my only child. I tried to give all my children their individual attention and I sacrificed my social life just so that I could raise my children to become adults with principles and this is the thanks I get. It's bullshit."

"If and when you need me, I'm here."

Cheryl looked at Oates. "Well, I don't need you to be here for no one else but me. My children are raised and soon they will be living their own lives. Now it's time for Cheryl to live hers."

Chapter 22

Regrets

It was 6:30 P.M. when Porsha answered the phone. After she hung up, she didn't look too happy about the call.

"Preeeecious!" she yelled from the living room.

Precious ran out of the bedroom and gave her sister an evil glare. "What? Why are you yellin' my name out like that?" she replied with an attitude.

Standing there with her right hand on her hip, Porsha looked pissed off. "Did you go to school today?"

Precious rolled her eyes. "Yeah, I went to school today!" she lied. She had decided to cut school again and go back to Kody's house for another session of sex. Precious loved the way Kody made her feel and she couldn't resist him.

"Well, accordin' to the recordin' on the phone, your ass didn't go to school yesterday or today!"

Precious sucked her teeth and plopped on the couch. "They are lyin'."

"Oh, yeah? Well, they left a number for Mommy to call them back if they needed more information. So if you don't tell me the truth about why you didn't go to school and where you were, trust and believe I'm gonna blow you up as soon as Mommy hits that door!"

Precious sighed. "Okay, I was hangin' out with Malika," she said. That was only half of the truth. She was with Malika the day before.

"Malika? It figures. Why do you still hang with that chickenhead anyway? She is not goin' to do anything but bring you down!"

"Malika is my friend, Porsha. We've been friends since we were little girls. Don't get mad because you don't have as many friends as I do!"

"Mad? Mad at what? The so-called friends that I had done already had two and three babies before they were twenty-one years old and they are hatin' on me because I wanna get an education! I mean, why would I want to be around them? I want to be around people that's doin' somethin' with their lives. Even if I didn't go to college, I don't want no sorry-ass people around me!"

"Oh, yeah? So what if you go to college! You still live in the ghetto! And look at how you dress!" Precious yelled, referring to Porsha's preppy outfit. "The problem is you think that you're better and you are just as ghetto as the rest of us!"

Porsha laughed. "No, bitch, you see, I have to talk like that around here because if I was to talk to y'all dummies the way that I talk with the people at school? Ha, y'all ghettofied motherfuckers would try to say I'm actin' white! And I'm far from bein' a white person! I am a proud African American woman who loves her people! But, unfortunately, talkin' properly is what stupid-ass, ignorant 'ninjas' like yourself call talkin' 'white' or tryin' to act like I'm better than somebody!"

Precious rolled her eyes. She was no match for Porsha's intellect. "So I'm still waitin' for you to tell me where you were and why you weren't in school?" Porsha asked again.

"We were around the way and that's all you need to know," Precious replied with an attitude.

"Really?" Porsha laughed. "Well, I wasn't goin' to say anything to you because I didn't want to hurt your feelings, but since you have such a fucked-up attitude, I think you should know this about your so-called 'friend,' Malika. First of all, Malika is goin' around runnin' her mouth about how y'all were hangin' out with Kody and dark-skinned Eric from 320 yesterday. She is tellin' everybody that y'all had an orgy, that you and her had lesbian sex and all that. Then I heard from one of my friends—yes, I said 'friend'—that there is a tape floatin' around of you and Malika havin' sex with Kody and Eric at Kody's house!"

"Nah-ah!" Precious yelled. "We wasn't doin' nothin' with them boys!"

"Sorry, sweetheart, but those aren't boys! Those are men! They're older than Poet and you're runnin' around with them? Better yet, how are they runnin' around with sixteen-year-old girls? And if that tape shit is true, when Poet finds out about this, you already know that's your ass!"

"Already know what, Porsha? Poet is not my damn daddy! I can do what I want and I can fuck who I want to fuck!"

Suddenly, Porsha looked toward door of their apartment. Precious turned around and her mother was standing in the doorway, staring at her. Precious plopped down on the couch and folded her arms.

"So, Miss Precious, what were you sayin'? You can do what you want and you can do what else?" she asked, putting her bags down on the sofa and standing over Precious.

"Um, I didn't say nothin', Mommy," she said. Her eyes were welling up with tears.

"Oh, you said something all right!" Cheryl exclaimed. "I want you to repeat what you said."

Precious looked at Porsha and hesitated. "I said that I can do what I want and I can fuh . . . fuh . . ." she stammered.

Cheryl gave her a look of death. "I'm waiting," she said.

"I said that I can fuck who I want to," Precious responded.

Cheryl slapped her daughter so hard that Porsha's hand went to her own cheek. Cheryl then grabbed Precious by her shirt collar.

"So is this how you talk when I'm not around? You're out here having sex now? Is that what you're doing, little girl? Answer me!" she yelled.

Precious was scared to death. "No, Mommy, no! Me and Porsha was just arguin'!"

"You are lying to me!" Cheryl screamed.

Cheryl pulled off her belt and began beating Precious all over the house. It was a sight to see as she chased her offspring throughout the apartment while giving her whacks all over her body with the thick leather belt. Cheryl was unrelenting in the way that she was punishing Precious, but in so many ways the girl needed it.

"Mommy, please, noooo!" Precious screamed as the belt made contact with her bare skin. She was crying uncontrollably.

After two minutes had passed, Cheryl finally let up. She was out of breath and every muscle in her arms felt like it had been strained. Porsha peeked around the wall of the kitchen. She managed to tiptoe into the bedroom and close the door.

Cheryl finally got a second wind and instantly began yelling at the crying Precious, who was laid across the living room floor.

"I don't condone any whores living in my house!" she said. "I raised all of y'all to respect yourselves. I expect you, Porsha, and that damn Poet to walk out of here and act like you came from somebody that got the sense that God gave them! If you wanna lay up with the whole neighborhood and if 'fucking' anybody that you want to makes you happy, pack your shit and get out of my house! I'm not having no got-damn babies come through this doorway! Is that understood, Precious Niasha Washington?"

"Yes, Mommy, yes!" she replied, still crying from pain and humiliation.

Cheryl threw the belt on the floor, gathered her things, and walked into her bedroom. She fell across her bed and cried silent tears for herself.

Cheryl felt that she had done everything to ensure that her children never felt the loss of their father, and in return she got a whore for a daughter and a criminal for a son. She loved her children and she was blessed to have all them in her lives but she realized that it was time for her to let go and let God. They were old enough to know better. The pathways that they chose at that point in their lives were going to be their decision and not hers. They already knew the answers that she had drilled into their hard heads all of their lives.

Cheryl wiped her tears and stood up to undress. What she needed was a nice shower and some alone time. But she really didn't want to be alone. She looked at her watch. It was seven o'clock in the evening and it was a Friday. She needed an out and she had the perfect person to give that to her.

Cheryl picked up her cell phone and dialed Oates's number. The phone rang twice before he picked up.

"Hello, sweetie, did you make it home okay?" he asked, turning down the music in the background.

"Yeah, I did. I'm home now." They both paused. "Um, Shareef, I'm sorry to bother you but I was wondering if—"

Oates cut her off because he knew exactly what she wanted to say. "I'm on my way to get you. I will be there in a half an hour," he said.

"That's perfect. Call me when you're downstairs," she whispered, holding back her tears.

Cheryl quickly ran to the bathroom to take a shower. She needed to get out of that house and fast.

While her mother was preparing to go out, Precious walked into her bedroom, sobbing. Porsha was lying across her bed, doing her homework and purposely ignoring her.

"It's your fault that I got in trouble," Precious whispered.

Porsha turned her head to face her troubled little sister. "I know that you seriously don't believe that."

"Yes! Because if it wasn't for you arguin' with me, I wouldn't have never said what I said and Mommy wouldn't have heard me."

Porsha waved her off. "Please, little girl!" she replied. "Don't blame me for your whorish ways! You said that because that's the way you feel and if you wanna be the project nympho, then go right ahead. Unlike you, I wanna be somethin' someday and get the hell out of nasty Brownsville! Looks like you and your ten kids and eight baby daddies are goin' to be livin' here forever!"

Precious stood up. "Well, for your information, I ain't gonna be livin' here forever and I ain't gonna have no ten babies and eight baby daddies! Me and Mekhi—" she began.

Porsha stopped her from finishing her sentence. "You and who?" she asked, cupping her ear. "You and Mekhi are finished, darlin'! You just tramped yourself out to some of the grimiest dudes in the hood and now you're talkin' about you and Mekhi? After Khi hears about you and Malika with Eric and Kody, you are a done deal. Eric and Kody are supposed to be pimps so you might as well just start chargin' for your services! Then again, I'm sure that you don't have a problem with givin' away the cooch for free!"

Suddenly, Precious jumped on Porsha. She hit her older sister in the face. Porsha managed to get up from the bed and began pummeling Precious. She was getting the best of her younger sister when their mother walked into the room after hearing the commotion.

"What the hell is goin' on in here?" Cheryl yelled, after she managed to pull her daughters apart.

The towel that she had wrapped around her nude body had dropped to the floor. Cheryl was standing in between her feuding daughters in her birthday suit and she was very angry.

"This chickenhead started first!" screamed Porsha. "She tried to blame me for her big, dumb mouth!"

"No, Mommy, she keeps callin' me a ho!" Precious announced.

"Well, you are a ho, you slut! Mommy, you heard what she said earlier!"

"Both of y'all shut the hell up!" Cheryl yelled. "Sit down, now!" Both girls sat on their individual beds. "I don't know what's goin' on with you, Precious—" she said before she was interrupted.

"But, Mommy, I . . ." Precious started to complain, but the look that Cheryl gave her was enough to quiet her down.

"I don't give a shit who started what! Porsha, keep your big mouth shut, okay? Precious, you are skating on thin ice, baby girl! If I hear one more peep out of your little ass, I'm gonna beat you into a got-damn pulp, do you understand me?"

Precious crossed her arms in defiance. Porsha nodded her head at her mother. Cheryl went upside Precious's head and she uncrossed her arms.

"Do you understand me, child?"

Precious replied with a meek, "Yes."

"Good. Now I am getting dressed and going out tonight. I need some air. Don't know if I'm coming home, I just may spend the night out. But if I so much hear that you, Precious, leave this damn house any more tonight, I'm gonna come home and stomp a mudhole in your ass!"

"Yes, ma'am," Precious whispered, holding her head down.

Cheryl looked at her daughters one more time and exited their bedroom. She had to get dressed for her night out. Porsha and Precious glared at each other.

"I could have blown your ass up," Porsha said, low enough so that her mother couldn't hear what she was saying. "I could have really put your ass out there. You are so lucky, Precious."

Precious didn't look at Porsha. She didn't even answer her because she knew she was right. Her mother was on a warpath; first Poet and now her. Precious felt as if she was being targeted for everything that was going in their household and she didn't like it one bit.

Precious lay on the bed and turned her back to the upset Porsha, who was still mumbling under her breath. As soon as Porsha fell asleep, Precious was going to sneak out of the house. She had to see Mekhi to confirm if everything was still right between them. She felt too guilty to relax.

Later on that night, Mekhi was awakened by his ringing cell phone. He looked at the time. It was 11:32 P.M. He yawned and answered the call.

"Yo," he said.

"What's up, Mekhi?"

"Who is this?" he asked. He knew who it was.

"It's me, Precious," she said.

"Yeah, what's up, Presh," he said nonchalantly.

"What's the matter? Am I botherin' you?" she asked.

Mekhi sighed. "Look, let's get to the point."

"Why are you actin' so nasty to me, Mekhi? I know that I haven't seen you since we had our little disagreement but I just stayed away until everything calmed down between us."

"Is that right?"

"Yeah, that's right. Now I'm tryin' to understand where this attitude is comin' from."

Mekhi sat up in his bed. "You really wanna know why I'm actin' like this? Because accordin' to your brother, he saw you, Malika, Kody, and Eric from 320 the other day hangin' out with each other. You had them cats, Kody and Eric, feelin' all over your ass and shit like you was some ho. Sad part is you didn't even see your own brother sittin' in a car right across the street from y'all. He saw everything that went down!"

"He didn't see nothin'. He's lyin'!" Precious contested.

"Now what reason does he have to lie to me when Poet doesn't even know about me and you messin' around with each other? So the things that he told me couldn't have been a lie. Why are you messin' around with these dudes anyway? Everyone knows how they get down."

"I wasn't messin' around with them, Mekhi!"

"You're full of shit, Precious! You cut school that day and everything. But you know what? Since you wanna lie about it, keep doin' what you do. It seems like you just used me to pop the cherry."

Precious was silent on the other end of the phone. "Can I come see you, Mekhi? Please?"

He sucked his teeth. "I don't think that's a good idea, Presh. We're done."

"Oh, word?" she said. "You're gonna just cut me off like that?"

"Yeah, Presh, I'm cuttin' you off like that. I had no business messin' around with you in the first place."

"Oh, is that right? Well, maybe I should go ahead and tell my brother about us."

"Who do you think that he's goin' to believe, me or you?" There was another silent pause on the phone. "I thought so. Later."

Precious sat on the living room couch, seething in anger.

The nerve of Mekhi to cut me off, she thought.

Precious may have started out by baiting him to take her virginity, but in the end she really had feelings for him. But now that her brother ran his mouth about something Mekhi knew nothing about, she was mad. Poet was always ruining everything for her.

Suddenly, a smirk came over Precious's face. The problem with Mekhi was that he cared about what everyone thought about him, especially Poet. Since Mekhi wanted to cut her off because of what Poet had told him, then she was going to make them both pay and she had an idea on how she was going to do just that.

Chapter 23

Danger Emerges

It had been a week since the argument with his mother and Poet was tired of staying at Rakiyah's house. He was homesick and he missed his family. His sister Porsha called him every day that he had been gone. His mother or Precious hadn't even bothered to reach out to him to find out if he was alive or dead.

"Poet, are you goin' to be here when I get home from work?" asked Rakiyah.

"I don't know, Raki," he said with a sigh. "Why?"

She put her hand on her hip and began rolling her neck. "What the hell is wrong with you now? Ever since you've been stayin' here, you've been havin' the most fucked-up attitude toward me! You should be happy that I even 'let' you stay in my house!"

When she said that, Poet jumped in her face. "Yo, let me tell you somethin', bitch, I'm tired of you talkin' shit to me. You must really believe that I'm some kind of sucker, huh?"

"Whatever," she replied.

"Yeah, keep sayin' whatever, Rakiyah," he warned. "It would be in your best interest to just go to work before I stick my foot in your behind. And if I put my hands on you, I'm gonna end up killin' your ass!" he said through clenched teeth.

Rakiyah quieted down. She didn't know how to take Poet anymore. He was always quiet, like he was plotting something, and it made her nervous. Unfortunately, she didn't know how to communicate those feelings to him. At that point, she didn't feel that it was worth it. She just wanted him to leave.

Rakiyah nervously continued to prepare for her day. Twenty minutes later, she quickly gathered the rest of her things and walked toward the front door with her daughter in tow.

"Bye-bye, Poet," said Rakiyah's five-year-old daughter, Fallon. She ran in the bedroom and gave him a tight hug. He smiled at the little girl and hugged her back. While he was doing that, he gave Rakiyah a sinister look; a look that she would never forget.

Rakiyah snatched her daughter's hand. "Okay, Fallon, let's go. We don't wanna be late for school," she said, trying to avoid any more eye contact with Poet.

As soon as he heard the front door slam, Poet climbed back into the bed and attempted to doze off, but to no avail. After some tossing and turning for the next hour, he instantly hopped out of bed and began packing his things. Poet had overstayed his welcome. It was time to leave.

As he packed, a flashback of Kody and Eric feeling on his little sister popped into his head. A smirk came across his face as he thought about the promise that he made to himself.

Poet grabbed his things and headed out to the car. It was time for him to handle his business.

Later on that night, Poet was driving through his neighborhood. The night was clear and, as usual, throngs of people were hanging out on Rockaway Avenue. He even spotted a few of his cronies standing in front of Popeyes, but Poet didn't want to be bothered with them. He was on the prowl for his prey.

Just as Poet was about to pull up in front of Mekhi's building, he saw Kody and Eric walking down the block. He immediately parked the car and got out. He made sure his gun was tucked in the waistband of his jeans.

"What's up, Kody? E?" Poet said. They slapped each other five and just stood there for a few seconds without saying anything.

"What's up with you, Poet?" asked Kody. He couldn't look Poet in the eye.

"Ain't nothin' up. What are y'all dudes gettin' into tonight?" he asked, looking directly at Kody when he said it.

Eric chimed in. "We got these chicks that we're supposed to be meetin' up with tonight," he replied, clueless to the silent beef that Kody and Poet had with each other.

Poet looked at Eric and nodded his head. Eric didn't know him that well. He also knew that the only way that Eric would have known that Precious was his little sister was because Kody told him. For that reason alone, he was going to let Eric live. On the other hand, Kody knew him very well and he knew that Precious was his sister.

"For real? Sounds nice, real nice," Poet answered with a smug look on his face. He looked at Kody. "Meetin' up with some chicks, huh? Anybody I know?"

"Nah, nobody you know," Kody replied with a self-righteous attitude.

Poet chuckled. "Better not be nobody I fuckin' know," Poet said in a condesecending tone. "I know how much of a 'G' you are, Big Kody! Wouldn't want my lady to run into a cat like you, now would I? Me and her might end up havin' some serious problems!"

"Hmmph. You think so, son?" replied Kody while sneering at Poet.

"Or you just might be the one to have some problems," Poet said without cracking a smile.

Eric sensed some tension and attempted to break the ice.

"A'ight, Poet," Eric said, giving Poet a pound. "We're out. Guess we'll see you around the way."

Poet grinned. "I guess you will, E. Later, Kody."

Kody gave Poet a head nod and walked away. Poet spit on the ground and stood there until he saw the two men disappear around the corner.

"Disrespectful motherfucker," Poet said aloud as he walked toward Mekhi's building.

Poet wasn't too happy with the fact that Kody wasn't alone when they ran into each other, but it was okay. He knew where he lived, and as far as Poet was concerned, the man was as good as gone.

Later on that night, Kody and Eric were in the basement of Kody's house with three teenage prostitutes from the neighborhood. It was one o'clock in the morning and they were worn out from a few hours of sex and consuming alcohol. They all had just awakened from a brief nap and Eric insisted that Kody go to the store and get some more alcohol for them to drink.

"Come on, man, we're in my house, which means that you should be the one to go to the store, E!" Kody exclaimed.

Eric rolled his eyes. "Hell no! You're the star of this show, my dude! I'm just the hype man! You can go to the store!" The girls began giggling and Kody popped his friend on the head. Eric laughed.

"Man, fuck you!" Kody replied with a smile. "Okay, okay, I'm goin' to the store this time but next time, you're gonna have to go!"

Kody grabbed his house keys and walked out the door. He headed for the twenty-four-hour bodega located at the corner of Bristol and Livonia Avenue, which was a block away from his house. A few street-lights were out and the block was unusually dark that night. But Kody paid that no mind. He knew those streets so well that he could get to his destination with his eyes closed.

As Kody embarked on his local journey, he had no idea that someone was lurking in the shadows. It was Poet, waiting to get revenge on the unsuspecting Kody. He stood in a dark driveway a few doors down from Kody's house, holding a knife with a six-inch blade in his gloved hand. The blade of the knife glistened in the dark but, unfortunately, Kody couldn't see the weapon or his impending death coming.

Poet waited patiently as Kody walked a few feet from where he was standing. He wanted the man to walk ahead of him so that he could surprise Kody from the back. He was going to make sure that Kody felt every inch of the knife that was in his possession.

Suddenly, Poet jumped out from the dark and am-bushed Kody. Kody attempted to push Poet off him but he wasn't prepared for the ferocity of the kill.

"So you wanna fuck with young girls, huh?" Poet whispered as he viciously plunged the knife into Kody's defenseless body.

In a matter of seconds, Kody had already been stabbed in his upper body repeatedly and Poet took a swipe at his throat. Tears ran down Kody's cheeks as he wrapped his hands around his bleeding neck. As he fell to the concrete, he tried to call for help but was choking on his own blood. Poet smirked as he watched Kody's body flinch all over the sidewalk like a dying fish. The dark red blood seeped through the Kody's white T-shirt as his last breath was drawn.

After Kody went down, Poet looked around to see if anyone was watching him. He then jogged to the corner of Bristol and threw the bloody knife into the sewer. After that, he hurriedly walked down the block to his vehicle.

While walking back to his car, Poet pulled the black hoodie that he was wearing over his head. He stepped alongside a building and stepped out of the bloody sweats that he was wearing over his jeans. He opened the trunk of his car, which was nearby, and took out a black garbage bag. He put the bloody clothing into the bag, threw it back into the trunk and drove away. Once he was inside his car, Poet turned on the radio to 97.1. His adrenaline was at an all-time high as he rapped along with the Lil' Wayne song that was playing on the radio.

This time, the killing of Kody was much more personal, in comparison to the other murders that Poet had committed. Kody was a pedophile who preyed on vulnerable teenage girls and their promiscuous ways and, unfortunately, Precious was all of the above. Not only did Poet feel that he was warranted in killing Kody because he had to protect his sister, he was sure that he was also saving other teenage girls from falling victim to Kody and his exploitive ways.

Thinking about his family, Poet reached for his cell phone. He hesitated for a moment, but after a minute had passed, he finally dialed his mother's phone number. Poet was amazed at how he was more afraid of how his mother was going to react to him than he was while murdering Kody.

"Hello, Prince Poet," his mother answered. It sounded as if he had awakened her.

"Hey, Ma," he said. "I'm sorry for wakin' you up at this time of the night, but I was thinkin' about our argument and I just wanted to apologize to you about everything."

Cheryl sighed with relief. Even though she was still disappointed in him, she was relieved to hear her son's voice.

"Come home, Poet. Just come home. We can talk about this in the morning, baby," she said, before she hung up the phone.

Poet smiled as he made a U-turn in his car.

Chapter 24

The First Forty-eight

It was 3:00 A.M. when the police received a 911 call from a homeowner on Bristol Street. The flashing lights on the roof of the patrol cars were blinding, and the sirens had awakened almost everyone who lived in the surrounding homes. The report was about a dead body that was lying in their driveway. Residents of the quiet block had gathered outside to get a look at the body as well. Three patrol cars responded to the scene immediately, with the homicide unit following closely behind them.

Oates and Lewis were among the first detectives on the scene. Along with the uniformed officers, they looked around the crime scene for any evidence. From what they saw, there was no evidence that could be seen with the naked eye. The partners were exhausted from working on their other cases that were still unsolved, and now there was yet another murder in their jurisdiction.

Oates knelt down to get a closer look at the bloody body that was sprawled on the concrete. "Okay, so who is this guy?" he asked, yawning at the same time. He needed some Dunkin' Donuts coffee.

Lewis frowned and looked at the crowd of people who were standing around. He would have to ask them if they knew anything about the dead young man. Lewis knew from just looking at the stone-faced crowd that they weren't going to talk. Most of them were afraid to and didn't want to be involved. This was because they feared retaliation from the killer.

Lewis stood there, rubbing his goatee, while Oates continued to do a visual inspection of the body.

"Whoever stabbed this guy hit his ass up pretty good! He looks like Swiss cheese with all these holes in him. Damn, look at his throat."

Lewis looked at the clean slit on the man's neck. Then he looked at the spectators. The other detectives had arrived on the scene and were talking to the individuals in the crowd. Everyone they approached seemed to be shaking their heads. Lewis already knew what that meant. He shook his head in disgust.

"You know what kills me about black folks, O?" Oates stood up and faced his friend. "They're the main ones always talking about how police need to do more to protect their community but they don't do anything to help us. I am willing to bet that somebody in that damn crowd saw what happened out here and they're not saying anything, How the hell are we supposed to get these killers off the street if these people are withholding information from us?"

Oates sighed. "Brother, this has been going on like forever. That 'no snitching' bullshit is a pain in the ass to us, but abiding by that rule is what keeps these people alive. It's a vicious cycle so I can understand how they feel. They're scared for their lives."

Oates and Lewis waited for a search warrant so that they could enter the Bradford household. When they got inside the house, there were three teenage girls and a guy sitting in the living room with solemn looks on their faces.

"What's going on here?" asked Oates. He looked at the three girls. They looked very young. "How old are you, young ladies?" They looked at each other but no one answered him. Oates sighed. "I'm gonna ask y'all again—how old are you?"

The guy spoke up. "'Scuse me, Detective whatever your name is, what does their age got to do with my boy bein' killed? One of the neighbors knocked on this door and told me that Kody's been murdered! Shouldn't you be workin' on this homicide case instead of worryin' about how old somebody is?"

Oates looked at Lewis and smirked. "Oh, okay, I see what's got to happen here." He walked over to the young man. "Okay, everybody, let's see some identification."

The guy protested. "Come on, man! Why we gotta show ID? We ain't do shit!"

Oates glared at the man. "As far as I know, you could be the fucking murderer! You're in this man's house while he's out there dead on the sidewalk. Right now, you're a suspect! You told me to do my job and I'm doing just that!" He looked at all them. "So show me some got-damn ID—now!"

All four of them rushed to get some identification. The girls showed their New York State identification and Eric showed his driver's license. He was twenty-three years old and one of the girls was only fifteen. Oates assumed the other girls were just as young.

Oates looked at Eric's license. "Hmmm, let's see, Eric Bartlett, 320 Dumont Avenue, age twenty-three. LaShawn Edwards, 1907 Saratoga Avenue, age sixteen. Monica Fillmore, 1650 Saratoga Avenue, age seventeen, and Tashanna Patrick, 1650 Saratoga, age fifteen." He looked around the place. There were empty liquor and beer bottles all over the place. "Looks like

y'all were having a little party, huh?" No one responded
to him.

Lewis chimed in. "All of them need to come down to
the station, O. Since this dude . . . What's his name?"
Oates showed his partner the driver's license belonging to Eric. "Since Mr. Bartlett wants to run his damn
mouth, he's gonna be the first person to tell us what
happened with his boy. Or else, I see some statuatory
rape charges. What you think, O?"

Oates looked at his partner and then at Eric. "I can
see that too. But even though we might not do anything
to you, I don't know if I can vouch for the parents that
we're going to have to call to pick up their daughters."

One of the girls began crying instantly.

Eric sighed loudly. "C'mon, man! I don't need to
have this on my plate! I just got off parole!" He paced
around the room. "Take me down to the station. I can
give you some information. All I know is that Kody was
my boy. I would never do anything like that to him!"

Oates and Lewis looked at each other and smirked.
Their moment was interrupted by the howls of Kody's
father, who had just walked in the door of his home.
The partners stood by as friends and family members
attempted to restrain him. Oates shook his head and
eased out the door.

An hour later, at the precinct, the three girls were
released to their mothers. Oates noticed that not one of
the girls' fathers had come to the station. He shook his
head. The demise of the family structure in the African
American community was so obvious; it made him sick
to his stomach. The teenage girls Oates had detained
were a perfect example as to why fathers and positive
role models were so important.

For months, according to various complainants, there were always girls who appeared to be under the age of eighteen going in and out of the Bradford home at all hours of the night. Kody was being investigated for human trafficking and solicitation, but a killer with a vendetta got to him first. Now it was up to Oates and Lewis to find out who that person was.

Oates walked into the interrogation room by himself. He wanted to speak with Eric first to find out what could have possibly led up to the death of his friend, Kody. Eric looked nervous as Oates took a seat across from him.

"Look, Detective, um, I didn't catch your name," Eric began.

"The name is Oates."

"Okay, Detective Oates. That's word to my mother, I didn't kill Kody! He was my right-hand man and, to be honest, I don't have the balls to kill anybody! And those girls were Kody's friends. I was just there to chill!"

Oates rubbed his chin. "Look, dude, nobody is charging you with anything, okay? And the mothers of those girls that you claim that you were just hanging out with came to pick them up about fifteen minutes ago. I'm not saying that you did or didn't do anything with those girls but that's not why we're here right now. I need some information about Kody's death. I want you to tell me what you do know about his murder."

Eric leaned back in his chair and put his face in his hands. "Yo, Mr. Oates, I can't say that I know exactly who did it so technically I won't be snitchin'. But one person you may wanna talk to is this cat named Poet."

Oates frowned. He felt lightheaded. "Who?"

"Poet. Don't know the dude last name or nothin'. Just kinda see him around the way from time to time. I ain't got no beef with him but accordin' to my man, Kody, Poet was not feelin' him at all!"

"Is that right? Why wasn't he feeling him?"

"Well, I'm gonna keep it real. Poet got these two younger sisters, and I'm not gonna lie, they're bad as hell! I mean, they are real pretty—you know, long hair, pretty brown complexions, bangin' bodies, the whole nine. Most of the dudes in the projects wanna get at them. A couple of weeks ago, Kody hooked up with the younger sister, Precious, and her friend. We went back to Kody's house and you know one thing led to another and we did our thing. Now after that day, I heard that there was a rumor that goin' around the way about how me and Kody had had sex with Poet's sister and her friend. Come to find out, Precious's friend was the one that was runnin' her mouth about it. Maybe Poet heard about it, I'm not sure, but the way he acted when we ran into him earlier tonight proved that he heard somethin'. He was cool with me but this look that he gave Kody was a 'if looks could kill, you would be dead' type of look. Even though we stepped off without any incident, I knew that there was some beef between them two, you know what I'm sayin'?"

"So were there any harsh words exchanged between Kody and Poet?"

"I can't remember exactly what they said to each other but anybody could see that there was a little tension between the two. When we walked away, Kody put me on to why he thought Poet was a little salty with him."

"So are you saying that this fella, Poet, is the one that could have possibly murdered your friend?"

"Yo, Mr. Oates, real talk, if you would have been there earlier tonight, you should have seen the way that dude Poet got out his car and ran up on us! We didn't have no burners on us at the time, but if we did, that motherfucker would've been shot! He hopped out of his car like he was police or a detective or somethin'!" Eric said with a nervous chuckle.

Oates nodded his head. The mere mention of Poet's name made his heart drop. This was the third murder that he was implicated in and it was becoming a serious problem for Mr. Poet Washington. This time, Oates made a promise to keep his big mouth shut and not tell Cheryl anything. This time, he was going to let the chips fall where they may.

After some more questioning, Oates let Eric leave the stationhouse. He was not a suspect so they had no other choice. He walked over to Lewis, who was helping himself to some Dunkin' Donuts coffee and treats.

"Man, you're over here munching and sipping on coffee while I'm doing all the hard work!" Oates said with a laugh. He snatched up a powdered jelly donut and bit into it.

"Look, O, I'm tired! I had to leave some hot number lying in her bed to come here for this murder! I'm just trying to regain my momentum here!" he said, while chomping on a Boston cream donut. They both chuckled loudly. "So, what's up with that dude, Eric? Is he clean?" he asked while chewing with his mouth open.

Oates put the rest of the donut in his mouth. "Man, Mr. Bartlett and his friend Kody is everything short of being classified as pedophiles, man! They were running through the neighborhood screwing teenage girls! But how can you get mad at the guys if the girls are giving it up? I'm telling you, I would have to stick my foot in my daughter's ass for messing around with some grown man!"

"You and me both!" The partners shook their heads at the same time. "So what did he say about the murder?"

"He told me that earlier that night, Kody had a little run-in with guess who?"

Lewis looked confused. "Who?" he asked.

"Poet Washington."

"You gotta be fucking kidding me, O!"

Oates poured a cup of coffee and took a sip. "Nope. I'm not kidding. Poet is about to get picked up. I done heard this guy's name way too much and I'm beginning to think that he's the menace that we've been looking for these past few months."

Lewis sighed. "Damn, O. I'm sorry to hear that. What are you gonna do about Cheryl?"

"I'm not doing nothing about Cheryl, but I know what I'm gonna do about her son. We're about to get a search warrant."

Lewis and Oates finished up their coffee and proceeded to put in the paperwork for the warrant. Oates knew that Cheryl was going to be upset, but the law was the law. It was just unfortunate that her son didn't respect it.

Chapter 25

Deception

The next morning, Poet was awakened by the smell of his favorite breakfast: turkey bacon, eggs, and home fries. He got up and threw on a pair of pajama pants. After using the bathroom and washing his hands, he walked into the kitchen, where he saw his mother preparing the food. Poet walked up to her and gave her a big hug.

"I love you, Ma," he said.

Cheryl hugged him back. "I love you too, baby. How are you feeling this morning?"

Poet plopped down at the table. "I'm okay, Ma, I'm okay. Just got some things on my mind, I guess."

Cheryl put more bacon into the frying pan. "Like what, babe? Talk to your momma. I'm listening."

The things that were on Poet's mind couldn't be discussed with his mother. They were on good terms again and he wanted it to remain that way.

"It's nothin' major," he replied.

As Poet and Cheryl were talking, Porsha and Precious emerged from their bedroom. Porsha kissed Poet on the cheek and Precious sat in a chair across from him. She looked at Poet but didn't say a word to him.

"So, Porsha, how's school?" he asked.

Porsha sighed. "School is comin' along. I'm maintainin' a 3.0 average so I'm happy about that." She paused for a moment and looked at her big brother. "I'm glad that you're home, Poet. I missed you."

He kissed her on the cheek. "I missed you, too, baby girl."

Poet glanced at Precious and she still didn't say anything. He loved his baby sister but she was a little out of control. He had hoped that she would be more like Porsha.

"Good mornin', Precious," Poet finally said. "How are you?" he asked, biting into a piece of turkey bacon.

Precious kept her eyes on her plate. Her guilty conscience wouldn't allow her to look him in the eye. "I'm fine."

"That's what's up. If you're good then I'm good."

Precious sucked her teeth and rolled her eyes at him. "Anyway, Mommy, can I go with Malika today?" she asked.

Cheryl put her plate on the table and pulled the chair out to sit down. "Depends on where y'all goin'."

"We're goin' to the movies."

"What movies?"

"Linden Boulevard movie theatre," she said.

"Hell no!" Poet interjected. "You're not goin' there!"

Precious gave Cheryl a pleading look. "You heard your brother," her mother said.

Precious hopped up from the table. "That's why I hate this house! Every time I wanna do somethin', Poet always gotta put his two cents in! And, Mommy, you always let him do it!" She marched toward the bedroom. "I hate you, Poet! You should go back to wherever you came from and stay there!"

The bedroom door slammed. Cheryl got up from the table and walked to the bedroom. She opened the door and reprimanded her youngest daughter.

"You don't pay no bills in here, Precious Niasha Washington! Slam that door again and I'm gonna slam your ass!"

When Cheryl walked back into the kitchen, she sat with the snickering Poet and Porsha.

"What is her problem?" asked Porsha. "You're just tryin' to look out for her!"

Poet shoved some eggs into his mouth. "I don't know what's up with your baby daughter, Ma. She acts like she doesn't like me. Don't she know that I would really hurt somebody over her?"

Cheryl shook her head. "I don't know what her problem is and I don't care. All I know is that she better get a hold of some act right before I whoop her ass up in here! I'm the queen mother of this household!"

Later on that day, Precious got dressed to go outside. She needed to get away from her family; they were all getting on her nerves. It seemed as if everyone was always on her back about something and she was tired of it. She thought about what Kody had discussed with her and Malika the other day, and the prospect of having men pay her for sex wasn't such a bad idea after all. She figured that she could save up some money and move as far away from her family as possible.

Precious headed straight to the courtyard where a few of her friends had gathered. Some of them had tears in their eyes.

"What happened?" Precious asked. "Why are y'all cryin'?"

Malika, who was sitting on the bench, stood up and pulled Precious to the side. "Yo, Kody is dead," she said.

"He's what?" Precious said.

"Kody is dead!" Malika whispered loudly.

Precious looked over at her other friends, who were wiping their eyes. "Why are you pullin' me to the side if all of y'all know that Kody is dead? What is the big secret?"

Malika looked around and took Precious by the hand. "Because somebody came to me and said that your brother is the one that killed Kody because he heard that you was fuckin' with him."

"Why would they think that Poet killed Kody? And where did my name come from?"

"Remember the day that we were at Kody's house?" Precious nodded her head. "Come to find out Kody was tapin' us havin' sex with him and Eric. I heard that it's all over the projects and that somebody even saw us on the Internet!"

When Porsha told her about a sex tape that was circulating throughout the neighborhood, Precious didn't believe it. Now that it was confirmed by Malika, she was at her wits end.

"Oh, shit!" Precious said, covering her face with her hands. "Okay, so now we have a sex tape of us on the Internet. Why are all of them cryin'?" she asked, pointing to the rest of their friends.

"Because Kody and Eric were havin' sex with them and tapin' them too! You don't get it? They were messin' with a lot of these young girls in the projects, Precious!"

Precious tried to get her thoughts together. It was too much to take in at once. "Okay, so who is the person runnin' around sayin' that my brother killed Kody?"

Malika shrugged her shoulders. She looked upset. They both walked over to a bench and sat in silence.

Precious was scared. What if Poet really did kill Kody because of her? She knew that her brother had a bad temper, and she also knew how protective he was when it came to his family. But murder? Was Poet really capable of murder?

In a way, the thought of her brother killing someone because of her proved that he really did love her. When he acted as if he were her father, she would get highly upset. Precious didn't realize until that moment that Poet acted like that with her for a reason. Things were finally making sense. To think, she had even considered selling her body for money just to get away from the family she thought didn't care about her. Now with the Kody incident and the alleged sex tape circulating the projects and the Internet, it was evident that having an overprotective big brother like Poet wasn't such a bad thing after all.

After a few minutes had passed, Precious and Malika got up from where they were sitting and walked off from their other friends.

"What else did you hear about Kody?" Precious asked.

"I heard that Kody and Eric were at the house fuckin' with some chicks from Saratoga the night Kody was killed," Malika said. "I don't know them personally but Shaniqua M. from Seth Low knows one of the girls that was in the house that night. Shaniqua said that the girl told her that Kody walked outside his house to go to the store and whatnot, and he never made it back. Next thing they knew, a neighbor came and knocked on the door to tell them that Kody had been killed. Then a few minutes later, police was knockin' on Kody's door and when Eric opened it, the police said it had been a murder on the block. I heard that whoever killed Kody stabbed that cat up real good, too. They cut his throat and everything."

"Damn! My brother wouldn't do no shit like that, Malika! Poet is many things but he ain't no killer!"

Malika stopped walking. "How do you know what Poet is? You don't what your brother is capable of doin'! It's not like Poet is some punk and you don't even like him like that."

"Yeah, okay, but I don't see him doin' no stabbin'. Shootin' somebody, maybe, but stabbin' somebody and cuttin' their throat and whatnot? Nah, that ain't the Poet I know!"

"Well, maybe the Poet that you don't know is the person that killed Kody."

Precious covered her ears. She didn't want to hear any more foolishness. "Malika, do me a favor, let's just cut this conversation. I don't even wanna talk about that shit no more."

Meanwhile, Cheryl was in her bedroom trying to take a nap when she heard a knock on her apartment door. She reluctantly rolled out of bed to answer it.

"Who is it?" she asked, looking through the peephole.

"NYPD. Could we talk to you for a moment?"

Cheryl stood by the door with a stunned look on her face.

Why is NYPD knocking on my door? she thought.

Cheryl slowly cracked opened the apartment door. She was face to face with two African American detectives standing in the hallway.

"Good afternoon, ma'am, my name is Detective Hopewell from the Seventy-third Precinct, and this is my partner, Detective Mickens. How are you?" the tall man said.

"Um, I'm fine, I guess," she replied with a frown on her face. "May I help you?"

Detective Hopewell presented a piece of paper to Cheryl. She read it and tried to give it back to him. He didn't take it.

"This is a search warrant, Detective Hopewell. What do I need with this?"

"Does a Poet Washington live here, ma'am?" he asked.

"Yes, Poet's my son, but what is this about?"

"We need to search these premises, ma'am. There's been a murder and your son was implicated in the murder."

"The murder of who?" Cheryl asked, still blocking them from entering the premises.

"Terrence 'Pumpkin' Watts."

Cheryl shook her head and let the detectives in. When they stepped inside, two other detectives walked in behind them.

Detective Hopewell turned around. "Which bedroom does Poet sleep in?" he asked.

Cheryl pointed to the last bedroom toward the back of the apartment. She stood with her back against the wall. The tears fell from her eyes as she watched the police go through Poet's personal things. They turned over the mattress; they looked in the closet, and opened old sneaker boxes. By the time the police officers walked out of the room, they had a few small bags of evidence. Cheryl didn't know what was going on. She made a mental note to call Oates as soon as they left.

"Ma'am, I apologize for upsetting you, but we've been working on this case for a few weeks now and everything keeps coming back to your son."

"Is he going to be arrested?" she asked, with tears welling in her eyes.

"We're not sure. He's not the only suspect in this murder," Detective Hopewell replied. "We'll be leaving now but here is my card. Please tell your son to contact us as soon as possible. Have a good day, ma'am."

As soon they walked out of the door, Cheryl called Oates. He answered the phone on the first ring.

"Hello?" Oates said.

"Shareef, I don't believe that these detectives came into my house and searched Poet's room! My son didn't do anything!"

"Whoa, whoa!" exclaimed Oates. "Calm down, baby, calm down! What happened?"

"Your damn coworkers came into this apartment and turned my son's bedroom upside down! I don't know what the hell they were looking for but I don't appreciate this one bit! I didn't raise no murderer, Shareef, I just didn't!"

"Look, Cheryl, I didn't know—" he began, but she cut him off.

"Don't tell me you didn't know, Shareef! You could have done something to stop this! I don't want my baby to be arrested—he's innocent! You hear me? He is innocent!"

Cheryl hung up the phone without letting Oates reply to anything that she said. Even though she thought that Poet may have done some bad things in the streets, there was no way that she was going to make herself believe that her only son, her pride and joy, was capable of committing murder. At that moment, Cheryl made up her mind to defend her boy to the very end.

Chapter 26

A Harsh Reality

"Poet, come home right now!" his mother yelled into his cell phone. He held the phone away from his ear.

"Ma, I'm in the middle of somethin' right now," he said.

Poet watched as his supplier counted the money for the half kilo of cocaine that he was about to buy. He was looking to buy a few grams of heroin, too. Poet figured that since he was no longer working with Bone, he would branch out on his own. Now his mother was calling him with her drama in the midst of an important transaction.

"I don't give a shit about what you're in the middle of, Poet!" Cheryl screamed. "You need you to get your ass here and fast!"

"Okay, okay, Ma, I will call you right back," he said, hanging up the phone. Poet put all of the drugs in his North Face knapsack, gave the supplier a pound, and walked outside.

As Poet walked to his car, he spotted a guy stooping down beside a vehicle that was located across the street from where he was standing. Poet had his suspicions but proceeded to get into his car. He threw the bag onto the back seat and tightly held on to the gun that was tucked in the waistband of his jeans.

All of sudden, shots rang out. The bullets were coming at him from two different directions. Poet pulled out his 9 mm and began shooting in the direction of the man he had spotted first. While shooting at that man, Poet saw another man who was shooting at him from the left side. Poet dropped to the ground and ducked behind several cars, trying to avoid the bullets that were whizzing by his head. He managed to get off a few more shots before the two decided to run away.

Poet still had his gun in his hand as he watched the culprits disappear into the night. He fell back onto his car and tried to catch his breath. From underneath his baseball cap, sweat trickled down his face. He was still trying to make sense of what had just happened to him.

Poet crawled on the ground and opened the car door. He carefully slid into the driver's seat and began fumbling for his car keys. After finding them in his front pants pocket he started the car, but not before he began banging on the steering wheel. After a few seconds, Poet caught himself. He was fuming, but was more afraid than anything. What made it even more upsetting was Poet didn't know where the attack was coming from.

A half hour later, Bone got out of his car to speak to a few young men who were hanging out on Newport and Lott Avenue.

"What's up?" Bone said, greeting them with pounds and bear hugs.

After a brief talk with the small group of men, Preme pulled Bone to the side for a one-on-one conversation.

"Yo, Bee, we didn't hit that motherfucker," Preme said.

"Aw, c'mon, Preme," Bone said with a disappointed look on his face. "I need you to get at him, son! He done fucked up my business and whatnot—I had to pull out from crackhead Sha-Sha's crib because of this dumb motherfucker, man!"

Preme looked around to see if anyone was listening to their conversation. "Yo, I took that dude Sam with me, Bone, and he ain't no real sharpshooter. I'ma get this dude myself but it's gonna take a little time. We was shootin' at this dude, right, and he pulled out his ratchet and start bussin' off too! Poet isn't the amateur that I thought he was! I was shocked because I never saw Poet as being no real gangster!"

Bone sucked his teeth. "'Cause Poet ain't no real gangster and that's the fuckin' problem! And I know he killed Sha-Sha! I've moved out of that crib for like three weeks now and nobody ain't seen her show her face around there yet so you know that bitch is dead!" Bone shook his head. "And to think, I trusted the little bastard, too."

Bone felt bad about setting Poet up to be killed but his ex-protege had become a liability with all the rumors of him killing Pumpkin. Then when Sha-Sha went missing, it was more than Bone could take. Bone had managed to avoid prosecution all of these years and he refused to have some young, gunslinging fool spoil everything for him so Poet had to go.

Preme chuckled. "Damn, Bone. Sounds like you're hurtin'."

"Yeah, I am hurtin', Preme. Poet done fucked up my money and you know how I am about my money, Preme!"

Preme nodded his head in agreement. "I know."

"But make sure you take care of Poet real good for me. You're my hitman, boy, I know you're gonna clean that up for me."

Preme smiled and slapped Bone five. "Come on, Bone. You know I got you!"

After the shootout, the nervous Poet managed to make it back to his building in one piece. He pulled his bag out of the back seat and quickly walked toward his building. When he got upstairs, his mother was pacing back and forth like a madwoman. He had just come back home and now the bullshit was already beginning.

"What is going on with you, Poet?" his mother asked. The expression on her face told him that this was going to be serious.

"Ain't nothin' goin' on with me," he replied.

Cheryl tightened her jaw. "Okay, see, you need to stop right there. Stop before you tell me another fucking lie and I'm going to be mad as shit. Now, I'm gonna sit down on this couch and you are too, and I need for you to tell me the truth. Because what's gonna happen is, you're going to go to jail, Poet. Uh-huh, jail. I'm tired of being in the dark, I'm tired of you lying to me, and I'm ready to hear what's been really going on with you."

Poet walked toward his room. "I don't have to tell you nothin' because I ain't do nothin'!" When Poet opened the door to his bedroom, he got the shock of his life. His whole room was in disarray. "Yo, Ma! Who the hell did this to my room? Did you do this to my room?" he yelled.

Cheryl appeared in the doorway with a smirk on her face. "Oh, no, I didn't do a damn thing! No, not your momma! That was the courtesy of the homicide unit at the Seventy-third Precinct, baby!"

Poet looked at his mother and looked back at his room. It felt as if he was having heart palpitations.

"But, Ma, I didn't—"

Cheryl cut him off. She stood there with her arms crossed. "So are you still going to tell me that you haven't done shit?"

Poet dropped his bag and fell to his knees. He began to cry uncontrollably and Cheryl bent down with him. She held her son in her arms and started to weep as well.

Now that she saw him showing some emotion, Cheryl changed her tone. "Whatever it is, baby, we can try to work it out," she said, kissing him on the forehead.

"We can't work this one out, Ma. Not this one," Poet replied with tears in his eyes. "I've gone too far this time."

"If you killed Pumpkin, I'm sure that it was self-defense, right?" she asked, as she made him look her straight in the eye. "I'm sure that you and him got into a fight or something and you had to um, defend yourself, right?"

Poet shook his head. There was no use in his mother making excuses for him. He thought he was doing a good thing by getting rid of the human vermin who plagued their crime-ridden neighborhood. Now it seemed as if he had become just as much of a menace as Jerrod, the rapist; John-John, the thief; Pumpkin, the gangbanger; Sha-Sha, the crackhead; and Kody, the pedophile. The story was supposed to end with him being a hero, not some murderous maniac.

"I killed Pumpkin, Ma," Poet said, wiping his tears. "Yes, I killed him."

Cheryl sighed and held his hands. She saw a look in her son's eyes that she had never seen before.

"Prince Poet, I need you to be one hundred percent honest with me. Did you kill other people?" she asked.

He held his head down. "Yes, Mommy," he replied, sounding like a lost little boy.

"Who were they?"

"I killed a man that raped the girl in the staircase. I killed John-John for robbin' Mr. Leroy. I killed Pumpkin after we got into an argument. I had to take him out before he killed me. I killed Sha-Sha for stealin' Bone's drugs. I killed Kody. I killed him because he was pimpin' little girls. I killed him for Precious."

Cheryl tried to refrain from crying. She had to be strong for Poet, for herself, for her daughters. She could not believe that her beloved son, her sweet man-child, had just confessed to the murders of five people. It was so much for one person to bear, and she couldn't understand how Poet had been able to hold on to the horrible secrets for so long. And Cheryl felt equally responsible for what had transpired. She blamed herself for imposing so many expectations on her son, subconsciously looking for him to take the place of the absentee patriarch of their family.

As a mother, she was supposed to be the protector and she neglected to do that with the one child who needed her the most. And the denial of who Poet had actually become had her detached from reality. She had an idea that her son was always involved in illegalities, so when he was implicated in a murder Cheryl had to confront him about the horrible truth. She was sorry that she asked him but she had to know. Now it was her duty as a loving parent to give Poet the same support that he had given their family for so long.

"Well, we're going to try to work through this, okay?" Cheryl said. "The police only came here to search for evidence for the Pumpkin killing. Now where did you put the gun?"

"I got rid of it. I don't have any guns in my bedroom."

Cheryl looked at the knapsack. "What's in this bag, Poet?" she asked, reaching for it.

Suddenly, Poet came back to his senses and snatched the bag away from her grasp. He held it to his chest.

"Nothin'," he replied, looking as if his eyes were about to pop out of his head.

"The only way that I can help you is for you to be honest with me, Poet. I told you that. No more secrets."

Poet hesitated but slowly opened the bag to show her what was inside of it. Cheryl peeked inside of the bag and sighed loudly when she saw that it was drugs.

"Poet, I want that shit out of my house right now," she said. Cheryl shook her head. "Give that bag to me. I'm going to throw it down the incinerator."

They both stood up and Poet handed his mother the knapsack. His mother had a disappointed look on her face while holding the drugs tightly to her chest. She rubbed his face, and continued to talk to him.

"I thought that I was a good mother, Poet. I made so many sacrifices so that you and your sisters could have the best. I don't understand where I went wrong with you, with any of my children."

"Ma, you are a good mother! I just . . . I just . . ."

"I wanna help you, baby, but where do I start? If they catch up to you, you're going to jail!" she cried. Cheryl broke down and dropped the knapsack to the floor.

Poet embraced his mother as she sobbed uncontrollably. He wanted to leave but he didn't have anywhere to go. He wasn't going back to Rakiyah's house; he knew that she deserved better. He was afraid to go too far away from home so he decided that he would go to Mekhi's house for a few days just to get his mind right. He needed to lay low.

After making sure that Cheryl had calmed down, he went into his bedroom to inspect the damage. The detectives had searched everything. He knew that they would probably be coming for him soon so he had to start making some plans. He quickly began to put his things back in order so that he could get the hell out of there.

When Poet finished cleaning up his room, he grabbed the knapsack filled with drugs and walked out of the house. He got into his car and realized that his days of riding around in the Camry were almost over. The next stop was to get rid of the drugs that he had on him. Poet knew that he could get a nice amount of money for the half kilo of cocaine and the couple of grams of heroin that he had purchased. He called up a few connects that he knew and when they asked what the damage was, he upped the prices. They agreed to meet him to make their purchases.

After getting rid of the drugs, Poet made some more phone calls then took a drive to Flatbush. He knew some Rastafarians from Vanderveer Houses who would be more than willing to buy the car right there on the spot for $8,500. Poet needed as much money as he could get his hands on. It looked like he was going to need a good lawyer, if a lawyer could help him.

After meeting up with the Rastafarians, Poet walked into a bodega and purchased a Red Bull. He felt himself fighting a losing battle with exhaustion and he needed a burst of energy. After that, he caught a cab to a nearby motel. He couldn't go home and he needed a place to count his money.

Two hours later, Poet was in the Surfside Motel, counting over $30,000 in cash. He also counted another $20,000 that was hidden in a small lockbox inside of his car before he got rid of it. After Poet was finished, he looked at the over $50,000 in cash that was spread out on the bed. Poet just shook his head. He had all of that money and he knew that he wasn't going to be able to spend it the way he wanted to.

Poet plopped on the bed and covered his face with his hands. He looked at the money again. Then he had an idea. He was going to give all of that money to his mother. She would need it more than he did. Poet figured that there was no use in trying to obtain a lawyer for his freedom. Although he still felt that the murders he had committed were justifiable, he would cop out to whatever time they had to offer him. Poet knew that a black man's trial for multiple murders was a battle that was almost impossible to win. But he wasn't going to turn himself in just yet; the cops would just have to catch him.

Chapter 27

Growing Up Too Fast

The next day, Precious was awakened by an angry voice in the living room. She walked out of her bedroom to see what was going on. Her mother was pacing back and forth, cussing to herself.

"Are you okay, Mommy?" she said, rubbing the sleep out of her eyes. "What's the matter?"

Cheryl was holding a note in her hand. She handed her daughter the letter without saying anything. It was a letter from Poet.

Precious sat down on the couch and read the letter. "Poet's not comin' back here, is he?" she asked.

"That's what the letter said. I don't know where he is. He must have snuck in here in the middle of the night, left me that letter, and left all of this money."

Precious looked at the stacks of money that were piled up in three Nike sneakers boxes.

"Wow, how much money is that?"

Cheryl rolled her eyes. "I don't know and I don't care. I would trade all of that money to have Poet back here with us."

"Why did he leave?"

"The cops are looking for him, Precious."

Precious's heart skipped a beat. Unaware of the other killings, she couldn't help but wonder if her brother really did kill Kody.

"They must be lookin' for him because he killed Kody." Precious covered her mouth, instantly regretting what she said.

Cheryl pretended that she didn't know what Precious was talking about. She knew all about the Kody murder because Poet had just confessed everything to her the day before. She remembered Poet saying that he had killed Kody because of Precious. Now she wanted to hear what Precious had to say about it.

"Poet killed Kody? Who the hell is Kody?"

"This guy that lives on Bristol. They found him lyin' in somebody's driveway all stabbed up and his throat was cut."

"But why would you think that he killed Kody, Precious?"

Precious looked away from her mother's piercing stare. "Because of me."

"What about you?"

"Well, it was a rumor goin' around that Kody and I were dealin' with each other and supposedly Poet had stepped to him about it and that was all she wrote. But I don't believe that Poet did anything to him. That's just the rumor."

Cheryl put her hand over her mouth and began to cry. A part of her didn't want to believe Poet's confession. Now that Precious had confirmed Kody's killing, she realized that her son may have been on a mission—a killing mission.

"What is going on? Why is my Prince Poet doing this?" she asked herself. She sat in the loveseat across from Precious and looked at the money.

Cheryl knew that there was nothing that she could do for her child. His legal defense would cost hundreds of thousands of dollars and O.J. Simpson's lawyer money was not something that they had. There would have to be some major technicality and a miracle from God in order for Poet to beat those murder cases. With those strikes against him, he didn't have a chance.

"Precious, please do me a favor, baby. Get dressed and go to Mekhi's house to see if Poet has been by there. His cell phone service is cut off and I cannot get in touch with him. Maybe Mekhi would know some information."

Precious smiled. "Okay, Mommy, I will. Let me throw some clothes on."

Precious ran to the closet and quickly threw on some clothes. She washed her face, brushed her teeth, and pulled her long hair into a neat ponytail. Her mother was still in the living room when she walked out the door. Precious quickly ran down the stairs and out of the building. The sooner she got to Mekhi's house, the more time they would have with each other. Even with all the drama going on, Poet's whereabouts weren't even an afterthought in Precious's immature mind.

When Precious arrived at Mekhi's door, she rang the bell like three times before he answered it. He was yawning loudly and stretching when he opened the door. When he saw Precious standing there, he sucked his teeth.

"Didn't I tell you not to come over here anymore?" he said with an attitude.

"Yeah, you told me that but I'm not comin' here for myself, Khi," she replied with a smirk on her face. She stood on her tiptoes in order to look over his shoulder and inside of the apartment. "Could I come inside for a minute?" she asked. "I really need to talk to you."

Mekhi sighed and reluctantly invited her into the house. "You can come in but stop right there in that living room."

He locked the door and followed her to the sofa. They both sat down at the same time.

"Okay, what do you want?" he asked, while yawning in the process.

"My mother wanted to know if you've seen my brother."

"Nah, I haven't seen Poet since the other night. Why? What happened?"

Precious sighed. "Poet left home because the police came there lookin' for him. He left my mother some note tellin' her that he's sorry about everything. He left her some money, too."

Mekhi shook his head. "Well, he's not here. I called him last night but he didn't return my phone calls."

"Well, do you know anything about him killin' Kody or Pumpkin? I keep hearin' these rumors about that," she said.

Mekhi hopped up from the sofa. He didn't give her any eye contact. "I don't know anything about that shit. I don't know what you're talkin' about."

Precious frowned. "You know somethin', Mekhi! I can tell that you know somethin' about it!" Precious announced.

"I don't know about nothin'," he said. He turned around and gave Precious a nasty look. "Look, if your brother calls me, I'll tell him to call Miss Cheryl, okay?"

Precious stood up and stood in front of Mekhi. She was close enough to smell his morning breath. She kissed him on the lips and he didn't resist.

"I'm sorry for the way I've been actin' toward you, Khi. I just want you to know that I really do care for you."

Mekhi held Precious by her arms. "Yo, Presh, I have to tell you somethin'," he said.

Precious didn't want anything spoiling their moment. She had to seize the opportunity.

"I don't want to hear nothin', Khi," she replied, pulling down his sweats.

Precious smiled when she noticed the bulge in his boxer briefs. She got to her knees and began giving him a blow job right in the middle of the living room. Mekhi was nervous that his grandmother would come home early from church, walk in the house, and catch them in the act. But it felt too good for him to stop her.

With the exception of the television in his bedroom, the only other sounds that could be heard were slurping noises. He moaned softly and looked down at his best friend's sister with adoration in his eyes. He loved Precious although their situation was extremely complicated.

Precious was working Mekhi's rod like a professional. She nibbled on the head of his erect penis. She made jerking motions with her right hand while she licked and sucked on his dick. Mekhi's eyes were rolled in the back of his head and his knees felt weak. Precious smiled to herself. The effect that she had on Mekhi only made her want him even more.

She pushed him onto the couch and began taking off her clothes. Mekhi tried to protest but he was too caught up in the moment. She slid out of the sweat suit that she was wearing. Precious had the curvaceous body of an adult woman and there was no way he could resist her. Precious took off her panties and slid onto Mekhi's hard dick. He closed his eyes and enjoyed every stroke.

Precious knew that she was working her magic on him once again. She had learned some new tricks from the deceased Kody and now she wanted to show Mekhi that she was a big girl. He began to moan again and so did she, as she felt the shaft of his penis going in and out of her wet pussy. Mekhi grabbed her ass, maneuvering his way inside of her. She felt him going deeper and deeper, hitting all kinds of nerve endings that she never knew were there. From the looks of things, Mekhi had been holding back. Tonight on that sofa he was giving her everything he had and she loved every minute of it.

Precious rode him until her body began to shudder with pleasure. It felt so good it brought tears to her eyes. Then Mekhi turned her on her back. He entered her and began slowly stroking her eager pussy. They gave each other wet, sloppy kisses while they made love to each other. After about twenty minutes of pure ecstasy, Mekhi exploded inside of Precious's tight vagina.

Both of them were out of breath as they got up to get dressed. Precious felt Mekhi's semen oozing out of her but she didn't care. She didn't seem to care that no protection was used. She smiled at the thought of her having their baby.

Precious realized that she had been there for some time and her mother had called her cell phone twice in a row. She had to leave before someone got suspicious.

Precious leaned over Mekhi and they shared an intimate kiss. He followed her to the door. When she stepped into the hallway, he stopped her and they began to kiss again.

"That felt good," Mekhi said, after they came up for air.

Precious gave him a faint smile. "I'm sorry for bein' jealous of you and Poet's relationship. He's your best friend and I was actin' real selfish."

"Let's forget about all that and start over, okay?" said Mekhi.

"That sounds cool. This time, I'm not gonna beef about anything. Our secret is safe with me. No more bullshit, right?" They gave each other a pound and a hug.

"No more. When we're together, it's all about us. By the way, that pussy was real good," he said, giving her another kiss on the lips.

Precious blushed. "Shut up, silly!" she replied with a laugh. "I'm gonna call you later, and in the meantime, if my brother calls you, please tell him to call my mother. She's worried about him."

"Okay, I will do that. You know that I love you, right?"

Precious smiled at him and opened the elevator door. "I know you do. And I love you too, Khi. Later." As Precious got on to the elevator, Mekhi closed the door to his apartment.

Poet peeked out of the staircase and into the empty hallway. He had overheard the entire conversation between his best friend and his little sister. Out of all the people he trusted, he couldn't believe that Mekhi, the man he considered his brother, had violated him in the worst way. Now Poet was about to prove to everyone that he had nothing to lose. Before he settled in for a lifetime in prison, he was going to make an example out of the one person he never thought would betray him.

Chapter 28

Betrayal

After discovering that he had been betrayed by Mekhi and Precious, Poet had to walk up to the roof to get some fresh air. While on the roof of Mekhi's building, he looked out at his surroundings. There were buildings everywhere and the bright lights of Manhattan could be seen from where he was standing. As usual, the customary sounds of ambulance, police, and fire sirens could be heard in the distance.

Poet realized that living in that neighborhood was his grim existence. By growing up in Brownsville, fatherless and poor, he felt that he didn't have a chance in hell. It was even more heartbreaking that he felt like doing the wrong thing was his only option if he wanted to survive. And he thought that he was making his mother so proud of him by helping her with the finances. He also thought that being a good brother was being extremely overprotective of his younger sisters.

For two and half months, he had been on an unexplained murder spree. He had single-handedly assisted in terrorizing his own neighborhood with the random killings that he had committed. But he didn't feel one iota of remorse because of this. He was more upset that his mother had found out about his misdeeds.

Poet pulled out a cigarette from an old pack of Newports that he found in the pocket of his denim jacket.

He lit it up and pulled on it like it was the last time he was going to smoke. Now he had one more person to kill and that person was Mekhi. It was going hurt his heart but he had to do it. It had taken almost twenty years to realize that their friendship was nothing but a lie.

After Precious left his house, Mekhi felt as if a weight had been lifted. He thought that Precious would have ratted him out to Poet after the altercation they had. The guilt weighed heavily on Mekhi but the satisfaction of being with Precious outweighed those feelings.

Later on that night, it was about 9:00 P.M. when Mekhi heard another tap on the door of his apartment. He dragged himself out of bed to find out who it was. When he walked to the door, he looked through the peephole and saw that there were two black men in suits standing in the hallway. He knew exactly who they were. They were homicide detectives. Mekhi sighed loudly and opened the door.

"Good evening, this is Detective Mickens and I'm Detective Hopewell from the homicide unit at the Seventy-third Precinct. Are you Mekhi Porter?" the tall, dark-skinned man asked.

Mekhi figured that they were going to ask him about Poet. "Yeah, that's me," he replied. Mekhi looked down at the floor then back up at the detectives.

"We didn't want to bother you but may we come in?" Hopewell asked.

Mekhi looked down the hallway and saw that his grandmother's bedroom door was ajar with the television on. He gave the detectives the signal to wait there while walked to the room to make sure that she was sound asleep and snoring. Mekhi checked on her then walked back to the front to let the detectives in. He guided them to the living room and they sat on the sofa.

Detective Hopewell looked around the neat apartment, admiring the beautiful hand-painted drawings that were on the walls.

"The artwork that you have here is very impressive. May I ask where you got it from?" he asked.

Mekhi blushed. "That's my work."

The detectives seemed impressed. "Okay, Mr. Porter! You should be proud of yourself! Are you in school for art?" Mickens asked.

Mekhi held his head down. "No, I'm not."

"Well, you should be," Mickens said. "You're a talented young man."

"I've heard that from my family, but not too many people know that I have a love for art, except for my family and close friends."

"Speaking of close friends, we're here to ask you about one close friend in particular," Hopewell said. "Um, do you know Mr. Poet Washington?"

Mekhi felt his chest tighten. "Yeah, I know Poet."

"Who is Poet to you?"

"He's a very good friend of mine."

"Have you heard about him being involved in a murder? Or two?"

Mekhi shook his head. "Nah, I didn't know that."

Hopewell looked at Mickens and smirked. "Okay, let me get this straight. Poet is a very good friend of yours but you don't know anything about him being involved in a murder—or two? I thought friends are supposed to tell each other everything."

Mekhi had to use his words carefully. "We do tell each other everything, sir, and if he did anything like killin' somebody, I would have been the first person that he would have told. But he never told me anything like that. That's how I know that he didn't do anything."

"Hmmm, that's strange," said Hopewell, with a suspicious look on his face. "We're here to tell you that your so-called friend Poet is a suspect in the murder of Terrence 'Pumpkin' Watts. Weren't you around when they had an argument with each other? They had an argument on the same day that Watts was killed."

"I don't remember—" Mekhi said.

Detective Mickens cut him off. "Come on, Mr. Porter! Don't give us that shit! We've had several eyewitnesses that put you there at the time Pumpkin and Poet had the argument! You were there! And I'm positive that if Poet killed him, you know all about it!"

Mekhi was unmoved. They wanted him to snitch on his friend but he wasn't going to do it.

"Like I said, Poet is my boy. If he had any intentions on killin' somebody, then he would have told me that he was goin' to do it. That's what I'm tellin' you. Poet has never said anything to me about killin' Pumpkin or anybody else for that matter. So I don't know what y'all talkin' about. Sorry."

Mickens and Hopewell looked at each other. They knew that Mekhi was probably lying for his friend. That's what they had expected him to do. Mekhi was holding his friend down to the very end.

"So you don't know where Poet is right now? Is he in this house?" Hopewell asked.

"Nah, he's not here."

"Do you mind if we looked around?"

Mekhi sighed. "I told you that Poet wasn't here! Plus, don't y'all police need a search warrant for that?"

A smug expression came over Detective Hopewell's face. "Look, Porter, we don't want to have to drag your ass into this murder case! Either you're going to prove to me that Poet isn't in this house or you're coming down to the stationhouse with us for a real interrogation. Might just decide to hold your ass for obstruction of justice or, even better, conspiracy! Who's to say that you and your boy Poet didn't plan to take out Pumpkin Watts that day, huh?"

Mekhi's jaw tightened. Hopewell had him by the balls and he knew it. He wasn't going to snitch on Poet but letting the detectives take a quick look of the apartment wouldn't hurt.

Mekhi showed them to his bedroom and he opened the closet door. When they saw that his room was empty, they crept into his grandmother's room while she was sound asleep. Mekhi prayed that she didn't wake up. Miss Addie continued to snore while they looked around her small bedroom. There was no sign of Poet. After the detectives checked the entire apartment, they concluded that Mekhi was telling the truth. Hopewell went into his wallet and handed Mekhi a business card with his name and phone number on it.

"If your friend comes here anytime soon or you speak to him, tell him to holler at me. Or maybe you would wanna holler at me if you see him. Harboring a fugitive is against the law, so stay out of trouble, Porter. We're watching you too."

Hopewell and Mickens walked out of Mekhi's house as quickly as they had walked in. When he locked the door behind them, he slid down the wall onto the floor. As Mekhi softly banged his head against the wall, he thought about all the unnecessary stress that the Washington siblings were causing him. Between Poet and Precious, he was a nervous wreck.

Still sitting on the roof of Mekhi's building, Poet was unsure of what to do next. With the exception of a large bottle of water in his knapsack, he hadn't eaten all day and was urinating all over the roof floor. He was sure that the police had a warrant for his arrest by now, and after the shootout the other day he realized that his life was in danger as well. All of the indecencies he had been trying to avoid after living in Brownsville all of his life were now his dismal reality. Poet was officially a criminal.

Hunger and fatigue finally got the best of Poet and he worked up the nerve to knock on Mekhi's door. It was a little after ten o'clock at night and sleeping on the rooftop or staircase of the building was not an option for him. The comforts of his bed and his mother's home-cooked meals were definitely going to be missed. Too bad he had taken all of that for granted.

After a few knocks, Mekhi opened the door and told Poet to hurry inside. Poet took one look at his friend and saw that he had a worried expression on his face.

"What's up, Khi?" he asked. "Why does it look like you got the weight of the world on your shoulders, man?"

Mekhi did have a lot of pressure on him. He was trying to be a loyal friend to Poet, and the secret fling with Precious had his conscience racked with guilt. Not to mention, Poet's situation had put him in precarious position. It angered him to see Poet standing in the middle of his living room with not a care in the world.

"Yo, homicide detectives came to my house tonight lookin' for you, man. You just missed them," Mekhi whispered in annoyance. He looked toward his grandmother's room. "They searched my crib and everything lookin' for you!"

Poet smirked and plopped down on the couch. "Fuck them *police*, son! You didn't have to let them search shit! Did they have a search warrant?"

Mekhi shook his head. "It ain't even about them havin' a search warrant! It's about you havin' me caught up in some bullshit that I had nothin' to do with!"

Poet stood back up. "Fuck do you mean by that, Khi?"

"Those cops were askin' me all this shit about you and, of course, bein' that you're my man, I didn't tell them shit! Then they proceeded to tell me that if I didn't let them search my crib to make sure that you weren't in here hidin' somewhere, they were going to charge me with obstruction of justice or even conspiracy to murder! Yo, man, I'm not goin' to jail, so you better think about what you're gonna do!"

Suddenly, Poet walked over to Mekhi and pulled out a gun on him. He grabbed Mekhi by the neck and put the gun to his temple.

"We've been homies all of our lives, right?"

Mekhi nodded his head in fear. Poet saw the tears forming in the eyes of his friend but that didn't deter him from making sure he got his point across. He pressed the gun against Mekhi's temple even harder.

"I will fuckin' kill you, son. I will splatter your brains all over this fuckin' living room if you decide to rat me out to the police. If the police come here again, you better come up with somethin' real good to make them motherfuckers go away. I need a few days to get my thoughts together and I'm gonna need to stay here with you and Grandma, do you hear me?" Poet said through clenched teeth.

Mekhi nodded again. He was scared shitless. Poet pulled back from him and pushed him onto the couch. He still held the gun in his hand.

"Now you need to find a way to explain to Grandma that I'm gonna be here for a little while. I don't need her to be callin' my mother and runnin' her mouth and all that, so you better come up with somethin', or else I'm gonna have to kill her too."

Mekhi looked at Poet with contempt in his eyes. "So this is what this shit has come to? This is how you're treatin' somebody that you consider a brother for most of his life?" he asked.

Poet laughed. "Brother?" He laughed again and waved the gun in Mekhi's face. "You ain't my fuckin' brother! How are you my brother when you're runnin' around here fuckin' my little sister behind my back?"

Mekhi fell back on the couch with a surprised look on his face.

"Yeah, Khi, I overheard you and Precious talkin' to each other in the hallway earlier today. She was tellin' you how much she loves you and you're tellin' her that she got some good pussy. I mean, what the fuck were you thinkin', huh?"

"Yo, Po, I didn't mean to hurt you, son. It's just that—" he began.

Poet pointed the gun in his face. "Well, you did and now you owe me. You're lucky that I'm not blowin' your head off right in this living room, you fuckin' pervert! My sister is a dumb little bitch but at least she's only sixteen. She has an excuse for bein' a dumb little bitch. What's your excuse, motherfucker? You're a grown-ass man fuckin' around with a sixteen-year-old girl— you're supposed to be in jail anyway! You're a rapist! You remembered what happened to Kody, don't you?"

Mekhi clenched his jaw. There was no way that he could be mad at Poet. He had been caught red-handed.

Mekhi held his hands in the air. "Okay, okay, Po, you got me, man. I'm so sorry, man. It's just that I always had these feelings for Precious, feelings that I had no control over and, I don't know, things just happened between us."

"I don't wanna hear that shit, Khi. You knew better! All of the times that I left you and Precious alone—all that time, you were havin' sex with her! You made me look like a fuckin' fool!"

They both paused for a moment. After a few minutes, Poet put his gun away. He was tired. Everything was coming down on him at one time and his mind was racing. He felt psychotic.

"Look, Khi, I'm not feelin' your punk ass right now but I need a place to rest my head. I need some rest."

Mekhi wiped the beads of sweat from his forehead and got up from the couch. He pulled out a comforter, sheet, and a pillow. He laid them out on the couch.

Poet looked at Mekhi strangely. "Who's sleepin' on the couch?" he asked.

The frightened Mekhi sighed. "Go in my room and relax. I'm gonna sleep out here. I owe you that much."

Poet made an attempt to smile. "That's what I thought."

When Poet walked out of the living room, Mekhi made himself comfortable on the couch/bed. Once he heard his bedroom door close, he reached into his pocket and looked at the card that Detective Hopewell had given him. Snitching on Poet didn't seem like such a bad idea after all.

Chapter 29

It's Not Only Business, It's Personal

In Queens, Oates stepped out of the shower. He must have looked at his cell phone like fifty times before he realized that Cheryl Washington wasn't going to call him back. He was still clueless as to why she went off on him. From what he remembered, he was the one who gave her the heads-up on her wayward son and his exploits in the first place.

"So much for being a compassionate man," he said aloud.

He sighed with disappointment as he came to the conclusion that there was no pleasing a woman. He dried himself off and threw the damp towel on top of the wicker hamper in his bathroom.

Oates walked into his bedroom. He slid into his bathrobe and proceeded to walk upstairs to the kitchen to raid his liquor cabinet. He needed a stiff drink to mellow him out.

After pouring some Cîroc vodka and pineapple juice into a glass, Oates walked into the living room and turned on the television. He skipped through channels, bypassing the news. He heard enough bad news at work and watching it on television just made it all the more depressing. Right now, he needed to unwind.

As Oates watched some basketball on the ESPN channel, he decided to walk down to his bedroom and get his phone. While he was walking back to the living room, he got a phone call. He looked at the caller ID and smiled. It was Cheryl. He hesitated to answer, wondering if she was calling to cuss him out again.

"Hello?" Oates answered, as he lay back on his couch.

"Hey, Shareef," Cheryl replied.

"Hey," Oates said. He didn't want to appear too excited to hear from her, although he was happy as hell.

"What are you doing?" she asked.

"I'm chilling out at home," he said while picking up the remote and surfing through the channels. He yawned loud enough so that she could hear it.

"Did I catch you at a bad time?"

Oates sighed. "Nah, you didn't."

"Shareef, I just called to apologize to you about the other day. I went off on you when I shouldn't have. I really do appreciate everything that you've done for me."

"Do you really? That's hard to tell."

"Ouch. I deserved that."

Oates sat up. Now it was his turn to get angry. "Cheryl, you and I have not known each other very long but I like you a lot. I admired the fact that you are a single mother raising three children on her own; a woman who doesn't mind working hard to make sure that her family is taken care of. I'm sure that you're confident enough in your parenting skills to know that you have done a good job considering these circumstances. When you went off on me about Poet, I understood that you were upset. It's just that you turned everything that I was telling you into me having something against your son. You made it seem like I was intentionally trying to make your life miserable."

Oates paused for a brief second then continued. "Do you understand that the things that I told you about Poet went against everything that I stand for as detective? I don't understand why you would want to treat me like I'm the enemy."

Cheryl was silent. Oates could feel the tension through the phone. He knew that she was thinking about what to say.

"You are so right and I apologize. I've been thinking about everything you told me. I had an idea that Poet was into illegal things and I have to admit that I was in denial. I wanted to be the perfect parent, and trying to be that way don't always make perfect children. And, Shareef, I know that you take great pride in your job. You're not the bad guy. Your job is to help solve murders, to give the victims' families closure. I was being selfish and I feel bad about that."

Oates sighed. "But let me ask you a question: what do you want from me?"

"At first, I felt like I wasn't good enough for you. I mean, you're a detective; you can have any woman you want. I have all these kids and I live in the projects. I don't make a lot of money. I asked myself, 'Why did he choose me?' Honestly, I haven't stopped thinking about you since the first day I met you."

"And I haven't stopped thinking about you. I never stopped wanting to be with you, Cheryl." Oates took a deep breath. "I just want you to know that I'm here to help you, not hurt you."

"I believe that."

"Good, baby. Look, I don't mean to change the subject, but what is going on with Poet? Where is he hiding?"

"He's being sought for questioning but no one knows where he is, not even me. He could be right here in this neighborhood but I haven't heard a word from him in about a day or two. He left me some note, telling me that he was going to be okay. But at this point, what can

I do? I did everything that I can to keep him from going in this direction and look at the thanks I get. I just can't believe this shit is happening."

"I got your back, baby. Let's just get past this dilemma with Poet first before we start getting back to us. You understand what I'm saying, right?"

Cheryl sighed. "You're right, Shareef. I know that it's nothing personal, it's business. You have a job to do so I completely understand."

"Yes, I do, but getting this situation rectified and being there for you is what I want to do. And don't worry. I got your back," he said with a smile.

"Thank you so much, baby. I'm gonna need all the support that I can get. This is like a nightmare."

"It seems that way but maybe it's a reasonable excuse for the decisions that Poet made. I'm your friend first, Cheryl, and don't you forget it."

"Before I go, I just wanted to tell you that I miss you so much, Shareef."

"I miss you too. I'm gonna call you tomorrow."

"You promise?" she asked.

"I promise."

They said their good-byes and he disconnected the call. Oates grabbed a blanket from the linen closet and went to lie back down on his couch. He had received the phone call that he had been waiting for, so he turned off his phone. Oates turned up the volume on the television and proceeded to go back to watching the game.

The next day, Oates went to work feeling rejuvenated. He was intent on closing out some of the open cases they had lingering. They had made a few arrests earlier in the week but he was still concerned about the Kody Bradford case. The man was found dead with multiple stab wounds and his throat was slit from ear to ear. There were no more witnesses who had come forward about the murder yet and Oates was beginning to get frustrated. Kody's friend, Eric, had given him some information, but they were going to need more evidence to support the claim.

When he arrived at his desk, Lewis was already there making phone calls. Oates silently prayed for leads.

"What's up, O? Eric Bartlett called me earlier. He's on his way over here with a copy of some videotape or DVD," he said. "He claims that it's evidence."

Oates took off his suit jacket and put it across the back of his chair. He rolled up his shirt sleeves and sat at his tattered desk.

"A videotape? DVD?"

Lewis stood up. "Yeah, one of those. This was recorded a week or two before Kody was killed."

"So what is the tape about?" asked Oates.

"Man, I didn't even ask because I have an idea of what the tape is about. You know that Kody and his boy Eric is into young meat."

"Sad but true." Oates looked over some paperwork. "So when is he coming?"

"He should be walking through that door as we speak."

Lewis's desk phone rang. "Hello? My witness is here? Okay, thanks for calling. You can send them right up."

Oates smiled and rubbed his hands together. "Wow, good detective work, homie!"

Lewis gave him a pound. "Just trying to be like you when I grow up, man!"

Oates and Lewis looked at the doorway, and instead of Eric, they were surprised to see a teenage girl walking toward them with a DVD in her hand. They sure hadn't expected a girl to have the evidence.

"Are you Detective Lewis?" the girl asked. She looked to be no older than sixteen years old.

Lewis looked back at Oates. "Um, yes, sweetheart, I'm Detective Lewis. Are you here to give me some evidence on the Kody Bradford murder?"

She looked down at the DVD that she held in her right hand. "Yes. Eric told me to bring this to you. He's the one that gave me a copy of it."

"Why would Eric tell you to bring it to us?"

"Because he thinks that Poet might have killed Kody and he wanted to me to show y'all why he thinks that Poet did it."

Lewis asked the teen her name, took the DVD from her, and told her to sit in a seat by his desk. He gestured for Oates to follow him to another room in the precinct. Inside of the room, there was a small television and a DVD player.

Lewis put the DVD inside of the player and sat in a chair beside Oates. When the DVD began playing, there was a man who introduced himself on the tape.

"What up, what up, what up, my dudes!" the man said. "This is K.O. and, as usual, I got a nice surprise for you. Some lovely young ladies are gonna show y'all what they're workin' with and, who knows, maybe some of y'all cats like to get in on the party. Just so y'all dudes know before you start thinkin' that the 'p' is for free, it's one hundred fifty dollars for a fuck, seventy-five dollars for a blow job, and if you want some special treatment, I got a special runnin'—two hundred dollars for everything. Girl-on-girl sex charges apply."

Lewis and Oates looked at each other. "Hmmph, so that's Kody. This bastard was trafficking these little girls! Never heard of DVD pimping!" Lewis said.

Oates shook his head. "I'm not surprised, Lew. These dudes aren't that bright and, obviously, they don't have any respect for womankind, man, I swear. If I wasn't a cop, shit like this would make me wanna blow a motherfucker's head off!" Lewis agreed.

As they continued to watch the DVD, they both had disgusted looks on their faces. About ten minutes into it, both detectives had had enough. Just as Lewis was about to cut off the television, Oates stopped him. He heard Kody call out a familiar name. They stepped back to watch the remainder of the sexual interlude between Kody and the mystery girl.

"Yeah, Precious, I love this pussy, baby," Kody said on the DVD. "Is that why your mother named you Precious, baby? You think Poet's gonna be mad at me for fuckin' his little sister?"

Oates put his hand to his mouth as he heard Precious scream the word "yes" to everything Kody asked her. From the looks of the video, he couldn't tell if she was enjoying the sex or if she was in pain. Kody had her in the doggie style position and Precious's face was turned to the camera. Kody had a devilish smirk on his face. Oates could see why Poet would have wanted to kill him.

Then it hit him. Thinking about all the other murders that were committed in that neighborhood, Oates began to put two and two together. The two murders that Poet was being accused of were finally making sense to him. Without a doubt, they were all miscreants and troublemakers, living in a neighborhood that was already swarmed with criminals. Oates believed that Pumpkin and Kody probably deserved what they got. But could Poet be responsible for Jerrod Timmons's and John Moxley's murders as well?

Watching the tape, Oates felt sick. Precious was Poet's youngest sister and Cheryl's sixteen-year-old daughter. He hated to be the bearer of bad news but he was torn. Should he just do good police work and proceed with his duties as an officer? Or was he at liberty to tell Cheryl about his new discovery? After all, Oates was a father. He would have wanted someone to inform him of something like this when it came to his own daughter. He wanted to give Cheryl the opportunity to save Precious from a dismal life of promiscuity. Morally, it was the right thing for him to do.

Lewis looked at the tape for a few more minutes and turned off the DVD player.

"My heart can't take no more of this shit, man," Lewis said. "If that was my got-damn daughter, I would have put a bullet in that dude's head myself! Did you see that shit, O?"

Oates plopped in a chair and put his head on the desk. "Man, this is the most stressful investigation that I have ever had in my life."

Lewis walked over to his partner and put his hand on his shoulder. "You all right, O? What's wrong?"

Oates looked up and wiped his face. "That young girl on the tape was Cheryl's youngest daughter, man. First her damn son and now the daughter! I feel so bad for this woman, Lew. Damn!"

"Look, O, I know that you got some kind of feeling for this woman. I hate to be the one to say this but whatever feeling that is, from the looks of things, you might have to let that one fall by the wayside. I just don't see anything good coming from this union and it's not even because of her. It's her kids!"

Oates looked up at Lewis. "Well, I'm feeling Cheryl and I want to make her happy. If that means dealing with her children and all their problems then it is what it is, man. I don't give a fuck anymore. I'm tired of being alone."

Lewis smiled. "Man, you've been my partner for the last ten years and you've been my friend for longer than that. I can feel your pain. Even though my wife and I are in the midst of a divorce, it's times like this I miss being married to her. Shit, if I meet the right woman, I ain't gonna lie, I would probably do it again. Whatever you decide to do, man, I got your back."

Oates and Lewis gave each other a manly hug. Then it was back to business. Lewis removed the DVD from the player and walked out of the room. Oates followed closely behind him. By the time they walked to their desks, the witness was gone. Lewis asked the other officers if they had seen the young lady walk out. Everyone had been too distracted to pay any attention to her. Oates went to his desk and shuffled through some papers, when he noticed a sheet of paper with a number on it.

"Hey, Lew, look at this," Oates said, calling Lewis over to his desk. "The girl that was here left this phone number and a name. Should I go ahead and give her a call?"

Lewis looked at the number. "I'll call her. She probably got cold feet and ran up outta here." He pulled out his Nextel phone and began dialing the number. He smiled at Oates when the girl answered.

"Hello? Malika? How are you, sweetie? Detective Lewis here," he said.

Chapter 30

Unwanted Celebrity

Meanwhile, Precious was sitting in her bedroom, bored to death. Earlier that day, her guidance counselor, Ms. Jenkins, had chewed her out about her slipping grades.

But Precious didn't care about that. She was a young, curious teenager who was more interested in sex and men. She had too many new and exciting things happening to her to think about doing some stupid homework. She only had one more year of high school to go and she was finished. So why should she worry about school?

She looked away from the television and looked at her sister. She was on her own bed doing some paper for one of her classes.

"Porsha, do you think that we'll ever see Poet again?" she asked out of the blue.

Porsha closed her textbook and sighed. "I don't know. I just hope that whatever is goin' on out there, he can get through it. I miss havin' my brother around."

Precious sucked her teeth. "I don't want him to get into any trouble but I don't know if I really miss him, either. He was always tryin' to act like he was my father!"

Porsha looked at her naïve younger sister and shook her head. "You just don't get it, do you? Our brother is on the run for a murder. We haven't heard from him so we don't even know if he's dead or if he's alive!"

"Well, I was hearin' mad stuff about Poet. I heard that he killed that dude Kody too—" Precious began.

"Kody who? Isn't that the guy that you made the sex tape with?" Porsha asked with a disgusted look on her face.

Precious sucked her teeth. "I don't know what you're talkin' about, Porsha," she replied while rolling her eyes. "Anyway, we were talkin' about Poet. I don't miss him. I hope that the rumors aren't true but I also feel like if he did the crime then he gotta do the time."

"You're a cold-hearted little girl, Precious. Poet may possibly go to jail for a very long time. That's only if he's lucky enough to get through this without bein' killed by the cops or some of these wannabe gangsters around here. And for your information, the reason that Poet was hard on us is because he wants us to respect ourselves and be with someone that's gonna respect us too. I appreciate his concern. We don't have no father up in this house and, to me, Poet was the closest thing to havin' a father around."

Precious waved her off. "Yeah, I figured you would say that. You kill me always tryin' to act like you're some goody two-shoes. I know that you're Poet's favorite sister and everything but, damn, you really believe that he is our father! Well, he's not my father and he couldn't tell me what to do."

"And that's part of your problem now. Nobody can't tell you nothin'. You walk around here thinkin' just because you're cute and you got that little stinkin' twat between your legs that everybody is supposed to kiss your ass or let you do what you want. But I'm sorry, Miss Precious, there are rules in life. The bottom line is you don't have to care about me, Mommy, or Poet and you don't have to listen to nothin' we say, but I am tellin' you that them people out there don't give a fuck about you. We love you and it's sad because you don't really seem like you care about us or your damn self. I hope you find some peace, little girl, because you're in for a rude awakening."

Porsha went back to her school work, leaving Precious to absorb her words of wisdom. Precious sucked her teeth again. She wasn't ready to grasp the seriousness of her promiscuous behavior or her attitude. Porsha could think that Poet was her "daddy" all she wanted. Precious never knew her father so she had no idea of what a father was supposed to act like.

An hour later, Precious was walking up the steps to Mekhi's second floor apartment. When she knocked on Mekhi's door, she heard shuffling inside. As she was about to put her ear to the door, Mekhi opened it.

"What was you about to do?" he asked with an annoyed look on his face.

Precious was confused. The day before, they had buried the hatchet. Now it seemed as if they were back to square one.

"Can I come in?" she asked.

Mekhi seemed hesitant to let her inside. "Well, I don't know about that, Precious."

Precious was about to get upset. "Why? Do you have another chick in there or somethin'?"

Mekhi nervously looked toward the back of the apartment. "Yo, Presh, I'll have to explain it to you another time. Look, I gotta go." Then he slammed the door in her face.

Precious was shocked. She didn't understand what was going on. She kicked Mekhi's door with the bottom of her foot and ran down the stairs.

"Did you get rid of the person at the door?" Poet asked when Mekhi walked back into the bedroom.

"Yeah, I did," he replied with an attitude. Mekhi felt bad about not letting Precious inside of his house, but there was no way that he could let her know that her brother was staying there.

"Who was that anyway?"

"It wasn't the cops if that's what you wanted to know."

Poet smirked. "Man, you're a trip. How do you have an attitude with me when you were the one fuckin' with my little sister?"

"I don't have no attitude with you, man. Let's not bring that up no more, okay?" Mekhi said. "We need to figure out what's your next move."

"What you mean, what's my next move? I'm stayin' here!"

"You can't stay here forever, son. You got the police lookin' for you, detectives comin' to my house—" Mekhi said.

"I'm not tryin' to hear nothin' about no police, man!"

"I don't understand you, Po. You know that you did all of the shit that you're bein' accused of so why don't you just turn yourself in?"

"The only thing that you're worried about is you bein' charged with somethin', aren't you?"

Mekhi sighed. There was no use in saying anything else to Poet. It was obvious that his childhood friend had turned into someone he didn't know. He was convinced that Poet had finally snapped.

Mekhi was tired of being held hostage in his own house and Poet wasn't trying to let him out of his sight. "Well, I'm outta here. Tired of bein' caged up in this house like a fuckin' animal. The police ain't lookin' for me."

Poet lay back on Mekhi's bed. "Yo, Khi, please don't make me have to look for you, man. I'm not really trustin' you but I'm sure that you will make the right decision and get back in this house to check Grandma; you wouldn't want anything to happen to her. And don't forget the only reason that I haven't killed your ass yet, 'brother,' is because I need a place to stay until I get all of this shit figured out."

Mekhi looked at Poet but didn't say a word. He grabbed his Yankees baseball cap from the dresser and walked out the door.

As Mekhi walked down the block, he pulled Detective Hopewell's card out of his back pocket. As he continued down Rockaway Avenue, he began dialing the number on the card.

"Detective Hopewell, Seventy-third Precinct."

"Um, yes, sir, how are you? Um, this is Mekhi Porter," he said, nervously looking over his shoulder.

"How you doing, Mr. Porter?"

"Well, I'm not doin' so good, Detective."

"What do you mean, you're not doing so good?"

"Because I'm about to snitch on someone who's been like a brother to me damn near all of our lives." Mekhi wiped a single tear from his eye.

"Look, little brother, don't look at it like that. Personally, I think that you're doing the right thing and I'm not just saying this because I'm a detective. You just might be saving many lives here, including your own."

"But I ain't no snitch, Detective. I'm just tired of all this. If Poet stays out here any longer, I don't know what's goin' to happen to him or me."

"Do you know where he is now?" Hopewell asked.

Mekhi sighed. He turned down Newport Avenue. "He's at my house."

"You got to be kidding me! Are you serious?"

Mekhi swallowed. "Yes, I'm serious," he whispered, shaking his head.

"Okay, Mr. Porter. I appreciate that. And, don't worry, you did a good thing. I know that you care about your friend but unfortunately, when you break the law, there's a price that you have to pay."

"I gotta go but when are y'all goin' to pick him up? He's got to get out of my house, man."

"We're on our way now."

Mekhi hung up the phone and began punching himself in the head. He was experiencing so many emotions. He felt guilt, anger, sadness, and extreme relief all at one time.

Little did Mekhi know he was being watched. Sitting in a car across the street from where he was standing were Bone and Little Preme.

"Ain't this somethin'?" said Preme. "We haven't seen this dude, Khi, since all this shit went down with his boy. What do you want me to do, Bone?"

Bone rubbed his chin. "I'm gonna call that motherfucker over here to the car. He might just know where Poet is." Bone rolled down his driver's side window. "Aye yooo, Khi!" he yelled.

Mekhi turned around. He saw Bone and his heart stopped. He didn't know whether to walk to the car or run away.

"Come here, boy," Bone ordered.

Mekhi cautiously walked across the street to the Dodge Charger. His knees felt as if they were about to give out.

"What's up with you?" Bone asked. "Haven't seen you in a minute. Where's your boy, Poet?"

Mekhi shrugged his shoulders. "I don't know," he replied.

"What you mean you don't know?" Preme asked.
"And why the hell was you standin' over there punchin'
yourself in the head? You're losin' your fuckin' mind or
somethin'?"

"Nah, I just got a lot of shit goin' on right now," Mekhi answered.

Bone and Preme laughed. "Yo," Preme began. "Your
boy, Poet? He know what it is. He knows we're lookin'
for him, too. You tell him . . . As a matter of fact, Khi,
get in the fuckin' car, man."

When Mekhi hesitated, Preme reached over Bone
and put a gun in his face. "I said, get in this car before I
blow your head off."

Bone had a smirk on his face. Preme was his enforcer
and he did all of Bone's dirty work. They wanted to get
to Poet before the police caught up with him. There was
no telling what Poet would say once he was in custody
and that was what they were afraid of. There were too
many people hating on their operation, and with Poet
catching a case, they felt that they would only be one
step closer to being indicted on all kinds of charges.

Mekhi opened the car door and eased into the back
seat. He was nervous as hell. Detectives were about to
go to his house and now he was sitting in the car with
Poet's potential murderers. Mekhi was pretty sure that
Bone had heard about Poet killing Sha-Sha, Pumpkin,
and possibly Kody.

They pulled off and headed for the projects. Bone
was a talker and he was unusually quiet this car ride.
Preme was doing all the talking.

"Yo, Khi, man, you know, I think you're a cool cat
but you need to watch the motherfuckers you roll with.
Your boy, Poet, is a grimy-ass dude, and right now he's
caught up in a lot of bullshit. Now he got you caught up
in it too. Let me ask you a question, son. Are you willin'
to take this bullet for your boy?"

Mekhi couldn't find the words to answer Preme. He knew that Poet's murder spree was going to backfire but Mekhi never thought that it was going to blow up in his face. Here he was sitting in the back seat of his former boss' car with the crazy hitman, Preme, threatening his life. This was all because Poet wanted to be a self-proclaimed superhero.

"I didn't do nothin', Preme," Mekhi pleaded with him, ready to beg for mercy if he had to. He shouldn't have to go down because of Poet's stupidity and carelessness.

Preme turned around in the passenger seat with the gun stuck directly in Mekhi's face.

"I don't give a fuck if you did anything or not. Your boy, Poet, is an idiot and you must be one too if you fuck with that dude. Now," Preme began while racking his gun. Mekhi closed his eyes. "Where the fuck is Poet? Tell us where he at or die, motherfucker!"

Mekhi felt like his air supply was being cut off. His mind was racing. "Um, um, Poet is at my house."

Preme smiled. "Word? You heard that, Bone? Off to Khi's house, we go!"

"Preme, Preme, listen. Y'all can't go to my house, man!"

Preme pushed the gun against Mekhi's nose. "Fuck you mean, we can't go to your crib? Didn't you just say that Poet was at your house?" he yelled.

Bone stopped at a stoplight. He turned around and looked at Mekhi with the screw face. "Don't make us have to murder your ass, Khi!" he said.

"Nah, Bone, it ain't even like that! It's just that the police are headed to my crib right now!"

Preme moved the gun out of Mekhi's face. He looked confused. "How do you know that the police are comin' to your house if you're not at home?" Preme began squinting at him. "Wait a minute, did you tell on Poet, Khi?"

Mekhi held his head down. "It ain't even like that, Preme."

Bone and Preme looked at each other and shook their heads. They didn't know what to think about their passenger.

"I'm just tellin' y'all this because I don't want us to go to my crib and my buildin' is swarmin' with one time."

"You snitched on your man, son?" Preme asked again, with a disgusted look on his face.

Mekhi became agitated. "Look, Preme, I had no choice, okay? Poet is on some bullshit right now. I don't know what he's capable of doin' to me or my family, man. So I just let him stay. From the looks of it, he's not turnin' himself in so I had to take desperate measures and do what I have to do for me and my family. Now y'all dudes are tryin' to kill this dude when he already got it bad. The cops are lookin' for him. Other cats in the hood want to take him outta here and now y'all wanna lay him down too. That's too much heat for everyone involved, man! "

Preme put his gun down and turned around in the passenger seat as Bone continued to drive.

"This fool does have a point, Bone," Preme said. "We don't need to get that dude. He's got enough problems."

Bone shook his head. "Nah, man, you don't understand! If Poet gets locked up, you don't know what he could tell the police about us just to save his own ass!"

Preme looked at Mekhi. "Yo, Khi, you're gonna have to get Poet out of your crib, man."

"Get him out of my crib? How am I gonna do that?"

Preme put the gun back in Mekhi's face. "I don't know but you better think of somethin'! Either you get Poet to come out of your crib so that we can kill his ass or you die too!"

When they arrived at their destination, Bone pulled over a block away from Mekhi's building. Preme continued with his tirade.

"Get that dude out here within the next fifteen minutes or else we're comin' for you!" Preme exclaimed.

Mekhi eased out of the back seat and began walking toward his building. He looked back a few times and the car was still idling in the same spot. Bone and Preme wanted Poet dead and Mekhi was about to sell his best friend out. He had already snitched on him, which he felt bad about doing, but setting Poet up to be murdered was ten times worse. But he had a choice to make. It was either him or Poet. He had to think of a way to get Poet out of his house.

Mekhi looked around and found it strange that the cops weren't in front of his building yet. He walked up the two flights of steps to his apartment and unlocked the door. When he walked inside, all that could be heard was the television in his grandmother's room. It was 9:30 at night so he figured that she was asleep. Mekhi walked into her room first.

"Nana," he whispered. She didn't answer. Mekhi walked to the other side of the bed. "Nana?"

Mekhi shook his grandmother softly and her limp hand fell on the side of the bed. Mekhi took a step back and put his hand over his mouth. He put two fingers on the side of her neck. He couldn't feel her pulse. He was taken aback when he realized that his grandmother was dead.

Mekhi felt the tears run down his cheeks. He couldn't contain his anger. He immediately walked out of the bedroom and burst into his room. Poet was gone. There was no sign of him anywhere. Mekhi looked under the bed and in all the closets. Poet was not there. He was frantic.

"I'm gonna kill this motherfucker!" Mekhi said aloud. He ran to the house phone to call an ambulance for his grandmother. He didn't know what was going on.

"Nine–one–one, what's the emergency?" the operator said.

"I'm gonna need an ambulance to 340 Tilden Avenue between Rockaway and Dumont, number 2F," Mekhi said. "My grandmother is not breathin'!"

"Okay, I'm contacting an ambulance right now," the operator patiently replied. "You stay calm. They're on their way now—" The operator's voice was drowned out by a banging on the door.

"Open the door! It's the police!" said a male voice. There was more banging. Then Mekhi's cell phone started ringing. It was Preme. Amid everything that was going on, Mekhi answered the phone.

"Yo, what's up, Khi?" he asked. "Where is Poet at? We're waitin'!"

"Man, Poet ain't here and I think this dude did somethin' to my grandmother! And the fuckin' cops are tryin' to break down my door!"

Mekhi threw the cell phone on his bed and ran to the door. When he unlocked it, several cops rushed in, knocking him to the ground. They were in every corner of the small apartment with their guns drawn, looking for their suspect. Two cops had Mekhi lying face down on the floor with his arms pinned behind his back. After the last cop walked in, Detectives Hopewell and Mickens walked in behind them.

One of the cops yelled for someone to come into the grandmother's room. While they were in the room, the paramedics and uniformed police officers showed up at the door. They had a stretcher and their equipment with them as well.

"What is going on here?" asked Hopewell. "This is like a fuckin' circus right now!"

Mekhi attempted to hold his head up. The cops who were holding him down picked him up so that he could face Hopewell and Mickens.

"Detective, my grandmother might be dead! Poet was here with her when I left to walk outside to call you! I don't know what I was thinkin', leavin' her here with this crazy dude!" Mekhi began to burst out in tears. "I think he killed her! Oh my God! I think he killed her!"

Mekhi was inconsolable. The cops let him go when they saw that he was harmless.

"Poet was here, Detective! I promise you that he was right here! He did somethin' to my Nana and left out of the house!"

One of the paramedics came into the living room. "We have an African American female, DOA, appears to be cardiac arrest. . . ."

Mekhi fainted.

Chapter 31

Evil Lurks

Right after Mekhi had walked out of the house ear-lier, Poet began to get suspicious of his whereabouts. After all, Mekhi was seeing Precious behind his back and never uttered a word to him about it. After dis-covering his disloyalty, their circle of trust had been broken.

Poet got up from the bed and threw on the sweat-pants he had been wearing for the last few days. As he was about to pick up his gun from the nightstand, Mekhi's grandmother, Miss Addie, burst into the room without knocking. Startled, Poet pointed the gun at her but didn't shoot.

When Poet pointed the gun at her, Miss Addie was scared out of her wits. She felt a sharp pain shooting through her chest. As she took her last breath, she just knew that she had been shot. She was experiencing a pain in her chest that she had never felt before.

Poet ran over to the woman and attempted to help her when he realized that she was having a heart at-tack. But there was nothing that he could do for her. He was on the run from the police and, unfortunately for Miss Addie, he had to focus on his present situation. Poet tried to move the unconscious woman when he saw that she had become very still.

"Miss Addie?" he whispered, shaking her in the process. "Miss Addie? Please don't die on me! Please!" When Miss Addie did not respond, he knew that she was gone.

Miss Addie Porter was a heavyset woman, and due to bad dieting and stress, she had not been doing very well. She had suffered with high blood pressure and cholesterol for years but her refusal to do anything about her health issues caused her heart to fail. Miss Addie's dead weight was another problem for Poet. Not wanting to leave her sprawled out on the floor, he struggled to put Miss Addie in her bed.

A half hour later, Poet finally managed to get her into her bed and under the covers. He turned on the television and kissed her softly on the forehead.

For a fleeting moment, Poet remembered that Miss Addie was more like a grandmother to him as well. She was also someone's mother and her death only made Poet think about the beloved matriarch of his own family, who was more than likely to be sick with worry about his well-being. After making sure that Miss Addie was comfortable in her final resting place, Poet snapped back to reality. Now his world was spinning out of control and he was in so deep that he didn't know how to come out of it. The black cloud that was looming over his head was about to explode.

Poet put the gun into his jacket pocket. He snatched Miss Addie's house keys from the dresser in her bedroom. He casually walked out of the house and locked the door behind him. He threw the keys in the incinerator because at that point they were useless to him. He wasn't ever coming to back to that house again.

Poet lingered in the staircase for a moment and tried to regroup. The fear of being arrested or possibly killed consumed him. But he had to remind himself that if he

was capable of killing five people, then he should have
no fear facing his own death.

Poet put the hood of his jacket on his head and
walked out of the building. He cased his surroundings
before he continued on his journey. It was nine o'clock
at night on a Sunday and it was pretty quiet. He proceeded to walk toward Livonia Avenue. He cut through
the housing projects, avoiding Rockaway Avenue at all
costs where he was sure that he would be noticed by
someone. Poet had to find another place to lay up until
he figured out his next move.

Suddenly, he had an idea, although he didn't think
that it was a good one. He had the key to Sha-Sha's old
apartment, which was probably abandoned by now. He
knew that Bone was coming nowhere near his old spot
because of the heavy police presence.

As Poet was making his way to Sha-Sha's house,
taking shortcuts and backstreets to his destination,
as usual he heard police and ambulance sirens in the
distance. For some reason or another, he knew that by
that time Mekhi had probably come home and found
out that Miss Addie was dead. Poet wished that there
was a way that he could tell his friend that he hadn't
done anything to hurt his grandmother, but it was no
time to get all sentimental. Poet was on a path of de-
struction.

When Poet got to the door of Sha-Sha's apartment,
he pulled out his set of keys. He fumbled with the lock
for a minute and, surprisingly, no one had dropped the
cylinder yet. Bone had paid Sha-Sha's rent for the year
so the New York City Housing Authority was probably
unaware of the unoccupied apartment.

Poet stepped in and looked around. He slowly shut
the door behind him and turned the double-bolted
lock. He was afraid of turning on the lights for fear that

someone would notice it. He walked around the apartment in the dark, almost tripping over furniture. After fumbling in the kitchen drawer, he found a candle. He lit the candle with the lighter and used the light to make his way toward the bedrooms.

They hadn't been in the apartment in the last two weeks but there were still fresh sheets on the beds. He remembered when he or Mekhi would get tired of packaging they would go into one of the bedrooms to take a nap. Poet took off his jacket and put the candle on the nightstand. He lay back onto the queen-sized bed and thought about how Sha-Sha never did experience a good night's rest in that comfortable bed. It was a shame because she was barely allowed in her own apartment.

As he dozed off, Poet's thoughts were racing. Would it have been fair for someone to have lodged a bullet in his head for his indiscretions? Now he had become a murderer and did some things that he avoided for most of his life.

An hour later, Poet was awakened by the sound of people talking loudly outside of the bedroom window. He rubbed the sleep out of his eyes and slowly walked to the window to see what was going on. It was just a bunch of rowdy teenagers walking past the building.

"Same old dirty-ass neighborhood," Poet said aloud, as if he believed that his reality was just a dream.

Poet plopped down on the bed and put on his boots. He sat there for a moment and played with idea of surrendering to the police. He had cut his other phone service off because he couldn't bring himself to listen to the pleas of his mother and sister Porsha on his voice mail. He pulled out his prepaid cell phone and turned it on. Poet sighed as he searched his contact list for one phone number in particular. He knew that once he dialed any number, he was going to be locked up. But considering all the stress that he was going through to elude the cops, Poet felt that he had no other choice at that point.

The phone rang and was picked up on the first ring. "Detective Oates here."

"How you doin', Detective Oates?"

"May I ask whose calling?" asked Oates.

"It's me, Poet." There was a silence on the other end. "Hello?" Poet said.

Poet listened to the noise in the background and it sounded as if Oates was moving into a quieter area.

"Is this really you, Poet?"

"Yeah, it's me."

"Where are you? Your mother is worried sick about you!" Oates said in a voice one decibel higher than a whisper.

"I know, I know, but I'm scared, man. Dudes are tryin' to kill me out here."

Oates was on the other end of the phone, shaking his head. He looked over his shoulder. He thought he heard someone fumbling with the door of the room he was in.

"Who's trying to kill you?"

"Bone, Preme, some Blood cats from my hood, I don't know, Detective Oates, man. I fucked up, man!" Poet replied, pacing around the bedroom and rubbing his head in despair.

"I wanna help you but you're going to have to tell me the truth. I'm gonna need you to start talking to me about what's going on with you and you can call me Shareef."

Poet sat on the edge of the bed. "Okay, okay, Shareef. Well, it's like this. I'm the one that killed the dude that raped the girl in my buildin'. I killed John-John for robbin' Mr. Leroy. I killed Pumpkin because I just didn't like the cat. I killed Sha-Sha, the crackhead, for tryin' to steal some of my people's drugs. I killed Kody because I found out that he was havin' sex with my my little sister and prostitutin' a lot of other little young girls in the hood. I didn't kill Miss Addie though—she died of a heart attack."

"Who's Miss Addie, Poet?"

"Miss Addie is my boy Mekhi's grandmother. I have been stayin' at Mekhi's crib for the last day or so and Miss Addie just happened to walk into Khi's bedroom without knockin'. I pointed my gun at her, thinkin' that she was the police comin' for me and I . . . I guess she got scared. Next thing I know she was clutchin' her chest and fallin' to the floor."

"Oh, God."

"I didn't mean to hurt her, man. Out of all the people that I killed, I really didn't mean for Miss Addie to die, Detective . . . I mean, Shareef. You gotta believe me, man!"

Oates sighed. "I believe you, Poet, I believe you." There was a slight pause. "What made you wanna kill these people?"

"I hated them, man! I hate these motherfuckers out here! They're the ones that fuck up the hood that I'm livin' in. They're the reason that people around here feel afraid to come outside of their apartments and the kids can't even play in peace anymore."

"But, Poet, listen to what you're saying. Aren't you a drug dealer? What makes you so different from these people?"

Poet was silent. "You're right. And I get that now. I realize that I'm not no different from any of the people that I killed. Do you know how hard I tried to avoid this type of lifestyle, man? I couldn't get no decent job so I had to resort to sellin' drugs. I just got so tired of seein' my mother strugglin' by herself. My moms is a beast, though—she's my fuckin' hero. My father is a piece of shit; a real creep. Who I really should have killed was his ass. He's probably out here right now druggin', robbin', or fuckin' somebody's daughter, not givin' one fuck about his own kids and havin' the time of his life because he's doin' exactly what he wants to do. I despise him for that."

"But Poet, don't you see that you were your mother's saving grace? You had the opportunity to be a better man than your father was for your mother and your two sisters. I'm sure that you could have gone to school, got a good education, a good job, and got you and your family out of this neighborhood. Don't you think that that would have been a better option than selling drugs and killing people?"

Poet sucked his teeth. He didn't have an answer for Oates. "Where were you a few years ago, Shareef? You would have been a real good look for my mother. Truthfully, you would have been a good look for all of us."

"Considering the way everything is going for you right now, I wish I could have met your mother then too. You seem like you're a smart young man with a good heart but, truthfully, you can't save the world, man. I'm a police officer and I know that. You have to put God first, then yourself, then your family. The weight of the world was not meant to be carried on human shoulders."

Poet began to cry. "I know, I know, but I done fucked up my life, Shareef. My mother is disappointed in me and I let my sisters down. And after all this, come to find out my best friend, my right-hand, my brother, Mekhi, betrayed me! I can't take no more of this shit, man!"

Oates felt sorry for Poet. But at that point it was out of his hands. It was up to the judicial system and, from the looks of it; Poet didn't have a fighting chance.

"Look, son, I know you've made some mistakes. In some ways, what you've done may be heroic to some people. But the law is the law. That's just the way it goes." Poet sniffled on the other end. "So how are you going to do this, Poet?" asked Oates. "You can't keep running forever."

Poet regained his composure. "I'm scared to come out of this house."

"Where are you, man? Do you want me to come and get you?"

"Okay," Poet replied. He gave Oates the address.

"I will be there in like fifteen minutes. Don't you move, okay?"

"I won't, man, I won't," Poet said.

Oates hung up the phone and ran out of the interrogation room. He approached his partner, Lewis, who was on the phone, still trying to get leads on the Kody Bradford case.

"Lew, hang up the phone. I have to talk to you," said Oates. Lewis frowned and put his hand up. "No, listen to me, Lew. You gotta hang up the phone right now!"

Lewis hung up the phone and stared at Oates. "Man, this shit better be good! I was just about to get another break in the Bradford case—" he began.

Oates cut him off. "It's no need for that. I just got a phone call from Poet Washington."

Lewis's eyes widened. "Poet Washington? Isn't that your friend's son—the same little motherfucker who's been giving us the runaround for the last few weeks?"

"Exactly. He took it upon himself to call me and we had a conversation about what's been going on with him. Let's just say he gave me a confession."

"So what did he say?" asked the excited Lewis.

"He admitted to killing Timmons, Moxley, Watts, Bradford, and somebody named Sha-Sha."

Lewis blinked. "You mean to tell me this boy done killed five people, O?"

"Five."

"Oh, shit! Did he tell you why he did it?"

"Let's put it like this: the boy has some serious, deep-rooted personal issues. Now, as far as him being a little nutty in the head, he may very well be that, too. I detected an antisocial disorder and maybe a little narcissism in there as well."

Lewis frowned. "Narcissism? Antisocial disorder? C'mon, man, this ain't psychology 101!"

Oates put on his blazer. "Well, I'm about to go pick him up."

Lewis grabbed his jacket too. "And I'm comin' with you. You're not going anywhere near that kid by yourself."

"You're right. Just follow behind me. I need him to think that I'm by myself."

Lewis and Oates walked outside and got into two different cars. Meanwhile, Poet anxiously waited for Oates's arrival.

Chapter 32

Catch Me If You Can

Meanwhile, Bone and Preme saw all of the police activity by Mekhi's building and quickly pulled off. They didn't need any attention directed toward them.

"Yo, Poet is really gonna make me air his ass out," said Preme. "He got so much heat on the hood right now . . . Fuck that, where his mother and them live at?"

Bone shrugged his shoulders. "I don't know, man. We ain't fuckin' with that dude's moms. That's a violation."

Preme was getting more hyper by the minute. He was an official gangster and all of his beefs were settled with bullets.

"Well, we're gonna have to do somethin'. This dude is goin' to be in police custody in a minute and we don't need him to be tellin' on none of us. My motto is dead people don't tell."

Bone sighed. He was getting tired of all the murder one talk. He just wanted to go home to his wife and children. Even though Poet wasn't the man he thought he was, he secretly admired the younger man for having more heart than he ever did. Bone knew that if Poet did kill Sha-Sha, he probably did it to not only save his own ass but he thought that he was helping Bone, too. Secretly, he believed that if Poet did get arrested, he wasn't going to tell on him. Preme was probably more concerned about that than he was, and in a minute Preme was about to be on his own.

"Look, Preme. I'm about to drop you off to your car and I'm outta here. It's gettin' late and its too much police activity out here for me. I'm goin' home to wifey and the kids."

Preme rolled his eyes at Bone. "So you're just gonna let this dude get away with all the heat that he's bringin' to us?"

Bone was quiet. He didn't feel like talking much. Poet was one of the younger dudes he had admiration for and he was sad that it had come to this. He didn't want to see anyone who worked for him caught up, but everyone didn't have the mental capacity to survive in the streets. It was obvious that Poet was one of them. It was funny because Bone would have thought that Mekhi would have been the one to fall victim to the streets. He was so wrong.

Bone continued the silence for the short car ride to Preme's car. Preme got out of the car without so much as a good-bye. At that point, Bone didn't care. He had a sick feeling in his stomach—the same feeling he always got when he knew that there was trouble ahead. Bone shook his head, turned his car around, and headed toward home.

Preme got into his car and pulled off. He was upset with the fact that Bone had flipped on him about killing Poet. As he was driving through the block where Sha-Sha used to live, something caught his eye. Who was standing right in front of the building with a hood on his head? It was nobody but Poet himself.

"Is that who I think it is?" Preme said aloud.

It was dark outside so he had to look again to make sure that his eyes weren't steering him wrong. It was Poet. He pulled over to the side and got out of his car.

Poet looked as if he was waiting for someone. Preme pulled out his gun and hid it under his lightweight jacket to conceal it. He looked around to see if anyone was in the area. As far as he could see the street looked deserted. From where he was walking from, Poet's back was to him. It was perfectly set up. Preme slowly crept up behind the unsuspecting Poet. He was only a few feet away when a Chevy Impala pulled up. Preme quickly ducked behind some stairs and watched as Poet got into the passenger side of the vehicle. The unmarked Chevy could only mean one thing.

"Damn. The fuckin' police," Preme said to himself.

As he watched them pull off, Preme exhaled and held his chest. He was a thug but he wasn't anyone's fool. A few more seconds and he would have executed Poet right in front of the police. Preme put his gun away and walked back toward his car. He pulled off thinking that Bone was on point—again. Preme headed home without any incident.

Poet cowered in the passenger seat of the Impala. He covered his face with his hood, hoping that no one would notice him in the police vehicle. Oates was silent for a few moments, not wanting to force Poet to talk to him but it did seem as if Poet felt some type of remorse for what he did. Or did he?

"Thank you for pickin' me up, man," Poet said without looking at Oates. "I'm tired of runnin'."

Oates shook his head. "I know you are."

"I just wanna get this shit over with. I can't be in these streets anymore."

"No, it's not safe being out here. You're like a sitting duck right now."

"I think I need a lawyer."

"We'll make sure you have a lawyer present."

"Are you gonna tell them other detectives about what I confessed to you?" Poet asked.

"No, I'm not, Poet. I'm gonna leave the confessing part up to you. When we get to the stationhouse, I want you to write it down on paper for me. I think that admitting to what you did and showing remorse about it is much better than trying to fight this case. It's too much of a gamble."

Poet attempted to smile. He was too overwhelmed to discuss the particulars of his situation.

"You really care about my mother, don't you?" Poet asked.

Oates managed to smile as well. "Yes, I do. I think she's a phenomenal lady."

"That she is. And I can tell that you care about her. I think that you'll be good for my moms. She is really feelin' you too."

"I would go out of my way to make sure your mother is happy."

"I can see that because you're doin' a lot more for me than anyone has ever done and that was takin' the time to listen to me. I appreciate that and I appreciate you havin' enough respect for my mother to talk to me."

Oates nodded his head. "It was no problem. I just wish that I could have been there for you before all of this happened."

Poet looked at Oates then looked out the window and sighed. "I know."

They pulled up to the precinct and Oates pulled in a parking spot for authorized vehicles. Poet got out of the car and Oates walked over to him and put handcuffs on him. A few seconds later, Lewis pulled into a spot a few feet away and got out of the car. He walked over to Oates and the handcuffed Poet.

As they crossed the street to walk inside the stationhouse, Mekhi was standing in front of the precinct with a smug look on his face.

"What's up, Poet?" Mekhi said.

Poet shook his head, not knowing what to expect. "What's up, Khi? I'm turnin' myself in."

"Word? Well, I think that was a good idea. I've been waitin' in front of this precinct to meet up with you."

"I don't understand. How did you know that I was gonna be at the precinct?" Poet asked with a confused look on his face.

Normally, Oates wouldn't have allowed anyone to talk to a perpetrator who was in custody, but Poet was an exception. He was Cheryl's son. Lewis walked inside the stationhouse while Oates and Poet stood there, waiting for Mekhi to finish speaking to his friend.

Mekhi chuckled. "Well, it's like this, Po. After I finished tellin' them what I knew about all of the murders, you were as good as locked up anyway." Before Poet could absorb that he had been snitched on, Mekhi burst into tears. "Why did you have to kill my grandmother, Po?" he whispered.

"I didn't kill her, Khi!" Poet said. Oates sensed some trouble and immediately began pulling Poet toward the precinct doors. "She had a—" he began, but Poet wasn't able to finish his explanation.

In a matter of seconds, Mekhi pulled out a gun. Oates was taken aback by the gesture and went to reach for his own gun. But it was too late. Mekhi had managed to let off one round, hitting Poet in the chest. When Poet fell back against Oates, Mekhi began running down the block. Uniformed police officers rushed outside and grabbed the wounded Poet while Oates and a few other officers chased Mekhi down the block.

A certified sharpshooter and an avid track runner in college, Oates was only a few feet away when he shot Mekhi. When Mekhi went down face first, Oates knew that he was hit. He stopped running and slowly walked up to Mekhi's injured body with his gun still pointed at him. Oates saw blood coming from the back of Mekhi's head. He knelt down and he saw that he had hit the younger man in the back of his neck. The bullet had entered Mekhi's neck, and went through his throat. Mekhi was slowly losing consciousness.

A minute later, the two officers who had been running with Oates walked over. They looked down at Mekhi and immediately began radioing for assistance. Emergency Medical Service had been notified for both Mekhi and Poet. Another minute later, Lewis walked over to Oates, who was standing against the wall of a residential building, trying to catch his breath. Lewis slowly removed the gun from the shocked Oates's hands. He knew that his partner would have to be treated for trauma.

"It's okay, O," Lewis said while patting his partner's back. "You had to do what you had to do."

Oates began crying softly. Lewis had never seen him like that before, and pulled him away from the small crowd of officers and spectators who had gathered around Mekhi's motionless body. If it weren't for the gun that Mekhi had in his hand, the partners knew that the residents would have been all over the police for the shooting of who they may have thought was an innocent man.

The ambulances arrived for Poet and Mekhi and the paramedics removed them from the scene. Another ambulance came by a minute later and Oates stepped inside of it. He was definitely experiencing some type of distress from the incidents and was unable to talk to the attending paramedics. He had to be taken to Brookdale Hospital, along with the victims, and Lewis went with him.

Chapter 33

Game Over

It was shortly after midnight when Cheryl walked into Brookdale Hospital with a solemn look on her face. Porsha and Precious were lagging closely behind. The eyes of all three of the Washington women were bloodshot from crying. Everything that was happening to them seemed like a bad dream.

Reporters were standing outside of the hospital, hoping to get a glimpse of any law enforcement official to give them information about the two best friends. The story was a hot commodity and they all wanted to be the first one to break the news.

After asking some nurses for information, Cheryl was led to her son's bed. There were all sorts of tubes connected to his body. She thought he looked more peaceful than he ever did. Cheryl held his hand and looked into the face of her eldest child. A feeling of sadness swept over her body. It was a shame that his life had come to this.

"Poet?" she whispered softly. "Poet, it's me, Mommy." There was no reply and tears flowed from Cheryl's eyes. "I know, baby, I know. You look so peaceful. I will always love you, my son, Prince Poet." Cheryl chuckled. "You were every bit of a prince to me, baby, and you are a hero to me now, I don't care what these people say about you. You're not a monster. I know you love us. Your sisters? They're going to be fine, baby, don't you worry. They love you too. You just rest, okay? You just rest."

All of a sudden, Cheryl felt a breeze. She looked at her two daughters and they began to cry. They had felt it too. Poet had passed away.

The flatline on the monitor made a loud, continuous noise. Cheryl and the girls stepped to the side as the team of doctors and nurses came to tend to Poet. One of the nurses came by the bed with a defibrillator machine and she gave it to the doctor. They pumped Poet's chest and attempted to restart his heart, but to no avail.

The doctor looked at Cheryl and she nodded her head at him. Little did they know, she knew that Poet had passed before they even started working on him.

"Good-bye, baby," she said to herself. "Mommy will see you in heaven."

The doctor pulled Cheryl to the side to discuss what happened. Porsha and Precious sat in the chairs and comforted each other. Precious was crying harder than anyone.

If only I could turn back the hands of time, she thought.

She would bring her brother back and she would love him like no other. Not appreciating him when he was alive would haunt her for the rest of her life.

"Do you know Mekhi Porter?" the doctor asked Cheryl.

She held her head down. "Yes, I do. He was my son's best friend and he's also the one that shot my son. I don't have the details as to why he did that yet."

The doctor shook his head. "Mr. Porter just died a few minutes before your son did."

Cheryl put her hand to her mouth. *What is going on?* she wondered.

She turned around to walk away and standing right in front of her was Oates. He looked disheveled and a look of despair was all over his face. Cheryl broke down in his arms, and the girls rushed over to hug him too. It was the first time they were meeting Oates and it was unfortunate that it had to be under those circumstances. They all stood in the middle of the emergency room crying like babies for their brother, son, and friend.

It was a few days after the passing of Poet and Mekhi. Cheryl tried to be strong while preparing for her son's burial. She was also able to contact Mekhi's aunts and uncles, who agreed that they would have a double funeral for the best friends. Sadly enough, the following day Cheryl had to attend yet another funeral for Mekhi's grandmother, whom she heard had died of a heart attack the same day that Mekhi and Poet was killed.

Throughout the ordeal, Oates had been more than supportive. Regrettably, he would have to carry the burden of responsibility when it came to Poet's death. He felt like he was accountable for the way that Poet was killed, but Cheryl never once blamed him.

Cheryl just felt relieved that her son's murderous wrath had come to an end. Besides death, there was no other way for her son to be released from his demons. Secretly, she would have rather buried her son than see him locked up in someone's prison for the rest of his life.

Then her daughter Precious came to her with another startling confession after the funeral arrangements were made.

"Mommy, can I talk to you for a moment?" Precious asked, slowly entering Cheryl's bedroom. Her mother was sprawled on her bed with a blank look on her face.

"Yes, Precious," she replied with a sigh. Her heart couldn't take any more bad news, but for some reason, she knew that there was more to come.

Precious sat on the side of her mother's bed. "Mommy, I have to be honest. I was involved with Mekhi."

Cheryl frowned. "Involved like how?" she asked.

"Involved as in sexually involved."

Cheryl shook her head. "I don't believe this," was all she could muster up to say.

"I know, Mommy. I wanted to tell you but I didn't know how to."

Cheryl sighed again. "So you were having sex with an adult man, because that's what Mekhi was, you know. He was like a son to me and brother to you. I don't understand how or why that happened."

Precious couldn't find the words to express how bad she felt. She held her head down.

"And remember the guy that people said that Poet killed? Well, I had sex with him too. Poet knew about it and, well, I guess he did what he thought he had to do to protect me."

Cheryl did not allow herself to be upset. After these deaths, she knew that it would have to be a new chapter in all of their lives. This included her having more patience and understanding when it came to her girls, especially Precious. She had lost one child to the streets and she didn't want to lose another one.

"How old was Kody, Precious?"

"He was twenty-five years old."

Cheryl flinched but she maintained her composure. "Did you use protection?"

"With Mekhi, yes, I did, except for one time, and Kody, um . . . um . . ." she stammered.

"Did you get your period for this month, Precious?"

"That was goin' be the next thing I wanted to talk about. No, I haven't got my period yet."

Cheryl was silent. The death of her son was now met with the possibility of the birth of her grandchild. But it wasn't in Precious's best interest to have a child at sixteen. She was only a year older than Precious when she had Poet and it had been a struggle ever since. If Precious was pregnant, Cheryl had already decided that she wasn't keeping it. She was going to make sure that her daughters had a bright future ahead of them, no matter what it was going to take.

"It's between Mekhi and Kody, huh?" Cheryl asked with her eyes closed.

Precious nodded her head. "Yes, it is."

"If you're pregnant, Precious, you're not keeping this baby. We're going to handle this situation as soon as possible. I wish that you would have come to talk to me about this. My poor heart can't take any more bad news right now."

"No, Mommy. There's no more bad news. I'm so sorry."

As Precious was about to get up from the bed, Cheryl grabbed her daughter's arm and pulled her close to her.

"Precious, baby, I always loved you. I don't want you to think anything less. Your father left this family and I just wanted you to know that it wasn't because of you. It was obvious that he wasn't strong enough to be a father to his children or a husband to me. From now on, promise me that you will always love your beautiful self. No man can love you the way that you love you. Remember that, okay?"

Precious nodded her head. "I will, Mommy. I will love me and respect myself from this day forward, in honor of my brother." She looked up. "I love you, Poet, and I'm gonna miss you. Thank you for always havin' my back."

They embraced each other and began rocking back and forth while crying over the tragic loss of Mekhi and Poet. Porsha walked into the bedroom and joined them too.

In Queens, Oates walked around in a daze. He hadn't been back to work since the incident with Poet and Mekhi had occurred. He shot a few perps in his career before, but having to shoot Mekhi Porter for killing Poet was something he never thought he would experience. It felt so personal. Oates was racked with guilt, feeling like he could have done something more to save the lives of the two young men.

Oates lay on the couch and turned on the television. It was daylight outside but he had every blind in the house closed. It was nearly pitch black inside of his home and he wanted it that way.

A few minutes after lying on the couch, Oates's phone rang.

"Hey, Shareef."

"Hey, Cheryl. How are you feeling?" he asked.

"I'm better. The arrangements were the easy part and that was hard. Now the burial and the grieving process is another story."

"I totally agree with you, babe. Damn."

"I just wanted to tell you that I appreciate you so much. You did everything that you could to make things easier for me and you were a godsend," she said.

"Aw, it was no problem, sweetheart. I know one thing, though, this is the most complicated case that I have ever had in my whole career."

"I can imagine."

"This case hit close to home. But I must say that I am glad that I was able to reach Poet. And he definitely approved of our friendship."

"Did he really?"

"Yes, he did. He even said that he knew that I really cared for you. He could tell. He said that he wished that I would have come around sooner."

Cheryl was sniffing on the other end. He knew that she was crying.

"I'm gonna miss him so much, Shareef," she said through tears. "He was such a loving child. He wanted the best for me and my daughters."

"Yes, he did."

"He never once thought about himself. Oh, God, this hurts so badly."

Oates wiped a tear from his face. He wished that he could be there to comfort Cheryl, but he knew that he had to stay away for a little while as they were investigating the incident. Oates knew that it would look bad if they were seen together.

"Don't cry, baby. We're going to be together real soon," Oates said.

When he said that, it sounded as if Cheryl had stopped crying. Oates smiled. He hoped that he made her feel better. It was the least that he could do.

There was silence between the both of them. "Oh, yeah, Cheryl?"

"Yes?" she replied.

"I love you, baby."

"And I love you too."

Oates smiled and he could tell that she was smiling too. Even after the death of her son, her happiness meant everything to him, and Cheryl Washington deserved every bit of it.

Chapter 34

The End of the Road

The following morning, Saint Paul's Baptist Church was filled with loved ones and friends as the reverend spoke at the podium.

"In these caskets are two young men, young men that never had the opportunity to experience the good things that life had in store for them. You have Mr. Prince Poet Washington: loving son, brother, and loyal friend who would go above and beyond to help his family and the people of his commuity."

Mr. Leroy blew his nose into his handkerchief. He shook his head as he thought about the night Poet helped him after John-John robbed him for his money. He would never forget Poet.

"He was a young man who valued family more than he did himself, and sacrificed his life to prove that."

Precious thought about how mean she was to the one man whom she knew truly loved her. She was out there looking for other men to give her what she already had at home with Poet. Although it was a sin, she knew that he had killed Kody defending her honor. That memory would be etched in her mind forever.

"He went to extremes to make sure that the lawless and sinful ones paid for hurting those that he did not know but loved anyway. He gave new meaning to the commandment 'love thy neighbor.'"

Erica, the fifteen-year-old rape victim of Jerrod Timmons, was seated in the back of the church with her mother and aunt. She heard about Poet's death and insisted on coming back to New York from North Carolina just to pay homage to the man who practically saved her life.

Sitting beside Erica and her family were the mothers of the teenage girls who were demoralized by Kody Bradford. They heard the rumors about how Poet may have possibly killed Kody to avenge the exploitation of his younger sister. They didn't agree with murder, but when someone harms a child, there's no empathy for the offender. The young girls who were victims or would have become victims of this type of crime were what brought the mothers out to the funeral to pay their respects to Poet.

"He wasn't perfect, but people loved this young man. He made an impact on all of those that he associated with."

Bone and his wife sat on the other side of the pew. He held his head down and let the tears flow. Guilt racked his body as he recaptured the moment when he and Preme wanted to kill Poet. Bone thought that Poet was a good person, even blamed himself for getting the impressionable young man involved in the drug game. After finding out about Poet's death, Bone had decided to change his life and get out the drug game for good. He had consulted with his lawyer and insisted on putting his money to good use by opening a community center for the neighborhood teenagers. Being in the foster system and Poet's death had inspired him to give back the right way.

Next to Bone were former Blood members and other innocent young men who were caught up in the vicious cycle of gang violence. The former members were in fear for their lives, thanks to the intimidation and power of Terrence "Pumpkin" Watts. The innocent men were either brutally beaten or disfigured after Pumpkin and his cronies succeeded in forcefully recruiting them into their gang. They heard about Poet being killed and made their way to the homegoing services to get a look at the person who made their lives so much safer now that the notorious Blood leader was dead.

"Like all of us, Poet had his demons. But he loved and he was loved and that was what was more important than anything else. His memory and his experiences will never be forgotten, for there is a lesson to be learned here. Hopefully, his death and the death of Mr. Mekhi Porter will make an impact on the youth of our crime-ridden neighborhood. In memory of Mekhi, we are featuring his artwork in the lobby of the church. Mekhi and Poet's high school, Thomas Jefferson, has agreed to rename their art program 'The Mekhi Porter Project' after the young man who will never have the chance to show the world his stupendous talent."

The congregation of people clapped after the announcement. In the solemn faces of the people from the community was a flicker of hope. They had grown tired of burying their sons and daughters, mothers and fathers. They knew about the situation that led up to the deaths of Mekhi and Poet, but the residents of Brownsville came out to support the families of the friends who grew up like brothers. They realized that the real problem was the separation of the community as a whole that caused these young men to go against each other. It was time that they stood together and create a united force against crime, violence, and guns.

As people filed in a single line to view the deceased young men lying in their caskets, they gave envelopes with sympathy cards that contained money to Cheryl, and Mekhi's aunts and uncles. Unfortunately, Mekhi's mother, Dana, never made it to the services. When Cheryl contacted Mekhi's aunts and uncles, they told her that Dana was too far gone on hallucinogens to even realize that she had left behind a talented young son, let alone know her own name. Mekhi was gone and he would never have any knowledge of his mother's addictions. The family knew that he would have been devastated to find out that his mother had absolutely no connection to him or reality.

After the services, people gathered around Mekhi's beautiful artwork on display in the church's lobby. There were about ten oil paintings that were on sale for fifty dollars apiece. As Precious made her way toward the paintings, she stopped when she saw one that caught her eye. She instantly began to cry and her mother walked over to comfort her.

When Cheryl looked at the picture, she was in awe. It was a beautiful portrait of Precious, and the likeness to her daughter was almost uncanny. Mekhi captured her aura, even her piercing stare. Cheryl walked over to the person collecting the money for the paintings and purchased the picture of Precious. Precious held on to the painting for dear life. Any memory of Mekhi was good for her. Any memory of Mekhi was also the memory of her brother's handsome face.

As the Porter and Washington families walked toward their waiting limousines, Oates appeared out of the crowd. He had been seated in one of the back pews, as far away from the caskets as possible. He hated funerals but had made it his business to attend that one. Before Cheryl could get into the vehicle, he touched her shoulder. She turned around and saw that it was him. They embraced each other and Cheryl wanted to cry again. But there were no more tears.

Oates held her face and kissed her on the lips. "Before you go to the burial, I need to make an offer to you. I've been thinking about this for the past few days."

Cheryl looked confused. "What offer?"

"I want you and the girls to come and live with me in Queens."

Cheryl was at a loss for words. "But, Shareef, you have your daughter and your family—" she began.

Oates cut her off. "Look, that's fine. I had a long talk with my daughter and she knows all about you and your situation. I told her how I felt about you. She's happy for me. She even wants to meet you and the girls. I just want you out of that fucking neighborhood. You and the girls deserve better and I'm ready to give it to you."

Tears began flowing down Cheryl's cheeks and Oates kissed her again. "Don't cry, baby," he said, comforting her. "I love you. I promised to take care of you. That's why I want you and the girls to start packing up your shit, and by next week this time, we're all going to be living in my house in Queens together."

She smiled and kissed Oates. "Okay, baby. I agree it's time for a change of atmosphere. Too bad Poet isn't here to come with us."

Oates looked up to the sky. "Don't worry, sweetheart. Poet is coming with us. He is going to be with us—always."

Cheryl kissed Oates on the cheek and he watched her get into the limo. He waved at them as they pulled off and sighed. At that moment, his partner, Lewis, walked over and laid his hand on his shoulder. Oates was surprised to see him there.

"You're a good man, O, and you deserve a good woman. I'm sorry if I doubted this before."

Oates looked at the limo turning the corner. "That's okay, Lew. I knew that Cheryl was the woman for me from the first time I saw her. Even her son told me in so many words that I was the man for her and that was all that mattered." He looked up in the sky and blew a kiss. "Don't worry, son. I'm going to give your mother everything that you tried to give her and more. She's finally going to be okay."

Oates knew that Poet had sacrificed his life thinking that he was protecting his family from the ills of society. But karma got a hold of him, and in return, he lost his life.

As Oates was heading back to Queens, he was distracted by a huge mural that was painted on the side of the corner bodega of Poet's block. It was a picture of Mekhi and Poet, holding each other's hands in the air. Underneath the pictures of the young men, it said, "GONE BUT NEVER FORGOTTON—R.I.P. KHI & THE KILLER POET." Oates stared at the mural in amazement.

The Killer Poet? Oates thought.

Oates was annoyed that the people of the community were glorifying the murders that Poet committed by giving him that nickname. He found the mural to be offensive, but wasn't really surprised by the brazenness of it.

Moving Cheryl and the girls out of Brownsville was the best idea that he had in a while. He didn't want them to have to be subjected to the distasteful wall painting, which was a constant reminder of why the two young men were dead in the first place.

"Some things will never change," he said aloud. "Never change."

Oates took one last look at the wall, wiped a tear from his eye, and pulled off.

Notes

Notes

Notes

ORDER FORM
URBAN BOOKS, LLC
78 E. Industry Ct
Deer Park, NY 11729

Name:(please print):_____

Address: _____

City/State: _____

Zip: _____

QTY	TITLES	PRICE

Shipping and handling-add $3.50 for 1st book, then $1.75 for each additional book.

Please send a check payable to:
Urban Books, LLC
Please allow 4-6 weeks for delivery

ORDER FORM
URBAN BOOKS, LLC
78 E. Industry Ct
Deer Park, NY 11729

Name: (please print):_____

Address: _____

City/State: _____

Zip: _____

QTY	TITLES	PRICE
	16 On The Block	$14.95
	A Girl From Flint	$14.95
	A Pimp's Life	$14.95
	Baltimore Chronicles	$14.95
	Baltimore Chronicles 2	$14.95
	Betrayal	$14.95
	Black Diamond	$14.95
	Black Diamond 2	$14.95
	Black Friday	$14.95
	Both Sides Of The Fence	$14.95
	Both Sides Of The Fence 2	$14.95
	California Connection	$14.95

Shipping and handling-add $3.50 for 1st book, then $1.75 for each additional book.

Please send a check payable to:

Urban Books, LLC

Please allow 4-6 weeks for delivery

ORDER FORM
URBAN BOOKS, LLC
78 E. Industry Ct
Deer Park, NY 11729

Name: (please print):_____

Address: _____

City/State: _____

Zip: _____

QTY	TITLES	PRICE
	California Connection 2	$14.95
	Cheesecake And Teardrops	$14.95
	Congratulations	$14.95
	Crazy In Love	$14.95
	Cyber Case	$14.95
	Denim Diaries	$14.95
	Diary Of A Mad First Lady	$14.95
	Diary Of A Stalker	$14.95
	Diary Of A Street Diva	$14.95
	Diary Of A Young Girl	$14.95
	Dirty Money	$14.95
	Dirty To The Grave	$14.95

Shipping and handling-add $3.50 for 1st book, then $1.75 for each additional book.
Please send a check payable to:
   Urban Books, LLC
Please allow 4-6 weeks for delivery

ORDER FORM
URBAN BOOKS, LLC
78 E. Industry Ct
Deer Park, NY 11729

Name:(please print):_____

Address: _____

City/State: _____

Zip: _____

QTY	TITLES	PRICE
	Gunz And Roses	$14.95
	Happily Ever Now	$14.95
	Hell Has No Fury	$14.95
	Hush	$14.95
	If It Isn't love	$14.95
	Kiss Kiss Bang Bang	$14.95
	Last Breath	$14.95
	Little Black Girl Lost	$14.95
	Little Black Girl Lost 2	$14.95
	Little Black Girl Lost 3	$14.95
	Little Black Girl Lost 4	$14.95
	Little Black Girl Lost 5	$14.95

Shipping and handling-add $3.50 for 1st book, then $1.75 for each additional book.
Please send a check payable to:
    Urban Books, LLC
Please allow 4-6 weeks for delivery

ORDER FORM
URBAN BOOKS, LLC
78 E. Industry Ct
Deer Park, NY 11729

Name: (please print):_____

Address: _____

City/State: _____

Zip: _____

QTY	TITLES	PRICE
	Loving Dasia	$14.95
	Material Girl	$14.95
	Moth To A Flame	$14.95
	Mr. High Maintenance	$14.95
	My Little Secret	$14.95
	Naughty	$14.95
	Naughty 2	$14.95
	Naughty 3	$14.95
	Queen Bee	$14.95
	Say It Ain't So	$14.95
	Snapped	$14.95
	Snow White	$14.95

Shipping and handling-add $3.50 for 1st book, then $1.75 for each additional book.
Please send a check payable to:
Urban Books, LLC
Please allow 4-6 weeks for delivery

ORDER FORM
URBAN BOOKS, LLC
78 E. Industry Ct
Deer Park, NY 11729

Name: (please print): _____

Address: _____

City/State: _____

Zip: _____

QTY	TITLES	PRICE
	Spoil Rotten	$14.95
	Supreme Clientele	$14.95
	The Cartel	$14.95
	The Cartel 2	$14.95
	The Cartel 3	$14.95
	The Dopefiend	$14.95
	The Dopeman Wife	$14.95
	The Prada Plan	$14.95
	The Prada Plan 2	$14.95
	Where There Is Smoke	$14.95
	Where There Is Smoke 2	$14.95

Shipping and handling-add $3.50 for 1st book, then $1.75 for each additional book.

Please send a check payable to:

Urban Books, LLC

Please allow 4-6 weeks for delivery

ORDER FORM
URBAN BOOKS, LLC
78 E. Industry Ct
Deer Park, NY 11729

Name:(please print):_____

Address: _____

City/State: _____

Zip: _____

QTY	TITLES	PRICE

Shipping and handling-add $3.50 for 1st book, then $1.75 for each additional book.

Please send a check payable to:

Urban Books, LLC

Please allow 4-6 weeks for delivery